I0733633

Lady Beast's Bridegroom

A Twist Upon a Regency Tale
Book 1

By Jude Knight

© Copyright 2023 by Jude Knight
Text by Jude Knight
Cover by Kim Killion

Dragonblade Publishing, Inc. is an imprint of Kathryn Le Veque Novels, Inc.
P.O. Box 23
Moreno Valley, CA 92556
ceo@dragonbladepublishing.com

Produced in the United States of America

First Edition January 2023
Trade Paperback Edition

Reproduction of any kind except where it pertains to short quotes in relation to advertising or promotion is strictly prohibited.

All Rights Reserved.

The characters and events portrayed in this book are fictitious. Any similarity to real persons, living or dead, is purely coincidental and not intended by the author.

ARE YOU SIGNED UP FOR DRAGONBLADE'S BLOG?

You'll get the latest news and information on exclusive giveaways, exclusive excerpts, coming releases, sales, free books, cover reveals and more.

Check out our complete list of authors, too!

No spam, no junk. That's a promise!

Sign Up Here

www.dragonbladepublishing.com

Dearest Reader;

Thank you for your support of a small press. At Dragonblade Publishing, we strive to bring you the highest quality Historical Romance from some of the best authors in the business. Without your support, there is no 'us', so we sincerely hope you adore these stories and find some new favorite authors along the way.

Happy Reading!

CEO, Dragonblade Publishing

DEDICATION

This book is dedicated to all those who have been rejected or mocked on the grounds of their appearance or of some other factor beyond their control. True love looks past such surface details and sees the person within. Dear reader, may you be surrounded by people who truly love you.

About the Book

A reclusive bride. A reluctant fortune hunter.

Lady Ariel lives retired in the country after being badly scarred by a fire that killed her mother and brother. Society gossips about her and calls her Lady Beast.

Her second cousin, who inherited her father's title but not his private wealth, wants to have her committed so he can manage—and steal—her fortune.

Only finding a husband will prevent the cousin from having his way.

Peter, Lord Ransome, has inherited his father's debts along with responsibility for a stepmother who loathes him, her daughters, and his own two half-sisters.

Only a wealthy bride will save his estate and his family, especially the sisters who have fled his stepmother.

Once wed, the Beau and the Beast find they have more in common than they thought, but their accord is shaken when their enemies rouse Society and the rabble against them.

In their struggles to survive deadly hatred, they find that their marriage offers more than they bargained for.

Chapter One

Greenmount, the Midlands, January 1817

"A N EMPTY THREAT," Mr. Richards insisted. "Your cousin has no authority to have you committed to an asylum for the insane, my lady."

The frown that creased his forehead and pinched his mouth hinted that her solicitor was not as certain as he wanted Lady Arial Bledisloe to believe. Arial shared his doubts. She lived secluded with her companion and her servants but read widely. She knew that the law tended to favor men over women, earls over commoners, and those with money over those without.

Her cousin—second cousin, to be precise—was a man and an earl. She was a commoner, with only a courtesy title. She did have money, but with two of three counts against her in the eyes of the law, the money her father had left to his only living child, rather than to his heir, became the essence of the problem.

To add insult to injury, Father had not appointed guardians to manage Arial's inheritance, but had trusted Arial to take whatever advice she needed and make her own decisions.

At first, Josiah, now Earl of Stancroft, had declined to believe it. Then he had confronted Arial and demanded that she hand everything over to him in return for a small allowance. After she refused, he ordered his lawyers to challenge the will. When they reported that they could find no legal pretext for such a move, he had come up with this.

"There are no grounds for finding you insane," Mr. Richards said, but his frown deepened as he resettled his glasses on his nose. "Even if he demands a committal hearing, he will fail."

"I am a woman, horribly scarred, and a known recluse," Arial pointed out, her voice calm though she felt far from it. "These may be grounds enough. Tell me the results of your research, Mr. Richards. Have you found anything we may use to discredit him?"

Mr. Richards shook his head. "Nothing apart from mismanagement, my lady. Failing to make money from his investments and lands shows stupidity, but stupidity is not a crime or even a scandal."

Arial grimaced. Stupidity might not be criminal, but it was dangerous. In the minds of her cousin and his wife, her continued existence was an affront, preventing them from living in the style to which they thought they were entitled.

Marjorie had said as much to Arial's face, on the one occasion she and Josiah had visited Arial here at Greenmount. "You don't need the money," she had complained. "You don't leave your property. You have no visitors."

Arial did not retort that she went to church every week, socialized within the local community, and occasionally enjoyed dinner with the squire and his wife, or the local countess and her aunt. To Marjorie, only London Society counted.

In any case, Marjorie did not pause to allow her time to comment. "You will never marry or have children. How can you, when you are so ugly that you are afraid to show your face? You might as well give us the money your father should have left us. It will all come to us eventually, anyway. We are your only living relatives."

Arial was stung by the accusation of cowardice and made reckless by Marjorie's unerring strike on her deepest sorrow, her lack of children. She had dropped the half-mask she wore to protect others from the sight of her and had had the dubious satisfaction of seeing Marjorie blanch and shrink back in her chair.

Josiah, made of sterner stuff, only swallowed hard, but neither he nor Marjorie looked directly at Arial for the rest of the visit, even when she outraged them by explaining her death would not serve them, since her will was made, and the bulk of her fortune had been left to some of the philanthropic organizations she supported, with small legacies to her faithful servants.

Remembering her visitors' faces, Arial told Mr. Richards, "Josiah will not give up. Not as long as he sees me as vulnerable."

Mr. Richards tapped his steepled fingers against his lips and then said, "Give me permission to discuss the matter with your neighbor, Sir Thomas Repton, my lady. He is the local magistrate, is he not? It would be as well for you to have someone at hand to protect you should Lord Stancroft take the law into his own hands."

It was good advice. Sir Thomas and his wife were among the few people she trusted. "I will send him an invitation for dinner tonight, if you will join us, Mr. Richards."

That decided and the message sent, Mr. Richards declared himself satisfied, but Arial had a plan of her own, the seed of which Marjorie herself had planted with her taunts.

"Sir Thomas's influence may suffice in the immediate crisis, Mr. Richards, but it will not inhibit Josiah in the long term. I need a husband. I want you to help me get one."

Mr. Richards resettled his glasses again and stared up into the corner of the room for good measure.

"You disagree?" Arial asked.

He cleared his throat, looked down at his hands, and again lifted his eyes to the corner—all signs he had something he needed to tell his client, and was unsure how she would receive it.

Arial put him out of his misery. "I would be no beauty, Mr. Richards, even without the fire. As it is, I cannot expect a man to choose me without a considerable incentive. I propose that you find a man who needs money. A great deal of money. Someone whose embarrassments are so compelling he will be prepared to marry Lady Caliban."

The unkind nickname predated her scars. A childhood acquaintance had claimed that she was misnamed. The girl claimed Arial looked nothing like the ethereal spirit Ariel from Shakespeare's play, *The Tempest*, but instead like the shambling beast Caliban from the same play.

Mr. Richards winced, whether at Arial's use of the nickname or her plan, she couldn't tell.

"I realize that a husband has the potential to be an even bigger problem than my cousin. I need you to investigate candidates, particularly as regards their character, and to draw up a marriage settlement that protects me as much as possible."

Faced with the parameters of the challenge, Mr. Richards's frown cleared. "And any children," he added. "Or did you mean it to be a white marriage, Lady Arial?"

Arial blushed. "My preference would be for a true marriage." If any man could be found who was prepared to bed her. "That would be a matter for negotiation."

Mr. Richards nodded several times, a sure sign that he was already beginning to think about ways and means, and his next words confirmed it. "My major reservation, my lady, is that a man in dire financial need is likely to be unreliable. I suggest we focus on men who have inherited a debt-ridden estate, but do not themselves share the habits of their progenitors."

"My thoughts exactly," Arial agreed. "A man of good character who, through no fault of his own, needs an immediate infusion of cash in order to save his estates and his dependents."

They spent another hour creating a list of attributes and parameters for Mr. Richards's search, before changing for dinner. Mr. Richards had joined Arial's companion, Clara Tulloch, by the time Arial came down. Clara had been Arial's governess and had stayed on as companion and dear friend when Arial left the schoolroom.

Sir Thomas and Lady Wilson soon arrived to join them. The magistrate had been a great friend of her father's and wholeheartedly agreed to block any attempt by Josiah to pre-empt the legal process.

In the morning, Richards would be on his way back to London. Arial would next see him when she arrived in London herself, in six weeks' time, to interview the candidates on his shortlist.

Arial quailed at the thought of venturing out of the safe haven she had created for herself. But she could not expect the candidates to take the two-day trip to Greenmount so she could make her selection, and the final choice was too important to be left even to so trusted an adviser as Mr. Richards.

London it would be, then.

Three Oaks Manor, Sussex

"DID YOU TELL Lady Ransome I wished to see her, Edwards?" Peter Ransome said to his butler. Or, rather, his stepmother's butler. The man fell short of open disrespect, but Peter knew it was Lady Ransome's orders that the man followed, rather than Peter's.

Edwards shifted uneasily and would not meet Peter's eyes with his own. "Yes, my lord. I gave her the message."

"And she said…?" Peter asked.

"Nothing, my lord. She ignored me. I repeated your message, and she told me to go away."

Peter frowned. "I see." It was possible. Or she told Edwards to say nothing and do nothing.

Peter supposed his stepmother expected him to go up and confront her in her private sitting room, but he was reluctant to meet her on her terms and her grounds. The altercation could not be long delayed. The bills that arrived on his desk an hour ago showed she was continuing to prepare for a London Season, even though he had explained the family's parlous financial straits.

Peter had left home for the army as soon as he was old enough, and even after returning to England, set himself up in London so he did not have to share a house with his stepmother. He wouldn't have visited, except that he could not entirely abandon his two half-sisters. Now, he regretted the distance he had imposed. Perhaps, if he'd spent more time with his father, he could have avoided the mess of debts the man left behind. Or at least seen them coming.

Paying his father's debts had proved impossible in the short term. Peter was making every possible economy, had mortgaged every piece of property his father had left unencumbered, and had sold almost all his horses and his little bachelor apartment.

Even so, he'd made the humiliating round of the creditors he'd been unable to pay to ask for more time. So far, they had accepted the pittance that was all he could offer and waited patiently for the rest, but if Lady Ransome continued spending as if the family was still wealthy, he would be unable to make the next payment on time and that patience would run out.

Ever since Peter gave up his rooms and moved back into Three Oaks Manor, the servants had been divided in their loyalties, uncertain whether to obey the long-time mistress of the house or the person who paid their wages. And Peter had not pressed the point, unwilling to take on yet another battle in the vast succession that had descended as soon as he inherited the viscountcy, its debts, and its dependents.

Things were going to have to change. "Edwards, when I give an order, I expect it to be carried out. Take William with you. Return to Lady Ransome and tell her that I wish to see her immediately. Tell her that I have asked the two of you to escort her to my study. If she does not come, you are to inform her I have told you to carry her."

"My lord!"

"Do you understand your instructions, Edwards?" They were instructions the man would not carry out, but Peter needed open rebellion in order to have cause to dismiss the man.

"But my lord, you cannot expect me to lay hands on Lady Ransome."

"If you tell her you are willing to do so, I doubt it will be necessary." Peter was confident that Edwards would do nothing of the sort, but it would put both Edwards and Lady Ransome on notice that Peter had lost patience with them. "Do you feel unable to continue in my service, Edwards?"

The implied threat was enough. Edwards marched off towards the back of the house, and returned a few minutes later with William following, to climb the stairs to the countess's private sitting room.

A few minutes later, he returned, looking even more uncomfortable. "She says she will not come, my lord. She says that, if I touch her, she will have me arrested. If you wish to speak with her, you must come to her, she says." He nibbled his upper lip. "You didn't really mean me to do it, did you, my lord?"

Peter was not surprised at the response. While waiting for Edwards, he had been thinking about his next move. "You will give her this note, Edwards."

That should fetch her. It was short and to the point: "I regret that you have refused to allow me to discuss the matter of our finances in person, Lady Ransome. Without such input I am forced to assume you have no intention of curtailing your spending to suit our circumstances. Therefore, I am currently sending notes to instruct Richards to cut off your allowance, the bank to freeze access to your account, and every shop you patronize to tell them I will no longer pay your bills. With every due respect. Ransome."

The butler bowed, and took the note, holding it at a distance as if it might bite. Which it might. "Edwards, be ready to duck when she reads it," Peter advised.

He waited, leaning against the door jamb, while Edwards,

trailed by William, returned up the stairs. A few seconds later, he heard a screech, and the sound of china or glass breaking, item after item hitting an immovable surface with sad consequences for the item. The ornaments in Lady Ransome's room were uniformly ugly, but he hoped none of the servants nor his sisters were within range.

When the door upstairs slammed, he retreated to his desk, and began writing on a scrap of paper. A nonsense succession of phrases and words, but he hoped it made him look busy and unconcerned about the temper tantrum approaching in a flurry of lace, flounces, and ribbons.

"Beau Ransome, how dare you! You cannot cut me off. It would be unconscionable. I am your mother! When I think how I have cherished you, loving you as if you were my own son, and now you turn on me like this. I have nourished a viper in my bosom!"

Peter had expected this speech, and ignored it, continuing to write.

"Your father would expect you to look after me. Was it not the express wish in his will? 'I trust my son to care for my wife and her daughters as I know he will care for his own sisters.' Unnatural son!" An admonition that would not have been necessary if Peter's father had not gambled away all his unentailed property as well as his wife's portion and the dowries he had promised to his stepdaughters.

Lady Ransome stamped her foot. When she lost her temper, the good looks that had captivated his father were not much in evidence. Usually, the blacks she wore to trumpet her widowhood formed a frame for her fragile porcelain beauty; she was a tiny sprite with golden hair and creamy skin, looking even more slender and ethereal in the funereal color. Now, she was so white with fury that her careful use of makeup was disclosed to all observers, hot red blotches of rouge coloring her cheeks, angry creases marring the perfection of her skin.

"You may be seated, Lady Ransome," Peter said.

"Are you listening to me, Beau? You cannot cut me off without any money. Your sisters and I are leaving for London in less than a week. I have bills to pay at the local dressmaker. I have to send a deposit with my orders to the London modistes. And that incompetent nitwit Richards has refused to hire a townhouse for me without your direct order. You must tell him immediately that I have your authority, Beau. I will not be told what to do by a mere servant. I do not understand why you sold our London townhouse. It was unutterably foolish, Beau, and your father would never have done such a stupid thing."

Peter would not react to her insistence on calling him by the foolish nickname he'd attracted as a schoolboy. "Handsome Ransome," they'd dubbed him. Then one wit changed it to Beau, and the name had stuck, though Peter liked it no better in French than in English.

His stepmother knew he hated it. *Which is why she uses it.*

"Richards is *my* solicitor, Lady Ransome. He has very properly alerted me to your plans, which were against my direct instructions. Let me, therefore, tell you again. We cannot afford for my stepsisters to have another London season this year. You will not be going to London."

She started to speak, but Peter ignored the dictates of courtesy and spoke over the top of her.

"By next year, or at least the following, if you make the necessary economies, I hope to be able to afford accommodations for you in one of the cheaper towns. Cheltenham, perhaps. Or Bristol. Not this year. And any other expenses will have to come from the generous stipend my father allocated for your support. If you cannot pay, the clothing you have ordered will have to be cancelled. If it has been delivered, it must be returned."

She yelled. She threatened dire social consequences. She hurled verbal abuse. When he refused to give in, she resorted to tears. When those failed, she retreated for long enough to fetch his stepsisters to wail and complain about the loss of the husbands they were sure to meet this year, though none had shown an interest in previous seasons—four for Laura and five for Pauline.

Peter continued, obdurate. Even if he could afford it, he would not have bent to their bullying. The generous allowance his father had willed to his second wife was perfectly adequate to her reasonable expenses. As it was, the allowance ate up money that should be going on debt repayment, and left nothing for necessary estate maintenance, let alone improvements. He had no choice but to continue to refuse the ladies a Season.

The three of them withdrew at last—to prepare for dinner, Peter assumed. Foreseeing another series of attacks over his meal, he sent Edwards to bring a tray to his bedchamber, and retired for the night.

The next three days were miserable, as Lady Ransome continued to cycle through the various approaches of attack, abuse, beg, weep, and wheedle. While the weather was wet and bleak, Peter went out every day to visit tenants, preferring the cold and the damp of the ride to the discomfort of his own house.

His stepmother even tried to enlist his half-sisters from the schoolroom to her cause, and they obediently parroted what she'd told them to say, ten-year-old Vivienne in an uncanny imitation of her mother's voice, and eleven-year-old Rosalind in a sepulchral monochrome that had him fighting down a grin. The girls caught his amusement despite his attempt to remain stern. They giggled. He lost the battle with his features and joined the merriment.

"But you should not mock the viscountess," he warned them. "If someone informs her, she will be cross."

Viv wrinkled her nose. "Only we three know, Peter. Mother was going to come and make sure we said what she told us to say, but Pauline told her you were more likely to give in if it was just us two."

"Your mother does not wish to believe I cannot afford to let her and your sisters go to London this year," Peter explained.

Viv sighed. "Are we very poor now, Peter? Will I need to scrub floors? Will we be able to keep Rose?"

"We are not so poor you will need to scrub floors, Viv," Peter assured her. "And Rose is our sister. Rose, darling, this is your home." In fact, Rose had already been installed in the nursery when Lord Ransome married the former Mrs. Turner and brought her and the Turner sisters home. Vivienne was born five months after the wedding, her robust good health hinting at the reason for the sudden marriage.

Lady Ransome disliked having her husband's base-born daughter raised with her own child, but had kept her opinion to herself while Peter's father was alive. Any mistreatment of Rose was the one thing that caused the former Lord Ransome to exert himself to lose his temper with his wife.

Perhaps Peter needed to throw things, shout, and threaten beatings.

Instead, he did his best to reassure the two girls.

By the third day, Lady Ransome was demanding he immediately seek out a wealthy heiress, marry her, and reinstate his stepmother's previous standard of living, "For the paltry allowance you are giving me, Beau, is totally inadequate to my consequence as the widow of an earl. Even your father, God rest his soul, was not so parsimonious, and I blame him entirely for failing to give dear Pauline and Laura the support—the setting, if you will—in which they could attract the proper kind of suitor."

Peter was not aware that either of his stepsisters had had any kind of suitor, proper or otherwise, in all the years since their debut. In his opinion, it was their personalities, so much like their mother's, which kept them single. He kept the thought to himself and merely replied to the only new element in her litany of complaints. "I do not intend to marry at this time."

"That is so like you, Beau. Always thinking of yourself. So selfish."

No wonder my father spent so much time at his club, or with his mistress, or anywhere that Lady Ransome was not.

His stepsisters also kept up the pressure, Laura in particular, alternately berating him and pleading. Pauline was more circumspect. He found her one evening in the nursery, whispering with his sisters, undoubtedly filling their heads with his stepmother's lies.

"Leave them alone, Pauline. It is wicked to involve them in your plots, and it won't make any difference."

His stepsister flushed. "I didn't… I wouldn't…"

He glared at her, and her eyes dropped as her color heightened still further. "I'll just be going then," she said, and sidled round him and out the door.

"You were not very nice to Pauline," Vivienne growled. Rose said nothing, but she wouldn't look at him. They didn't understand. He forced a smile and asked if they would like him to read their bedtime story.

The letter from his solicitor was as welcome as a reprieve from execution. It requested a meeting at Richard's offices in London.

"I have a proposition to put to you, my lord, which may resolve your current difficulties."

Peter couldn't imagine anything that would fix the viscountcy's finances except years of economies and hard work, but he packed a satchel with a change of linen, had a horse saddled, and set out for London.

Chapter Two

WITHIN FOUR WEEKS, Mr. Richards sent Arial a list of the candidates he had considered, and a detailed biography for each of those who met the criteria he and Arial had agreed.

No one responsible for his own indebtedness made the list. Mr. Richards also rejected men subject to the flaws of whomever had preceded them—gambling, drinking, wenching, or even just poor management.

The four men who made the final short-list were intelligent, capable, and responsible—at least in Mr. Richard's estimation. Two had inherited from profligate uncles, one from a remarkably stupid brother, and one from a father whose bad habits included gambling and drinking far beyond his capacity. On the information in his report, any of them might be suitable.

Arial hesitated over the last name—Peter Ransome, now Viscount Ransome. She knew him. Or, at least, she had known him once, when they were both children. Their fathers had been the best of friends, though her family's principal estate was in the Midlands and the Ransomes lived near the coast in Sussex.

They visited back and forth when in London for Parliament and often stayed at one another's estates during the remainder of the year. Indeed, the Ransomes had been staying with Arial's family on the night of the fire—Peter had lost his own mother to the flames, as Arial had lost her brother and her mother.

Perhaps that bereavement was why they never returned. By the time Arial was recovered enough to ask about them, the father and son were far away, back in their own home, five counties away.

It wasn't ancient history that bothered her. The estrangement could easily have been on her father's side—he and Mama had been highly sociable before the fire, spending months every year in London and more time at house parties around the country. When they were home, they usually had guests.

The fire changed that. After losing his wife and son, and nearly losing his daughter, her father retired to the Midlands, traveling to London only occasionally and for a night or two, when a particular vote in the House of Lords attracted his interest.

Even if Ransome senior had been the one to abandon the friendship, Peter bore no responsibility for that. He would have been thirteen or fourteen when she last saw him.

And beautiful. That was the problem. Peter Ransome, as a youth, had been the most perfectly formed individual she had ever seen. *Beau Ransome*, the boys at school called him, and he hated it. But it was true.

When she was ten, Arial had had a painful crush on Peter—painful because such a glorious male would never look at a pudgy, overgrown female like her.

He was fifteen years older now, so perhaps he had changed. She very much feared he would have changed for the better. How could a man who was the epitome of male beauty marry a female like her? She had never been pretty—she was too large for that, with a big nose and a square chin.

Sturdy, her nurse called her, being partial. Fat, said the Turner sisters, who lived next door to the Ransome estate. Her mother and Peter's thought it was nice for her to have company of girls her own age, so Laura and Pauline Turner were invited over whenever the earl visited his friend the viscount.

It had been Laura Turner who dubbed her *Lady Caliban*, even before the fire left her scarred and twisted into a monster. Beau Ransome would never marry such a one as her.

She sighed. From Mr. Richards's report, poor Peter had been left in a dreadful situation. The new Lord Ransome, said Mr. Richards, was determined to put his estates back into good heart, but he faced an uphill struggle.

His father had become a wastrel: a drunkard and a gambler who ignored his estates. And his second wife was as extravagant and careless as the viscount. That was another strike against Peter. His father had married Mrs. Turner, mother of Arial's persecutors.

Arial firmed her chin. She could not hold the Turner sisters against her old friend. Let Peter make his own decision. This was to be a marriage of equals. She could not offer a husband beauty, but she had other attributes. Her wealth, of course. But also, she kept an efficient house, was an excellent estate manager, and a skilled investor. She understood livestock, including horses, and ran a superb breeding program that was producing champions.

Added to that, as far as she could tell when it had not been tested, her reproductive system was in full working order. She was willing to do her part to produce heirs for her husband. More than willing. Her heart yearned for children.

She hoped her ugliness would not prevent the conception of such offspring. *Presumably, the necessary deed can be done in the dark, however.* The grim humor did little to calm the pounding of her heart at the mere thought of allowing another human being so close to her.

Better marriage than an asylum. Her response to Mr. Richards authorized him to go ahead and talk to his candidates. Arial then put the matter out of her mind as much as she could. Her next challenge would be the journey to London. She bent her mind to the logistics. It would be a procession of several carriages, with Arial, Clara, and their maids in one, the servants she was taking in another two, and the luggage in a fourth. Grooms, including the tough burly ex-soldiers that Sir Thomas had found to guard her, would act as outriders along the way.

They would need one overnight stay. She asked Sir Thomas about inns near the halfway point, and he gave her the names of three that might be able to accommodate her entire entourage, and that would offer her the privacy she needed.

"Do you know anything of these three?" she asked Clara, who went away once a year to visit her married sister.

The companion shook her head. "I have stayed at none of them, Arial. Would you like me to investigate?"

"Visit them, do you mean?" Arial liked the idea. She trusted Clara to understand what she needed.

Two days later, Clara, with a maid and an escort, left to visit all three and make a decision. The party would stay overnight at the inn Clara had favored with their booking and return the next day.

That afternoon, Josiah came.

A footman called the alarm. He had been returning from an errand when he saw the approaching carriage and riders. He arrived flushed and breathless, but managed to pant out, "It's Lord Stancroft, my lady. Come bringing trouble, I reckon. Got half a dozen men with him, and maybe more in the carriage."

Arial agreed. Josiah would not be bringing such a force for a social call. "Go for Sir Thomas. No, you are winded. Send someone fresh, at all speed. Make sure he knows how many people Josiah has with him."

From the window, she could see them coming down the drive. "Tell him to go through the orchard, Fredericks. He'll be out of sight from the driveway, then."

How long would she have to stall her cousin? It was ten minutes through the fields at a full run. Then Sir Thomas would have to have his horse saddled and collect his men before coming to the rescue. Twenty-five minutes, at least. She took a deep breath as her father had taught her. In through the nose, hold, and out through the mouth. Her heart kept pounding and her mind skittered from one thought to another.

She must protect the servants. Should she hide? Surely, he would just bluster and shout as he had before? But the carriage and its swirl of horses halted in front of the steps, and Josiah looked up at the house, a fierce grin evidencing no intention to talk. Though Arial was hidden in the shadow of the curtain, she trembled like a mouse before a cat.

He dismounted, as did his attendants. The guns that two of his men slid out of saddle holsters confirmed their evil intentions. One man opened the door of the carriage, and two women descended. Not ladies. They were soberly dressed in functional clothing with plain bonnets.

Josiah spoke to them. They, too, looked up at the house and Arial could see their faces. Women in their middle years, as tall as Josiah and broadly built, with hard stern faces.

Behind them, another person descended from the carriage, and Josiah turned away from the women to hail him and lead him up the steps to the front door.

A sound behind her had her spinning around, afraid the invaders had already found their way inside, but it was one of Sir Thomas's ex-soldiers with her butler hovering at his elbow. "My lady."

Arial swallowed and managed a semblance of calm. "Sergeant Miller. Barlowe."

"My lady, we mean to refuse them the house," Barlowe said. "Will you go upstairs? Preferably to a room where they will not expect to find you?"

Sergeant Miller assured her, "We'll try to keep them out. But if we cannot do so without bloodshed… We will protect you to the last man, my lady, but I'd rather just hold them off until Sir Thomas arrives."

Having something practical to do seemed to unfreeze Arial's brain. "I will hide in the attics, Sergeant. Feel free to tell them I am not at home."

Sergeant Miller grinned. "I'll leave that to Barlowe, my lady."

"I'll take my maid with me. If they do search the house, they are more likely to believe I am away from home if they cannot find Clara, me, or our maids. Do not risk yourselves or the servants to keep them out."

The men nodded as the knocker on the front door sounded a fierce rat-a-tat-tat.

Arial hurried upstairs, collecting Nancy, her maid, as she passed her bedchamber.

In the back corner of the attic, hidden behind trucks and boxes, they heard the invasion as nothing more than distant shouting, with the occasional thumping as door slammed or heavy people hurried up or down the stairs.

It seemed that hours had passed before they heard Sir Thomas's voice. "Lady Arial? We have sent them packing."

Downstairs, Arial was relieved to find that none of her servants had been hurt. Sergeant Miller and Barlowe had blocked Josiah until he ordered his men to shoot and had then stepped aside.

"He and his men searched the house, but Lord Stancroft told them not to break anything. Said he might be able to sell it, my lady."

The earl had only ten minutes before Sir Thomas arrived with half a dozen armed constables. "The earl insisted he was here out of concern for you," Sir Thomas explained. "I made it clear he acted illegally in invading your home and threatening your servants, and that his intention to—as he claimed—have a doctor examine you was also illegal, as he has no standing in the matter. I said any further attempts would be prosecuted to the extent of the law. Even if he were prepared to ignore me, the doctor he had in his pocket was more susceptible to reason. Particularly when I explained that you had appointed me and your solicitor as your trustees in the event you were incapacitated in any way, so Lord Stancroft would have no access to ready cash to pay his supporters no matter what happens to you."

Perhaps, Arial thought, that would discourage the awful man. If it kept him at bay long enough for her to find a husband, she could defeat him entirely.

The incident was not Josiah's last action against Arial that day, however. Later that afternoon, Clara arrived home, shaken, after being stopped by Josiah, who recognized the carriage. Fortunately, the coachman, guard, and outrider realized they were both outnumbered and outgunned, and did not fight back. Once Josiah found he'd caught the companion and her maid, and not Arial, he sneered a few insults and left. Arial reassured Clara that she was taking a small army of servants and guards when they left for London, but Clara was still nervous several days later when they finally set off.

Sir Thomas, having heard about Clara's frightening experience, insisted on sending another six men with them, including two armed constables.

In the event, they had no trouble, apart from people staring at a heavily veiled Arial as she walked through the busy courtyard and crowded inn to the sanctuary of the rooms Clara had hired and did the same excruciating trip in reverse the following morning. Pinned in place, the veil could not move, yet some part of Arial ignored all logic, certain that at any moment it would whisk aside, taking the half-mask she wore beneath it to reveal the horror of her face to a jeering world.

She ignored her damp palms and thundering heart, the knees that perversely wanted to give way and run, both at the same time. She forced herself not to hurry. But she was grateful beyond measure for Clara on one side, Sergeant Miller on the other, and others of her servants going ahead to ensure she had clear passage.

The ordeal needed only to be faced for the overnight stay. Otherwise, they looked after their own needs at discreet stops along the way, and nothing occurred to hamper their journey.

They arrived at the townhouse Richards had hired for her in the mid-afternoon, one ordeal over and another to come. Tomorrow, she would meet the first of the candidates.

THE ROOM PETER took for a couple of nights was clean and quiet, as London hotels went, which meant noisy by country standards. He was unaccustomed to London's noise, its odor, the constant movement and bustle, the smudge of coal dust ever present in the air, dulling the sky.

Even so, the trip felt like an escape, a few days of release from the constant bickering at Three Oaks. He felt guilty leaving Rose to the non-existent mercies of Lady Ransome, but he had advised the two schoolroom girls to play least in sight, and informed both their governess and the housekeeper he would hold them accountable if any servant dared to carry out an instruction that caused Rose or, for that matter, Viv, any injury or distress.

Last time he'd left the estate for a few days, Lady Ransome had instructed Rose was not to be fed. At least the old harpy did not dare to repeat her offense from after his father had died. Peter resigned his commission as soon as the news reached him and returned to England immediately. His stepmother had clearly not expected him. Rose had been turned from the house with nothing but the clothes she was wearing.

Fortunately, his house steward had taken her in. And on the most recent occasion, Viv had conspired with the cook to be fed double helpings so she could share with Rose.

"I promise you," Peter had told Lady Ransome after that incident, "whatever action you take against my sister Rosalind, I will take against you." He hoped it would help. But if it didn't, at least the servants were warned to support the girl, and not the viscountess.

His precautions should be enough, and he could do no more. He might as well try to enjoy his brief trip to the capital. After washing off the dust of the journey and changing into clean clothes, he set out in search of a dinner. He was just about to enter a pie shop that looked clean and was busy enough to hint at tolerable food when he was hailed.

"Peter! I thought you were buried for life in the country!" He turned to see Captain John Forsythe, who had served with Peter during the Peninsular campaign and later in Belgium. As tall as Peter himself, John had dark hair while Peter's was fair. John was altogether more massively constructed, so that he felt as strongly about the nickname "Bull" as Peter did about being called "Beau."

Strictly speaking, the man was Captain Lord John Forsythe, but he refused to use the honorific, saying he had done nothing to deserve it beyond being born in a marquess's family some years after his older brother.

John looked in the doorway of the pie shop and protested. "Not here, Peter. I can do better for you than that. I'm off to my club to have dinner. You will join me, of course."

"I thought I'd just pick up a pie," Peter told him.

"Not enough to keep body and soul together."

"I don't know," Peter protested. "Remember that pork pie in Belgium?" After Waterloo, that had been. A baker, delirious with joy at the defeat of Napoleon, had given them her entire day's baking as they passed her establishment on their way back into Brussels. After handing most of the haul out to the men they'd managed to bring back with them, John and Peter had shared the last pie.

"Pure heaven," John agreed. "But so is the roast beef at Westruthers, Peter. Come on. Eat with me. I want to know what you've been up to." His mouth twitched upward in a smile. "And I want to tell you about my betrothed."

"You are betrothed? John! When did that happen? Who is the unfortunate lady?" He fell into step beside his friend and listened to rhapsodies about the most perfect and lovely woman in the world all the way to the club and on through most of the two courses of a delicious meal.

Eventually, even John realized he was repeating himself. "I am sorry, Peter. You should have stopped me. You cannot be interested in where Belinda is buying her bridal clothes and what linen she has chosen for our new townhouse."

"I need to meet the lady for whom you have become interested in such things, John."

"Come with me tomorrow afternoon and I'll introduce you," John proposed, and when Peter demurred, saying that he would not want to play gooseberry, John said it was no such thing. "For I am never allowed to be alone with her, more is the pity. Even when I proposed, her mother sat on the other side of the room. And no wonder. She is a diamond, Peter, in every way. Do come along, for her drawing room will be crowded with callers and it will be good to have a friend of my own there."

And why not, after all? His appointment with Mr. Richards was at noon, so he was sure to be free by three o'clock. "Very well. I'll come and make the acquaintance of your paragon. When is the wedding?"

That set John off again. The date had been set for after the end of the Season, and none of John's representations had served to move it closer. "Her mother will not hear of it," he complained. "I promised we would remain in town so that Belinda could continue to enjoy the parties and so forth, but her mother insists. They will not even announce the betrothal or allow me to speak of it." He sighed.

"What does your betrothed say?" Peter wondered.

"Oh, that she cannot wait to be my wife, but she feels she owed it to her mama to abide by the lady's wishes. And I do see that. Belinda is the Weatheralls' only daughter, and Weatherall tells me that his wife and Belinda have spent all winter planning for the fun of the Season."

John managed not to raise his eyebrows. "I collect that Miss Weatherall is a young lady, just out?"

"This is her third Season, but she has had a hard time of it in other years, poor dear. Girls jealous of her beauty have been very cruel to her. I cannot help but admire her courage in returning. She is wonderful, Peter, and very mature for her age, I assure you. A great reader and feels just as she should on all the things important to me." His eyes stared into nothing, and his lips curved in a fatuous smile. "And as beautiful as the dawn."

He continued to extol the virtues of his beloved until Peter declared himself ready for bed after his days of travel, and they parted with an arrangement to meet the following afternoon.

Nonetheless, Peter lay awake for some time, his fatigue weighing his limbs but his brain still active. What could Richards possibly have to offer? And what was he to do about his stepmother?

Two fruitless lines of thought. He turned his mind to John and his Miss Weatherall. If the lady's regard for John was as high as John's for his Belinda, they were bound to be happy. And if a few of John's comments had given him pause, it was probably just the caution of a friend with reasons of his own to be suspicious of female wiles.

Through all their years at war together, John had talked of his dream, the dream for which he fought.

Whereas Peter had joined up to escape his father's toxic second marriage, John was driven by the conviction that Britain's enemies must be defeated to preserve the peace John longed for. He had a vision of raising a family in the country, of living the life of a wealthy squire on the estate he had from the uncle for whom he had been named.

He had a heartbreak in his past he would never discuss, but it had not broken his faith in the idea of a love match. Presumably, Belinda shared his longings, and in a few years' time, he and his wife would deep in love and surrounded by the children of his dream.

Despite Peter's skepticism about love matches, the pull of that future sank him deep into sleep and followed him into dreams of Three Oaks Manor ringing with the sound of children's voices and one low melodic female voice he didn't know—a voice that laughed and sang with the children. Peter found himself searching for them through halls and rooms subtly transformed— warmer, somehow. More like the home he remembered from before his mother died. But however fast he hurried, however quickly he turned corners or opened doors, he did not catch up.

Chapter Three

THE SENSE OF something just out of reach followed Peter into the morning. His appointment with Richards was at noon. He waited to be announced, feeling as he had sometimes before a battle: as if something momentous marched inexorably towards him, bring a change for better or for worse.

After civil greetings, Richards got straight to the point. "I have an opportunity for you, my lord. It will allow you to pay the estate's debts and leave money and to spare over to bring your lands back into full production. And you will also be able to do a great service for another person."

"It sounds too good to be true," Peter commented. "What is this service that brings such great rewards?"

His solicitor leaned forward a little, his eyes intent on Peter. "Another of my clients has commissioned me to find her a husband, Lord Ransome. Her need is urgent and imperative."

An obvious reason for haste occurred. "Pregnant, is she? I've no wish to make someone else's son my heir, Richards."

"No, my lord. My client is a lady and a maiden. I am authorized to explain her reasons, but only if you agree to consider the marriage. The lady does not wish her identity to be known or her circumstances to be discussed except with the candidates for her hand."

Peter's brows twitched upwards. "Candidates? I am not the only person to whom you are putting this proposition?"

"The lady commissioned me to select candidates and send them to her for interview, Lord Ransome. She will make the final decision." He nodded, firmly. "After all, she will live with the results."

"She, and her chosen groom," Peter pointed out. "I wish the lady well, Richards, but I am not minded to sell myself in such a way." He'd not sunk that low. Not yet.

Richards set his jaw, examining the blotter on his desk as if it contained some secret he could interpret if he stared for long enough. "You will forgive me, my lord, if I point out that your other choices are untenable. You have cut your outgoings to the bone, and yet you will still not have sufficient money to pay the mortgages when they fall due, let alone the other more pressing debts."

Peter protested, "You advised me not to let staff go nor to begin selling off everything that is not entailed!"

Richards nodded. "I advised you not to frighten your creditors by behaving as if you were insolvent. You and I needed time to come to terms with what might be done. But, my lord, you are insolvent. I must change my advice. If you will not consider an advantageous marriage, then you must make haste to sell whatever you can."

"It won't be enough!"

"No, my lord." Richards sat back in his seat, his hands in front of him on the desk, keeping his gaze steady.

Peter shivered, though the day was not cold. He had sunk lower than he knew, if a convenient marriage was his only option. "I daresay I could find an heiress on my own." He had a little time, surely? The mortgages were not due until next quarter day, and Richards could continue to put his creditors off a little longer.

The solicitor tipped his head in acknowledgement. "Yes, my lord. A wealthy merchant's daughter, perhaps."

Peter sighed. "You think I am cutting off my nose to spite my face. Very well, Richards. I will consider your lady. Tell me why I should agree to be one of the supplicants for her favor." He wrinkled his nose at the thought of being interviewed by the would-be bride, like a footman or a groom anxious to win a position.

Richards considered him for a moment, his eyes narrowing. "You know the lady, Lord Ransome. Or, at least, you knew her once."

Peter tried to think of a lady of his acquaintance who might seek a husband through a solicitor. No. He couldn't imagine who it might be.

Richards ignored his confusion. "My client was seriously injured some years ago and was left disfigured. She has lived secluded ever since. When her father died some eighteen months ago, his title went to a distant cousin, but he left his private wealth to his daughter. Since the will was read, the cousin has been attempting to challenge it. Failing that, he is now seeking to have my client declared insane and himself declared her guardian."

Peter snorted. At Richards's raised eyebrows, he protested, "Come on, Richards. Surely the lady exaggerates. This is the nineteenth century, and not one of those ridiculous novels that women read."

"On the contrary," Richards's gaze was steady and his voice cool. "The villain has already been thwarted by the lady's neighbor in an attempt at abduction. I have received a letter from the man, who is the local magistrate. I can assure you, my lord, that my client is in very real danger. She has no close family and her scars have kept her from the society which is her birth right. These are the reasons she has taken the unusual step of seeking a husband's protection through interview."

Despite himself, Peter's sympathy was stirred. The poor woman was even more alone than Peter. "You said I know your client."

"Knew, my lord. She remembers you from childhood. Your father and hers were friends, I believe. Before the fire that killed her mother and brother and left her scarred."

"Arial!"

"Lady Arial Bledisloe," Richards confirmed.

In Peter's memory, the ten-year-old girl smiled at him over a chess board, her eyes sparkling with glee as she put his king into check. She wasn't like the other girls he knew. She rode out around the countryside with him and their fathers, astride on a horse that was only a little large for her, since she was as tall as him and sturdy. She climbed trees and rowed boats and played cricket. She didn't fuss about her clothes or her hair.

He had liked her, though at thirteen he was not prepared to admit it. And he had always felt guilty for what he had done on the night of the fire, had always wished he could make it up to her.

His natural sympathy for a lady beleaguered on all sides deepened into a longing to serve and protect his old friend. Perhaps she would turn him down. But he must at least try.

"So, what happens next?" he asked Richards. "An interview, you said?"

Richards gave a thoughtful nod. "You are willing, then?"

"I promised to consider it. Lady Arial and I were friends, once."

"Very well, my lord. My instructions are to discuss the marriage settlements with you, and then, if you still wish to proceed, to set a time for you to meet Lady Arial."

THE FIRST CANDIDATE disqualified himself within ten minutes of being shown into the little parlor off the entrance hall that Arial was using for these interviews.

The hint of condescension in his manner grated from the first.

He won no points with his answer to her question about what he wanted from this marriage—her money to put into the businesses his uncle had mismanaged, so he could sell them as going concerns and live a life of leisure as a gentleman should.

He topped his dismal performance by announcing he would need to renegotiate some terms of her proposed marriage settlement, because women were not clever enough to keep control over their own money. He was astounded and not a little annoyed when Arial thanked him for his time and told him she did not think they would suit.

The second was courteous and charming. His uncle, an earl, had shot himself after losing everything in a speculation, and he sought marriage to an heiress as a way of relieving his older brother of responsibility for providing for him and his three younger sisters. "Buck can bring the estates back to solvency if he has only himself to worry about," he explained.

That wasn't quite what Arial was hoping for when she asked what he wanted from marrying her, but at least his answer was not entirely self-serving. She continued the interview. He would do, she thought. He had no complaint about the proposed financial arrangements. His comment on her continuing to manage her business and investment interests was that he couldn't understand why she wanted to, but he had no intention of interfering with her life.

That was slightly disconcerting—surely a husband and wife should interfere at least a little with one another's life? She had hoped for someone who would be in some sense, at least, a partner; perhaps a friend.

Which brought her to the vexed question of children. Or to be more precise (though only in her own mind) to the consummation of the marriage. Arial had already faced the possibility that she might be forced to accept a white marriage—one where she remained a virgin. She was, after all, ugly.

Her chest tightened and a vein at her temple throbbed, but she fought the sensations and kept her voice calm. "I would like you to give me children."

His eyes widened at the bald statement. "Ah. Well. Of course."

She barely heard him, focused as she was on forcing her suddenly leaden arms to move, to grasp the veil that protected him from having to look at her. "I need to show you what you are agreeing to," she murmured, as she lifted first the veil and then—when he did not react to the minor scarring disclosed—the shielding mask that covered the ravaged side of her face.

He stood, his hand over his mouth, his eyes so wide that the whites showed around them. "I am sorry," he mumbled. "So sorry. Sorry." He kept repeating the word as he backed towards the door and flung it behind him as he left the room. "Sorry."

So much for that. Arial sat forlorn and alone, numb with shame and disappointment, while the daylight faded. She only stirred when Clara Tulloch came looking for her and was startled to find her sitting in the dark. "Are you well, Arial?

Arial roused herself. "Quite well, thank you. I was just thinking." *Thinking that I have all this to do again tomorrow, with two more men. And I am afraid it will all be for nothing.*

PETER WALKED THROUGH the London streets, trying to think of some other way out of Arial's dilemma. He couldn't reconcile his dignity to the idea of selling himself to a rich wife. On the other hand, leaving Arial to the non-existent mercies of her cousin was impossible. He owed her his help.

He had come to no conclusion by three, the time appointed to meet John at his lodgings.

John's betrothed lived in a large townhouse in one of the finest parts of town. Several young ladies dotted the luxurious drawing room, but he knew which was Belinda immediately. Only one lady was dressed for the indoors. Only one was surrounded by gentlemen callers. Indeed, only one deserved the adjective *beautiful*, though Peter was willing to make allowances for a besotted man, and if John had looked at any of the other ladies, he might have doubted his immediate identification.

Belinda sparkled like the diamond John called her, and was just as hard, unless Peter completely missed his guess. When he and John were announced, she glanced over, not at John but at Peter, calculation in her gaze. As an older woman approached the two of them, Belinda turned away to laugh at some remark by one of her courtiers.

"Captain Lord John! Do introduce me to your friend." The mother was an older version of the daughter, her beauty even more polished, her adamantine soul less well-camouflaged. After his experience with his stepmother, Peter could detect a rapacious harpy at fifty paces.

"Mrs. Weatherall, allow me to present my friend, Lord Ransome. The viscount and I served together in the Horse Guard. Peter, Mrs. Weatherall, our hostess."

Peter knew his duty. He bowed and tossed the woman the food her sort most enjoyed: a compliment. "Mrs. Weatherall, my friend did not exaggerate when he told me how beautiful your daughter was, but he did not mention your own loveliness."

She giggled like a girl and tapped him lightly with her fan. "Oh, you. But Lord Ransome, I am almost your aunt, for your mother, Lady Ransome, is like a sister to me!"

It made sense that one such as this would be friends with his stepmother. He managed not to show his disgust, not then, and not later, when Belinda finally turned from her other admirers and ignored John while flirting with Peter. It almost overcame his good manners when she mentioned how much she admired the Turner sisters, Laura and Pauline, whom she insisted on referring to as his sisters. He recovered and turned the remark off with a comment about a brooch she was wearing.

The regulatory half hour for a call passed with glacial slowness, but at last he was able to take his polite leave. Before they were down the front steps of the townhouse, John was explaining that his love was not at her best. She was intimidated by Peter's title. She knew how good a friend Peter was and wanted to impress him for John's sake. Peter needed to give her a chance, and he would come to admire her as John did. Though not as much, of course.

Peter didn't know how to respond. What was his duty when his friend was about to make a terrible mistake? He would keep his peace, he decided. John's passionate defense of the budding virago showed a dawning awareness of her true nature. And if John was too much of a gentleman to withdraw from the betrothal, unannounced though it was, Miss Weatherall and her harridan of a mother would drop him the instant they had a better prospect in mind, for John was only a second son. Though, to be sure, John's elder brother had so far had only daughters.

Peter returned to his hotel as the sun set and the air chilled. The manager must have been watching for him, for he hadn't taken two steps inside before the man was at his elbow. "Lord Ransome, you have visitors, my lord, and they cannot stay here."

"Visitors?" Peter looked around the foyer but could see no-one he knew. The manager tugged at his arm. "I let them into your rooms, my lord. I thought it best. But it is most irregular. Most irregular."

Frowning, Peter followed the fussing man, but the mystery was solved when the manager used his master key to unlock Peter's door. There, one on each fireside chair, were his sisters, Viv and Rose. Their governess slipped from her perch on his bed at his entry, standing almost to attention.

"Peter," the two girls chorused, and ran into his arms, burying their faces in his coat so he could hear only the occasional word of the half-sobbed explanation that poured out of them.

The manager cleared his throat. "They cannot stay here," he repeated.

"No, of course," Peter agreed, his mind racing. "But they will stay while I make other arrangements for tonight. Tea. They must be hungry." He looked at the governess. "Have you had anything to eat?" She shook her head.

"Food. Whatever you can manage," he ordered the man. "And a pot of tea."

Grumbling, the manager left, closing the door on his way out.

"You won't send us back?" Viv lifted her head to plead with him, tears still running down her cheeks. "Mama sold Rose!"

"No, no, I won't send you back," he assured her, his eyes on the governess, who was nodding.

The two distraught girls quieted under his soothing pats, and he guided them over to the chairs, sitting in the larger of the two and settling a sister on each side of him, perched on the wooden arms.

"Sit down, Miss Pettigrew. Can you explain, please?"

"It is true, my lord. Edwards drove Lady Ransome and Miss Rosalind into Barnstable in the gig yesterday morning. I was suspicious, so I instructed a groom to follow them. Her ladyship indentured Miss Rosalind to the mantua maker and left her there. Harry, the groom, was not sure what to do, but Miss Rosalind climbed out of the window of the room where they had locked her, so he put her up before him on the horse and brought her home. I thought it best to escort both girls to you, sir." She blushed. "I only had sufficient money for the stagecoach, my lord. It was not proper, but I did my best to look after the girls."

"You did quite right," Peter agreed. Better than right. The governess had spent her own money to defend the girls who were his to protect. Lady Ransome had gone too far. He would have his stepmother out of his house if it was the last thing he did. No. It couldn't be the last thing he did. He had to live to stand between the two girls and that evil woman. She could not be allowed to have charge of them ever again.

For tonight, though, he had a problem. He couldn't keep two schoolgirls here. Even if the hotel catered for females, which it didn't, he had barely enough funds to feed them all, let alone to pay for a room for them. It would be just for tonight. He'd see Richards again in the morning—beg a loan if he had to. Where could he take them tonight? Maybe John could help. He hoped so. His other town-based friends were less than respectable and would be no help at all.

A knock on the door heralded a pair of maids with laden trays. The two girls allowed Miss Pettigrew to draw them away and chivvy them into washing their hands and faces.

"Girls, I am going out to find you a place to stay for the night," Peter told them.

They turned alarmed faces to him. "We want to stay with you," Viv declared, a hint of hysteria in her voice.

"I will try to find a place we can all stay," he promised. "If I cannot do that tonight, I will by tomorrow." Somehow.

Now that their faces were clean, though, he noticed something. He tilted Rose's face to the lamp. Sure enough, she had a large bruise over one cheek. A hand-shaped bruise. "Who slapped you, sweetheart?"

Rose's voice was little more than a thread, and he had to bend close to hear it. "Madame Le Roux. I told her you were my guardian and Lady Ransome had no right to bring me to her, and she slapped me. She said Lady Ransome owed her money and she had taken me in part payment of the debt. She said I was worth next to nothing, and no one wanted to hear the opinion of a bastard."

"She is a very stupid woman if that is what she thinks," Peter told the girl, doing his utmost to keep his anger from his voice. He would save it for his stepmother and her mantua maker. A pair of monsters to treat a child so.

After a few more assurances, he managed to disengage himself from the two girls. Then he had to soothe the manager, who stopped him as he strode through the lobby to once again insist the girls could not stay the night at the hotel. Peter stopped that conversation with an abrupt demand to know if the man doubted his word as a gentleman. "I am on my way to arrange accommodation for my sisters. You have my thanks for allowing them to wait in my room, and for arranging a meal for them, but do not imagine I would allow them to remain here."

The manager stepped out of his way, intimidated by the stern, cold voice, and Peter hurried on to John's lodgings. His friend wasn't home. Perhaps he was at the house of his betrothed? But the butler denied he was present and when Peter, in desperation, asked for Miss Weatherall, she listened impatiently to his explanation of his problem, and told him she could do nothing for him. Mrs. Weatherall arrived to hear the end of her rejection, and expostulated. "My dear! Lord Ransome…"

"Lord Ransome is penniless, Mama," Miss Weatherall said. "And wants to foist his half-sisters off on dear Lord John. Both of his half-sisters!"

Mrs. Weatherall was as outraged as her daughter. "What! Including his father's…?"

Miss Weatherall nodded, and the women treated him to identical glares, their scorn rendering their features ugly.

Peter bowed. "I shall bother you no more. I will see myself out." He was a fool to expect anyone who was friends with his stepmother to be of any help.

An hour had passed, and he was no nearer to finding shelter for his sisters for the night. In near despair, he tried to think of some other person in London with whom he was well enough acquainted to ask them the favor of a bed.

Chapter Four

ARIAL WAS CROSSING the landing above the entrance hall on her way to the dining room when the door knocker sounded. She paused to watch as Barlowe made his way to the door. *Whomever could it be?* Her breath caught at the thought that Josiah might have tracked her to London, then released in a sigh when her butler stepped back and allowed the caller to enter.

Not Josiah. This caller was taller, and the hair disclosed when he removed his hat was fair while Josiah's was dark.

Whatever he said must have convinced Barlowe to at least accept the calling card he was holding out, for her man took it and gestured towards the little parlor. Arial called out before the butler could come in search of her.

"What is it, Barlowe?"

Both men looked up at her call, and she stopped breathing again. The gentleman was beautiful, in an entirely masculine fashion—every line of his face sculpted to perfection, his blue eyes framed in lashes that were surprisingly dark, given that his hair glinted gold in the light from her candles.

And she knew him. He was a foot taller than he'd been at thirteen, with broad shoulders she could swear owed nothing to his overcoat, but his eyes had not changed. Why was Peter Ransome calling on her some eighteen hours before their appointment?

"Lord Ransome begs a moment of your time, Lady Arial," the butler said. "A matter of some urgency, he says."

Peter bowed. "My apologies for bursting in on you like this, my lady. But I need help, and I do not know where else to turn."

Arial's mind raced. Bailiffs at his heels? A gambling debt? An angry lover? Was she now to find the flaws that Beau Ransome hid beneath his perfect skin? *Well. Better get it over with, then.* She began to descend the stairs. "Tell someone to let Miss Tulloch know that I am delayed, please, Barlowe."

"Thank you." Peter stepped forward to offer her his arm. His left arm, of course, so he was on her blind side. Arial was struck with a longing for her father, the only other man to ever escort her in such a fashion. Every evening, from the day of her fifteenth birthday, they would meet in the parlor, and he would offer her his arm to conduct her into dinner. Papa had broken with convention and used his right arm so she could see him without turning her head past her shoulder.

This was another experience entirely, and not just because he was on her blind side. They reached the door to the small parlor, and she dropped his arm to step inside, still analyzing the difference. He was taller than Papa. That was part of it. Arial was used to looking men in the eye or looking down at them. Only a couple of her footmen, and footmen were usually tall, were an inch or two taller than her. One of Cousin Josiah's complaints against her was that she was taller than he was. "Unnaturally large for a woman," was the way he put it.

Perhaps Peter's height explained the physical sensations that walking on his arm gave her. Unnaturally hot. Quivery. Slightly breathless.

Distance was helping. She took a seat and waved him to another. A footman scurried in to light the room's wall sconces then took up station in the corner. Sent by Barlowe, no doubt, to protect the mistress of the house should the visitor prove to have nefarious intent.

"Thank you for seeing me, Lady Arial," Peter said. "May I express my sincere condolences on the death of your father? I remember him well. He was a fine man."

Arial nodded. "He was. I miss him every day. I was sorry to hear of your loss, as well, Lord Ransome. Your father was very kind to me when I was a child." She wasn't sure what else to say, when that same father had left Peter in such a difficult situation.

Peter inclined his head. He was looking her in the eye, showing no reaction to the fine scars on her chin and forehead and the half-mask that hid the right side of her face.

Arial waited for him to introduce the reason for his call. He said nothing, but his fine eyebrows drew together as he frowned. He opened his mouth and then shut it again. Arial, conscious of her companion waiting upstairs, decided to prompt him.

"Did you call to speak of my father, Lord Ransome? Or is this about our appointment tomorrow?"

"I beg your pardon, my lady." Peter grimaced. "I am imposing, calling at this hour and without an invitation. But I could not think of anyone else in London I could ask… I am afraid I am here to beg a favor. Of course, if you turn me out, you are well within your rights. You barely know me, and I will understand if you do not feel able to help." He ran out of words again, spreading his hands and clenching them again as if reaching out for a way to communicate what he wanted.

"I will not turn you away without listening to your request," Arial assured him. For the sake of appeasing her curiosity if nothing else.

"Please say 'no' if it will inconvenience you—but truly, they are very well-behaved. One might say unnaturally so. And their governess is with them, of course. They will be no trouble, I assure you, and tomorrow, when my solicitor's office opens, I will be able to make other arrangements, I hope." He looked at her, pleading with his eyes.

Arial blinked and gave her head a small shake, but she still could not make sense of what he was asking. "I am sorry. I don't understand. Who are very well-behaved, and what is it that you want me to do?"

Peter spread his hands again, a helpless gesture that somehow made him all the more appealing. "I did not explain, did I? I am sorry. I do not know whether I am on my head or my heels. My lady, I arrived back at my hotel this evening to find that my two young sisters and their governess had run away and come to find me."

He paused, as if expecting Arial to comment. *Run away? But they are well-behaved?* Arial did not know what to think, though her heart went out to Peter, who was clearly out of his depth. She managed a faint, "How enterprising."

"I should explain that my stepmother was to blame, and Miss Pettigrew did the right thing."

The former Mrs. Turner. Arial wondered about the details, but it must have been bad to send a governess fleeing with her charges.

Peter was still talking. "I need to find somewhere for them to stay for the night. The hotel I am in, it does not permit—it is not suitable for females, especially gently-born schoolgirls."

He grimaced. "You know my circumstances. I need not scruple to say I have little ready cash. Not enough to pay for suitable accommodation." He made the same helpless gesture again.

"You would like me to invite your sisters to be my guests for the night," Arial said, just to check that she understood him. The poor little girls. She could only imagine what they had been through. And poor Peter, too, swallowing his pride to make such a request of a lady he hardly knew.

"I have no right…" he began again, but she waved him to silence.

"Of course, bring them here. I shall give orders for bedrooms to be prepared. Will you stay with them? If they have been through a traumatic experience, they will need you close."

He frowned again and she pre-empted his objection. "There can be no impropriety, since I have my companion and you have your sisters and their governess."

His relieved smile was a reward in itself. "Thank you. They have already asked… Thank you." He stood. "I will go and fetch them. I can never thank you enough."

"Where must you pick them up? Is it far?"

"The Wyvern and Crow. In Clerkenwell. It is perhaps a thirty-minute walk, so we should be here in one hour, my lady."

"Henry, order the carriage. As quickly as possible please. It will be faster, Lord Ransome, and much easier with baggage. While we wait, please join me and my companion. We are about to dine. Problems are always easier to solve when one is not hungry."

He bowed again, standing as she did. "I regret, my lady, that I am not dressed for the evening. I have been chasing all over town…"

"We are old acquaintances, are we not? If I do not regard it, you need not." Barlowe appeared at the door, and she strode through into the entrance hall again as she gave her orders for dinner to be served immediately, and an extra place laid. "Also, please have rooms made up for the two Misses Ransome, their governess, and Lord Ransome. Are the two girls accustomed to sharing, my lord?"

"They would prefer it, I think," he said, as he once again offered his arm. She hesitated, then gathered her courage. Best to begin as she meant to go on. "May I take your other arm, my lord? I find it awkward to have you on my blind side."

His eyes, which had been firmly fixed on her single eye, darted to the blank space on the half-mask that covered where the other had once been. He looked away again and immediately winged the right arm. "Of course. The fire?"

"Indeed." She wondered how much to tell him. "A burning beam pinned me by the head for several minutes, I am told. I remember little about it, but the damage it left speaks for itself." She sighed, thinking of the would-be suitor earlier today, who had fled her presence and made it no further than a plant stand in the entrance hall before losing his lunch.

Peter placed his right hand over hers and gave a comforting squeeze. "When I saw the mask, I assumed that the scars beneath must be worse than those otherwise visible. I am truly sorry that you lost the sight on your right side."

Arial shrugged as they mounted the stairs. "I lived. For the most part, I consider that a blessing, particularly when I remember my father would have been all alone had I not done so. This way, Lord Ransome." She indicated the door to the dining room.

As they came into the room, Clara entered from the drawing room.

"Clara, this is Lord Ransome. He is a friend from my childhood and will be coming to stay for a few days with his sisters and their governess."

She turned to Peter. "Lord Ransome, Miss Tulloch is my companion and my dear friend."

Peter took a couple of steps forward, hand outstretched. "Surely, I remember you. Were you not that marvelous governess who made nature come alive for me when I visited the Stancroft estate as a boy?"

Clara allowed him to mime a kiss to her hand. And was that a blush? "I am flattered you remember me, my lord."

"How could I forget? I so envied Arial—Lady Arial—her fortune in having a teacher who made lessons interesting!"

DINNER COMPRISED A dozen or so dishes all served to the table at once. Peter attempted to serve the ladies. Arial told him he had no time for such ceremony and instructed him to feed himself. Even so, he was but halfway through the food on his plate when a footman arrived to announce that his transport was ready.

He half rose, then sat again, anxious to get back to his sisters but conscious it was the height of bad manners to leave the table halfway through the meal.

"Go," Arial said. "Clara and I do not regard it, and you will want to reassure your sisters as quickly as possible."

"One moment," Miss Tulloch commanded. She took a bread roll from a basket of them, sliced it open and buttered it. "Here," she said, passing it over. "Put your meat into that, my lord, and finish it in the carriage."

In the carriage, feeling much more optimistic now he was no longer hungry, Peter considered his impressions of his childhood friend and her companion.

The former governess had changed little in fifteen years. She was still a slight woman with sharp blue eyes in a plain but pleasant face, straight brown hair drawn back in a simple knot, and a no-nonsense manner. She had seemed old to his thirteen years, but she must have been in her forties back then, for she could not yet have turned sixty.

She and Arial were clearly friends, despite the age gap between them.

Would she remain with the household when Arial married? Peter, thinking back to the lively discussion over dinner, hoped she would, then caught the trend of his thoughts. Had he decided to offer for Arial, then?

His disgust at marrying for a fortune was no less. He had to ignore his pride, though, and protect his sisters. This was the only quick way to secure safety for his sisters, and the surest.

It helped to further soothe the raw hurt of being a fortune hunter that the lady needed the protection of his name and title. The idea of a convenient marriage had become a lot more palatable in the past hour or so.

She would not have been a beauty even without the scars he could see, and he shuddered to imagine the damage she kept hidden. That was all to the good. His stepmother and her younger daughter were beauties, and they were shrews.

He had not expected—did not even want—a love match. He had his father's example to show that romantic love was a fleeting thing, burning brightly for long enough to draw a person into foolishness, and leaving a lifetime of regret and problems.

He wanted a wife he could respect; a wife who respected him. Arial was kind, clever, and capable. Those were qualities that would wear much better than surface beauty. He could not quite picture them as lovers, but he could imagine them being friends.

Chapter Five

ARIAL, AT HER morning ablutions, was hoping that her third candidate would be more promising than yesterday's two, for she dreaded a future as Peter's wife. In her mind, her ideal husband was tolerant, intelligent, and kind—Peter was clearly all three. She had envisaged a relationship of mutual respect, in which she lived much as she had before, but with the added bonus of another person in the household, to meet at meals and perhaps to share an evening of music or cards with, on the occasions that he chose to stay home. A man with whom she might, in time, become friends.

She could never have that comfortable future with Peter. If only his outer beauty had covered an inner ugliness of spirit! A silly thought, for if he'd been arrogant or cruel or mean she could not afford to marry him. No point in exchanging one persecutor for another, and one, furthermore, with absolute legal rights over her.

Peter had begun to impress her when he swallowed his pride to ask for her help on behalf of his sisters, when he had, without hesitation, offered his left arm in lieu of his right, when he had greeted Clara with such remembered affection.

Then he had returned with the two girls and their governess. Watching his loving care of them had softened her still further.

After seeing her guests settled in, she had gone up to bed feeling more hopeful about the future than she'd been since her father died.

But a night's thinking had brought wiser counsel. Peter might be everything she dreamed of in a husband, but that made it all the more likely she would fall in love with him. Mr. Richards had reported he was reluctant to marry for money, but she thought he would come to it. She had learned enough to know he was driven by a strong sense of responsibility, and by love for his two half-sisters.

To marry someone whom she loved but who could never love her. Wouldn't that be a kind of living hell? Far more comfortable and less immediately dangerous than the one her cousin threatened, but lacerating to the soul, nonetheless.

At breakfast, Arial told Peter that she had another candidate to interview before she saw him. "The appointment is made, and it would be rude not to keep it."

He inclined his head. "Of course. And you would be foolish not to consider your options."

"Whatever I decide, you and your sisters are welcome to stay until you have had time to consider your own." It was an impulsive offer and a foolish one. If she married someone else, her husband would have the right to throw him out of the house.

He thanked her, but his reserve suggested he was thinking the same thing.

He would have every right to stay if I married him.

Afraid the insidiously welcome thought might show on what he could see of her face, Arial changed the subject. "Why not take your sisters sightseeing this morning? You can use the coach, and Cook can pack some food to take with you."

By mid-morning, they left Arial to wait for candidate three, who proved not to be her salvation. He had inherited family property from a brother who had been the most recent in a succession of bad managers and gamblers and was cheerfully open about his belief that finding a rich wife was a kind of gamble. He assured her he had abjure all wagers and games of chance since finding the mess his brother had left behind him, but sporting language peppered his conversation.

When she thanked him for coming and told him that she'd let him know, he shrugged and commented, "Which is a polite way of saying, 'thank you but no thank you.' Never mind, Lady Arial. I thought it was a long shot, for who in their senses would take a chance on a St. Aubyn? But something will turn up, I'm sure."

Arial told him she hoped it did, and watched him stroll, untroubled, out of her study and out of her life. Such a happy-go-lucky approach to life had its appeal, but not in a husband.

She refreshed herself with a cup of tea, taken at her desk while she tried to work her way through correspondence from her business managers. Her unsettled mind could not focus as it should, and so she put the papers away and instead pulled out a blank pad, which she ruled into two columns.

In one column, she listed the things she knew to Peter's favor. He had been a nice boy. Kind to a younger female child when he was not off tagging after the adult men or playing with the boys from the village. He was still kind—brave, too. She did not discount how hard it must have been to approach a stranger for the favor of accommodation for his sisters. According to Mr. Richards, he was thrifty, hard-working, and determined to do better by his land and his tenants than his father had before him.

At the top of the *against* column she noted his exceptional good looks. It was small of her, she knew, but she would have preferred a husband who did not attract admiring stares wherever he went. The contrast between her ugliness and his beauty could not fail to provoke stares and comments.

His kindness went into this column, too. She must, at all costs, guard her heart against reading too much meaning into good manners and an unwillingness to hurt.

His obnoxious relatives counted against him. They were not his fault, of course, but they were a factor that needed to be considered.

She sat for a long time, staring at the sheet of paper. One side was covered with points in favor of the match. The other had only those three points. It would depend on the interview, then. Perhaps he would turn her down, and then she would have to send Mr. Richards to hunt out another batch of reluctant fortune hunters. And she could not escape the conviction that she was running out of time.

She heard the sightseers return half an hour before the interview was due. A tap on her door heralded Clara, come with a message to say Peter had gone to freshen up, but would be at her disposal at the appointed time.

Arial asked for a fresh tea tray, and for Peter to be shown to her study when he was ready. It seemed wrong to treat a guest in her house as she had the other applicants and interview him in the little parlor downstairs.

He came at the same time as the tea, took the seat she indicated, and talked easily about his sisters' reaction to Hyde Park, the Houses of Parliament, the royal palaces, and other sights they had driven by. "We stopped at the Tower of London, which they found thrilling."

He fell silent after the maid brought him his tea and left the room, closing the door behind her at Arial's request.

"Lord Ransome," she began, "you know my reasons for seeking a marriage, and I believe I know yours. You want to repair the fortunes of your house, is that not so?"

He pressed his lips together as if catching back words, then must have decided to meet frankness with frankness. "I would not have put it like that. I want to secure the futures of those who depend on me—my sisters, servants, and tenants."

He hesitated again, then leaned forward, fixing her with his gaze. "Richards will have told you that my father left a mountain of debt when he died, mortgages on the estates just part of the whole mess. I can bring the estates back to profit, given time, but time is what I do not have." He rubbed a hand through his hair, a gesture of frustration that left him looking tousled and more attractive than ever.

"Your sisters?" Arial prompted.

He nodded. "My sisters. They cannot return to Three Oaks while my stepmother resides there. Either they or she must live elsewhere, and I do not have an elsewhere to offer."

He heaved a sigh. "I hope you will believe me when I say that I also want to be of service to you. Even without our past history, I would not want to abandon a lady in your circumstances. Given that I feel in some way responsible for your injuries—" He put up a hand at her shocked gasp. "I don't mean that the way it sounds. It is just…"

He stood to pace, not meeting her eye. "I should have been there. I crept out after dark. You may not remember, but I had a dog who was a ferocious rabbiter."

Arial nodded. "Sally. I remember." She remembered the argument he had had with his father and hers, over whether he should be allowed to go night-rabbiting. It was too dangerous, they had insisted.

"I was meeting some of the boys from the village. When the alarm went up…" He sighed again. "I've always wondered. If Sally and I were in my room, as we should have been, would she have given the alarm? Even if we'd not been in time to put out the fire, could I have got you and your brother out in time? Would Mother have lived, and your mother as well?"

He grimaced as he sat back down in his chair. "I know I can't change the past, but if I help you, perhaps I can redeem myself."

Arial was shaking her head. "You and Sally would probably have been the first on our floor to be overcome by the smoke, Peter. Your room was directly above it, and it was well aflame before it reached our floor. Indeed, my father used to wonder how you got out alive, since the floor to your room went up all at once."

Should she tell him how it started, or would that add even more guilt? Certainly, her father had never recovered from his own part in the disaster.

When she was Arial's governess, Clara used to say, "Tell the truth and shame the devil."

He insisted, "I may have been able to do something," and made up her mind.

"Have you not heard how the fire started? The report on the investigation was in my father's papers. He must have sent a copy to your father, for there was a letter…" A letter that rambled incoherently. Lord Ransome must have been drunk when he wrote it.

"Tell me."

"It began in the billiards room."

"But the billiards room was being redecorated. The door was locked."

How to put this? "According to the report, the outside doors had been left open to the terrace after we were sent to bed. A matter of allowing paint fumes to escape, I believe. The investigators believe that the fire started in the materials heaped in the corner. Wood scraps, turpentine, paint, offcuts from the wallpaper."

"I can guess the rest. Were our fathers drinking? I remember my mother had quarreled with my father over coming drunk to bed each night. They decided to take a look at the room, I suppose. Did one of them drop a candle?"

"Perhaps. Neither of them remembered doing so, but perhaps they left one alight in the room and it blew over, or perhaps sparks caught and smoldered and neither of them noticed." No need to say that her father had gone for a walk, leaving his friend smoking on the terrace. The report did not say, but Arial remembered angry words between the two friends that summer. "Neither of them was in the room when it went up in flames, and the conflagration in that room was complete. Before anyone noticed to give the alarm, the fire had taken too strong a hold. That room and the ones above on the next two floors were part of a single inferno."

"My mother's room. And the boys' side of the children's

floor."

Arial could not stop the tears spilling over onto her cheek, but she would continue on now that she had begun. "They think my mother must have tried to get John, my brother. They were found—" she swallowed hard—"what was left of them—huddled in the corner of the playroom, just yards from the door to the back stairs. But the stairs, too, were gone."

She felt Peter more than saw him through the veil of tears. He had crouched before her, holding her hands in his strong ones, gently stroking them with his thumbs. "Lord Stancroft saved you. I remember my father mentioning that."

She nodded and took a shuddering breath so that she could speak more calmly. "I was glad of it in time."

PETER WANTED TO pull her into his arms and comfort her as he would Viv or Rose. How she must have suffered. To lose a mother and a brother in such a way. Then months of pain from the burns. Or longer, most probably. She had lost an eye, too, she said.

He knew that she went veiled whenever she left her home, for his stepsisters had tittered about it, wondering aloud how much more beast-like she could have become, since she was no beauty to begin with. And he had seen that she wore that half-mask constantly, even here in her own home.

She withdrew her hands from his and wiped the eye that showed. Then she stiffened her spine, shoulders back, chin up, a soldier ready to face whatever came. "The fire was not your fault, and you do not owe me marriage," she declared.

Perhaps true, but it wasn't the point. Peter took his seat again. "Thank you for telling me what happened. It makes it easier, I think, to know I could have done nothing if I had been where I should." *How to put this?* Peter had never found it easy to put his thoughts into words, but he had to try. "I meant I wanted to help you because of my debt to you—or, rather, my family's debt to yours, given what you've told me. Also, because helping those unjustly persecuted is the right thing to do. I'd like to answer another question, if you do not mind, and ask it of you, too."

At her nod, he continued, "What do I want from marriage? I will tell you, and when I am done, I want to know: what do *you* want from marriage?"

From the slight widening of her eye, he concluded that he had surprised her. "Whatever our reasons for agreeing to wed, if we do agree, we will then be married, and marriage is for a lifetime. I want..." he struggled for words again, and then they came in a rush. "I want what I saw in your parents' life. A partner. A friend. Someone who is prepared to listen to me, to tell me if I am wrong, to praise me if I am right, to help me when I need it, and to take my help when they do. Someone who is at my side and on my side."

"I like that," Arial said, her voice soft. "I remember them like that, too."

"I know we are not making a love match, and perhaps that is to the good. I have seen love matches turn horribly wrong. By the time I came along, my parents no longer loved one another if they ever did. My father claimed that he loved Rose's mother, but then he abandoned her and married Mrs. Turner, whom he also claimed to love." He grimaced. "I would rather be wed to a friend than come to hate someone I thought I loved."

"What of children?" Arial asked.

Peter nodded. "I would like children." Even as he said the words, he wondered if she had misunderstood. Did she think he was offering only friendship? Did she hope to be a wife in name only? How could he ask a lady—and a sheltered maiden, at that— whether she understood the nature of the marital activities that resulted in children, and whether she intended to favor her acquired husband with access to her bed?

She was braver than him, it seemed, for though her voice cracked and caught on the words, she asked, "You are willing to bed me, then? Despite how I look?"

"I am," he assured her. And would have no trouble doing so. Her high-waisted gown did not disguise her lush figure.

"We can keep the room dark. I can wear my half mask when we…" She reddened as she waved her hand, her frankness not quite up to the task of naming the marital act.

Peter started to assure her that he wouldn't ask that of her, but she spoke before he could. "I think you need to see the full horror of my face before we make a commitment, Peter." She was fumbling with the strings of her mask.

He nodded, his mouth drying as his mind reviewed the wounds and the scars he had seen after injuries such as hers. War, unfortunately, offered too many opportunities for gruesome burns.

He detected pride in her gaze, a bit of fear, and some defiance. Her expression said as clearly as words that she expected rejection. But he had no difficulty keeping his face impassive. The damage was far from the worst he'd ever seen, and well-healed. But the lid drooped over an empty eye socket, and the burned skin had healed in lumps and knots of flesh. *The poor girl*. His heart hurt for all she must have suffered. "Does it pain you?" he asked.

Arial shook her head, then nodded. "It is mostly numb, but I get phantom pains at times, especially around where the eye should be. Nothing of any moment. I have a cream to use if the skin dries overmuch."

"Nothing of any moment" hinted at the pain she had lived through and left behind her. His admiration for her courage transmuted his pity into respect. She sat stiffly, one hand clenched on her mask, still waiting for him to do what? Revile her? Rush from the room? *How can I set her at ease?*

He passed her his cup. "May I have another?" he asked.

Her chin dropped before she caught the movement and composed herself. "Of course." She took the cup and busied herself over the tea makings. "You do not mind my face?"

"Only for what you have suffered, Arial. It does not change my mind about wishing to marry you, and it will not prevent me from... er... indulging our marital affections."

She nodded as she passed him his tea, a short, decisive movement of the head then settled back into her chair and focused for a moment on replacing the half mask. As soon as the worst of the scars were safely hidden, the tension went out of her. He had been going to suggest she didn't need the mask when they were together, but apparently, she felt better with it on. *Small steps, Peter.*

"Very well," she said, her tone brisk. "If you are willing, I am willing."

Very willing. His errant mind had wandered. Speculation about whether the burns had reached her body had drifted to the shape of her body under those layers of fabric. He dragged his attention back to the practicalities. "I take it you would like the ceremony as soon as possible?"

"Yes. I asked Richards about that. A common license would allow us to wed in your parish or in mine without posting the banns, or he has also made enquiries about a special license. If we can obtain one, we could marry immediately, here in London." She shrugged. "Richards knows the process." She would not argue for a special license, afraid to disclose the need for haste that drove her. Surely Richards was right, and her cousin would not attack her here in London? But she had not believed he would accost her in her house, either.

Peter, though, understood without being told. "The sooner you have a husband, the sooner your villainous cousin is disarmed, and the sooner, too, my bachelor status is amended so my stepmother cannot use it to argue for the return of my sisters."

Arial nodded, relieved that the benefits went both ways. "A special license, then?" she said.

"Shall I call on Richards and see if his enquiries have borne fruit?" Peter asked. "But first, let us tell my sisters and your companions the good news."

VIVIENNE AND ROSALIND expressed delight that their brother was to marry Arial, and relief that the couple wanted the two sisters to live with them. "You are to come to the wedding," Arial told them, "which we hope will be later today or tomorrow morning."

The girls looked at Miss Pettigrew in alarm. "But what will we wear?" Vivienne asked.

"I packed your best visiting gown," said Miss Pettigrew to Vivienne, and then both of them looked at Rosalind. "I don't fit into my visiting gown," Vivienne objected, "and Rose doesn't have one.

Miss Pettigrew's brows drew together. "I am afraid I was able to bring very little with us, and the girls have, in any case, grown out of everything they own." Indeed, the dresses they wore and the pinafores that covered those garments had been repeatedly mended, and were too tight and too short, more so on Rosalind than Vivienne, though Vivienne was the taller and sturdier of the two.

"You must have new gowns, of course," Arial agreed. "Clara, where might we find something suitable ready-made or near finished?"

Clara had no idea, but Miss Pettigrew had worked in London before being employed to teach the Ransome sisters. "We might try Smith's Emporium," she suggested.

"Then I propose an expedition," Arial said. She smiled at her soon-to-be sisters. "We shall see you outfitted for the wedding now, and then order you each a whole new wardrobe."

So, Clara and Miss Pettigrew rode away in the carriage with

two very excited girls, leaving Arial to contemplate Vivienne's parting words. "What shall you wear for your wedding, Lady Arial?"

Chapter Six

RICHARDS HAD DONE a sterling job of preparing the ground. When he and Peter arrived at Doctors Commons, they had no more than an hour's wait before they arrived in front of a cleric who questioned them narrowly, then scurried off with the papers. Another wait, but this time of only ten minutes before the man returned. "Your request is granted," they were told. "Your license is being prepared and will go up for the archbishop's seal during the afternoon. Return in the morning to collect it. The fee will be five pounds."

Richards counted out the notes while Peter asked, "If it will be ready, may we not return to collect it today?"

The man managed to both snort and sneer but agreed they could receive the license today if they returned no earlier than four but before five.

"You will need a vicar to wed you," Richards pointed out, as they exited the warren of offices to find that the weather had turned cold and blustery. "Let's take a cab back to my chambers. The vicar of the church on that street will oblige if he is available this evening."

The afternoon quickly disappeared. They paid the vicar's fee and arranged to collect him at five o'clock, sent a message to Arial to let her know that they had organized both license and minister, and then stopped at a coffee shop for a bite to eat before repairing to Richards's chambers so that Peter could sign the marriage settlements.

Richards suggested that their next stop should be a tailor to see if he had something part-made that might be suitable for the wedding, but watching the solicitor handing out Arial's money to one person after another on his behalf had set Peter's teeth on edge.

"I have suitable formal wear in my baggage at Lady Arial's," he informed the solicitor. "But that reminds me. The Ransome jewelry I sent for you to sell? You said you still had some of the pieces. Are there any rings suitable to give my lady?"

"I believe so," Richards said. "A good notion. Let us see."

The safe disgorged a small case containing a good two thirds of the items Peter had sent to the solicitor. "I have thus far sold the less well-known pieces," Richards explained.

"So as not to panic the creditors," Peter acknowledged.

"Also, in order to retain their value. If the jewelers know we are seeking purchasers for a large quantity of jewelry, they will assume the seller is in dire straits, and will offer a lower price."

Peter was sorting through the various bags, boxes, and cases. "I shall show these to Lady Arial, and she can decide what she wants to use and what can go back in the safe. Would you keep them, Richards, until I have arranged new accommodation for my father's widow?" He had sorted out several rings, and found a box to put them in. This, he slipped into his pocket.

"My mother's pearls." He held up the long string and set it to one side. "There should be a brooch that turns it into a choker. Ah, yes." The brooch joined the necklace. Peter looked through several more containers, to retrieve matching earrings, a bracelet, and a delicate tiara. "Perhaps Lady Arial might wish to wear these today. My father had them reset with diamonds for my mother, but the pearls themselves belonged to my great-grandmother." He grimaced. "I suppose they should be cleaned, and the clasps checked."

"I can organize that for you, my lord," Richards offered.

Peter began putting the jewelry back into the case. "Shall I leave you to it then, Richards? I am sure you have better things to do than keeping me company. I will go and see if I can find my friend, Captain Forsythe. I mean to ask him to witness my wedding. Shall I collect the license and meet you and the vicar across the road at the vicarage at five o'clock?"

That agreed, they parted. Peter called at John's lodgings and found his friend was out again. John's man Thorne had been his soldier-servant for years and knew Peter well from his time in the army. Perhaps that was why he was freer with his tongue than most servants. "I told him you called, my lord, and he went to your hotel. They said you had left and had not given them a direction."

Thorne was clearly in John's confidence. "When he gets back, tell him I was not sure where I would be staying or for how long, but I now have a fixed address for as long as I am in Town. Tell him—" *No, better still.* "Actually, don't tell him. I will write him a note with my direction. You may congratulate me, Thorne. I am getting married this evening, and I would like Captain Forsythe to stand up with me."

Thorne said all the right things while fetching what Peter needed to write a note. He had blotted it dry and handed it to Thorne when he heard a key in the outer door, and it opened.

"Peter!" John saw Peter and strode forward with his hand out. "Belinda told me about your sister. I am so sorry I was out yesterday evening. How did you manage? Did you find someone to take her? I went to your hotel, and they said you had left."

"I found a place for all of us to stay," Peter said. "Me and both sisters. In fact, it connects to the reason that I am here. I'm getting married this evening, and I wanted to ask you to stand up with me."

"I thought… I did not realize you were betrothed." As if the news had only just seeped into his consciousness, his eyes lit, and he began to smile. "Yes, of course, Peter. I would be proud to stand up with you. Where are you getting married? Do I know the bride? How long have you been courting?"

Peter hesitated. It wasn't John. He knew his friend would have his back whatever the circumstances. Beyond a doubt, though, anything Peter told John would be repeated to Miss Weatherall. "That is why I came to town," he explained. "To meet with my betrothed and her man of business. Lady Arial Bledisloe has done me the honor of accepting my offer. Her father, the Earl of Stancroft, was a close friend of my father's, and we knew one another when we were children."

"Congratulations. If this is what you want, I could not be more pleased. I am merely surprised you have never mentioned her." He barked a short laugh. "I suppose I was so full of my own news I did not let you get a word in edgewise. But what of your sisters? You will hardly want them with you if you are to be wed. I suppose you will be sending them back to their mother?" He flushed and added, "Lady Ransome's daughter, in any case. I suppose you might have to make other arrangements for the… um… your other sister."

Miss Weatherell had been talking, then. Peter had certainly spoken of his two sisters during the years he and John had served together, but he was fairly certain that he'd never mentioned the circumstances of Rose's birth.

"Viv and Rose will stay with me and Arial," he said, firmly.

"The lady doesn't mind?" John asked. "I mean that… um."

"That Rose is my father's daughter by his mistress? She doesn't hold that circumstance against the girl." His irritation must be seeping into his voice because John hastened to apologize.

"I beg your pardon. Even if it was any of my business, I'm the last person to hold a parent's peccadillos against a child. What time will you need me tonight? And where?"

Peter gave him the address. "I sent a message to Lady Arial to let her know I would be back by six o'clock with the vicar and the license, so I imagine we shall marry shortly after that."

John looked as if he had more questions, but if so, he thought better of asking them. Instead, he suggested that the two of them might go out for a celebratory drink. With over an hour to kill before he could pick up the license, Peter agreed.

AFTER THE SHOPPING party left, Arial sent for her maid. She should have thought of her wedding when she told Nancy what to pack. She had brought several changes of clothes suitable for traveling, half a dozen round gowns, and a single more formal gown suitable for changing into for dinner. It would have to be that, then, though it was in a sober dark blue, and she'd worn it the evening before when she dined with Peter.

She supposed it didn't matter. Peter was marrying her for her dowry and out of pity. What she wore would not change the reality of her ruined face and over-abundant form. Still, it was the only wedding she would ever have, and she wished her clothes to be pretty since she could not be.

But her maid Nancy had a surprise for her. She had exceeded her instructions, packing two other formal gowns, newly made to the current fashions by the village dressmaker, though with a higher neckline and three-quarter sleeves to hide the dark tracery of scars on her neck and arms. Clara, bless her, had talked Arial into purchasing one in a warm rose, and another in a shimmering gold.

Arial liked pretty dresses. She might tell herself it was futile— a monster in a silk dress was still a monster—but she had to be clothed, after all. So why not wear colors and styles that were pleasing to the eye?

She was delighted Nancy had thought ahead.

"I thought you might want to dress up if you are being courted, my lady. Either of these would be really lovely to wear for your wedding. And the new paisley shawl goes with both, if it's a bit cold like."

A message arrived from Peter to say all was arranged, and the wedding would be this evening. It was happening so fast. Peter also wrote that he wished to bring a friend with him—someone he knew from army days—so, there would be someone else to meet. A stranger who would stare, and who would perhaps disapprove of beautiful Peter throwing himself away on Lady Caliban.

Before she could fret herself to flinders, the shopping party returned. Rosalind's eyes were red from weeping, and tears welled again when Arial asked whether they had succeeded in finding something pretty to wear for the wedding. "Oh dear," Arial said to Clara. "Was there nothing available?"

"Yes," Clara told her. "We found them a lovely dress each for tonight, and another two for day wear. We also ordered some other items. Miss Pettigrew tells me they have nothing fit to wear. They will each need a completely new wardrobe, from inside out, from top to toe."

Rosalind wailed and buried her face on Vivienne's shoulder.

Miss Pettigrew explained, "Miss Rosalind is just a little over-whelmed."

Vivienne explained, "Rosalind has never had a new dress before."

Rosalind sobbed something. The words "a whole new ward-robe" were all Arial could distinguish.

Arial was unused to comforting a weeping girl, but if it was her, she would prefer plain-speaking. "Rosalind, you and Vivienne will be living with me and Peter from now on. You will never again have to wear hand-me-downs, or clothes that don't fit. You will be dressed and treated as befits the sister of a viscount. Now. Would you like to show me what you have purchased?"

They enjoyed a happy hour examining the new clothes. Clara and Miss Pettigrew had also purchased undergarments and stockings, and even a couple of sets of indoor slippers. "They will need shoes," Clara said. "Vivienne's are too small, and Rosalind's are too large and through at the heel, besides."

"My hand-me-downs," Vivienne explained. "Lady Arial, if it is going to be too expensive, we could maybe pick something up from the barrows for me? Rose has never had a new pair of shoes."

"The barrows?" Arial looked from Vivienne to Miss Pettigrew.

Miss Pettigrew blushed. "Second-hand clothes and shoes. They sell them in some of the markets. I couldn't afford anything more, but I couldn't let the girls go naked."

Arial was tempted to hug all three of them: both girls and the generous governess. Not that she knew them well-enough for such a gesture. "You don't need to worry about money, Vivienne. I can well afford to dress the two of you—or, after today, your brother can. It will give me great pleasure to make sure you have everything you need. Both of you."

Thinking to lighten the atmosphere, she suggested, "Let us order some tea and biscuits, and take a look at what I have to wear this evening. You can help me decide."

Discussing the relative merits of the rose and the gold, Rosalind recovered her balance, and shyly offered the opinion that the rose was pretty, but the gold was fit for a princess. "And a bride should be a bit like a princess, should she not?"

Vivienne's agreement was enthusiastic. Clara said, "She is quite right. It should be the gold." Even Miss Pettigrew and Nancy were nodding.

"The gold it is, then," Arial agreed.

"Do you have a mask to match?" Vivienne asked.

When she had been much younger, Arial had experimented with painting her papier-mâché masks in a flesh color, with an eye drawn in place of her own. The result had not been happy, the bland unmoving solid surface too much of a contrast against her own living flesh on the other side of her face. "All of my masks are like this one," she said, bracing herself for questions about why she kept half her face covered.

But Peter must've explained, for Vivienne merely said, "We should paint it gold, to go with the dress."

Rosalind's eyes lit up. "With flowers or swirls. Butterflies perhaps. Or, I know. Do you have some more of this lace?" She stroked the falls of delicate lace that trimmed the cuffs, hem, and neckline.

Arial began to shake her head, but Nancy said, "Yes, Miss. The dressmaker sent some so we could make repairs. I think I packed it." She disappeared into the dressing room and returned with a paper package. "Here it is."

Vivienne and Rosalind turned beseeching eyes onto Arial. Vivienne spoke for them both. "May we, my lady? May we, please?"

Miss Pettigrew added, "Rosalind is very talented."

Well, what was the harm? She had half a dozen spare masks, and it would give the girl something to do this afternoon, since at least two more hours must pass before they dressed for the wedding. "Very well. Clara, can you set them up somewhere with one of my masks and whatever else they need?"

Arial went back to her brooding about the unexpected guest and the risks she was taking that Peter might turn out to be a domestic tyrant. But Clara soon pulled her away from that to come and talk to Cook about a wedding supper, and one way or another the afternoon passed more easily than she expected. When it was time to fetch the girls from their painting, they refused to let Arial see the results.

"It has to dry," Vivienne explained.

Arial left the girls to their governess and went to have her bath. The knock on her bedroom door came three quarters of an hour later, when she was clothed again and sitting in front of her mirror while Nancy dressed her hair.

"It is the little misses, my lady," Nancy said, when she'd opened the door.

Arial checked that her mask—loosened to facilitate the hair

dressing—was fully in place and called, "Come in, girls."

Clara and Miss Pettigrew entered with the two girls. All in their best. All beaming. "Vivienne and Rosalind, you look wonderful," Arial told them. What a difference a well-fitting dress made. They looked like young ladies rather than neglected waifs, from their neatly plaited hair to the slippers that matched their dresses; their dresses matched their eyes—blue for Vivienne and green for Rosalind.

"You look lovely, too, my lady," Vivienne said.

"Call me Arial," Arial suggested. "After today, we shall be sisters, we three. I have always wanted a sister."

Vivienne and Rosalind looked at one another and nodded. Vivienne again took the spokesperson role. "We are so glad you are to be our sister, my lady. Arial. Will you call us Viv and Rose, like Peter does?"

"Of course, you darlings," Arial agreed.

Viv was holding her hands behind her back. Rose nudged her. Viv hissed, "I was just going to do it." She turned back to Arial. "We have your mask. We hope you like it." And she pulled it from behind her back as Arial composed herself to say something complimentary.

Chapter Seven

IT WAS A thing of beauty. They had left the background white and decorated it with gilded lines and swirls in a delicate filigree. Lace trimmed the top and side, attached behind the mask, and the edge was trimmed all around with tiny, paste jewels that caught the light and sparkled. Arial stared at it, entranced.

Her silence made Viv ask in an anxious tone, "Do you like it?"

"I love it." Why had it never occurred to her to adorn the mask, beyond that first failed attempt to mimic a face? She sat back down on the chair in front of the mirror and held the golden concoction up in front of her every-day, blank, white half-face. The transformation was astounding. Instead of the familiar half-person, half-monster she was used to seeing reflected, the woman in the mirror before her was fey, mysterious, and attractive.

She gazed for a long moment before the nervous fidgeting of the girls caught her attention. They were looking over her shoulder, their expressions saying, as clear as words, that they were waiting on her judgement.

As she turned to face them, Rose blurted, "We could have done better if we had had longer."

Viv spoke at the same time. "We could make one for each of your gowns, Arial. If you would like."

"I would like," Arial assured them. For her soon-to-be husband, as well as for herself. She could do nothing about her unfashionable curves except make the best of them, which her dressmaker had done. Peter would not need to blush for her appearance in that regard.

But faced with the ugly expanse of white where her face should be, people did not see her figure or her clothes. People would still stare, she knew. But perhaps in wonder rather than disgust. It was certainly worth a try.

There was another knock on the door. Nancy crossed the room to open it part-way and slipped outside to speak to the person in the passage. Arial, meanwhile, put the gold mask down, with some reluctance, and reached for the box of ribbons in her bottom drawer. Sure enough, as she remembered, the box contained ribbons in the colors of the girls' dresses—a light blue for Viv and green for Rose.

"A gift from me to you, to wear in your hair today," she told them.

Nancy returned as Clara was tying Rose's ribbon and Miss Pettigrew Viv's. "Lord Ransome has arrived, my lady, and is changing for the wedding. He will be fifteen minutes, Mr. Barlowe says. Mr. Richards and the vicar are in the parlor, and Mr. Barlowe is having refreshments served. Lord Ransome's friend is expected shortly."

"Thank you, Nancy. Will you finish my hair, please? Then you can help me with my mask, and we can go down."

Nancy held out a flat leather-bound box. "My lord asks that you wear these, my lady. They were his mother's."

Arial took and opened the box, a lump coming into her throat. The best she had expected from this marriage of convenience was politeness and tolerance. Instead, she had two new sisters and now this. His mother's jewelry. Even when he'd proclaimed that he wanted more than a mere civil arrangement, she had not expected the total acceptance that this implied.

She was stepping into his mother's place as Viscountess Ransome, and—was it too much to assume?—as mother of the next viscount. That is what these pretty pearl and diamond adornments said to her. "Look how well this goes with your mask," she told the girls, showing them the set.

"Right, then, my lady," said Nancy, briskly. "We'll have to rearrange the hair a little to fit the tiara."

Miss Pettigrew suggested leaving, but Arial insisted she wanted her sisters to stay with her and walk down with her when she was ready. It took only a few minutes to fix the tiara into her hair, and to put on the necklace, wrapped three times around her neck and fastened with the brooch so that a loop dropped towards the cleft between her breasts.

Arial touched the earrings in their box. "How will I wear these? My lobes are not pierced."

"I have an idea, my lady." Nancy found a couple of slender ribbons and threaded an earring on to one before using it to tie around the ear on Arial's good side. A pale peach, the ribbon was near invisible against her skin.

"We'll do the other and the mask behind the dressing screen," Arial decided, and led the way. When she stepped out, Nancy beaming behind her, the delight in the gazes of the two girls was heartening. Clara wiped away a tear, as she said, "My dear, you are so beautiful."

"You look like a fairy princess," Viv asserted.

Arial reserved judgement. She had always thought fairies to be frail little creatures, and no one had ever thought her frail, even before the fire. But when she stepped in front of the mirror, she had to concede there was much to be said for Viv's opinion. It was the gown, of course, and the jewels, and the mask. But she truly did present a gratifying appearance for her wedding. Two impossible things. She'd never thought to have a wedding. She'd never thought to know how it felt to see admiration in the eyes of others.

Would Peter, too, be pleased with how she looked?

"Let us go down," she said.

ARIAL RAN AN efficient household. They had had water steaming and ready when Peter arrived, and the butler set two footmen to filling the bath in his room with a swift word, before showing Mr. Richards and vicar into the drawing room, where he promised refreshments would be served.

Peter made quick work of his bath and went looking for his sisters as soon as he was dressed, keen to make sure they were still at ease with his decision to marry. He had just missed them, the maid who was tidying their room told him. They had gone to help Lady Arial dress for her wedding and would come downstairs when she did.

Peter suppressed a wince as he remembered the ill-fitting and worn dresses that were all they had with them. He had assumed they would not want to be seen by those outside of the household before he could arrange decent clothing for them both. Still, the vicar seemed like a nice fellow and John could be trusted to be kind.

Some of what he was thinking must have shown on his face, for the maid added, "Miss Tulloch and Miss Pettigrew took the young ladies shopping, my lord. It's little princesses they are, the pair of them."

The slight pinch to Peter's pride that he had not thought of his sisters' deplorable wardrobe and that the lack had been filled by his soon-to-be wife was swamped by warmth at Arial's care for them. "Your mistress is a wonderful lady," he told the maid.

"That she is, my lord." The maid bit her upper lip, then gave a sharp nod of decision before adding. "You will be good to her, Lord Ransome, will you not? I am speaking out of place, but we love her, you see?" She lowered her eyes, her cheeks flushed, standing before him as if waiting for judgement.

"She is an easy person to love," Peter commented. "I remember that about her from when we were children, and everything I have learned in the past day has confirmed that she has grown into a wonderful woman. You can tell the other servants that I shall try to be the husband she deserves."

The smile the maid gave him transformed her tired, middle-aged face. "I will, my lord. And bless you every day for it."

Peter went down to the parlor to join Richards and the vicar, a warmth in his heart and a smile on his face. But the smile faded when a knock on the door heralded John's arrival.

His friend had arrived with his betrothed and her mother.

The two Weatherall women ignored the butler even as they gave him their cloaks. They were too busy cataloguing all the details of the entry hall to notice a mere servant, or even Peter himself. This gave John time to make his apologies. "I hope it is all right that I brought Belinda and her mother. I know you said it was a small private ceremony, but I had promised to escort them this evening, and they insisted on coming with me in order to save time, since the ball we are attending is in this direction."

Mrs. Weatherall overheard. "Why should it not be all right? Lord Ransome is not ashamed of his bride, I trust."

Miss Weatherall's whisper was clearly audible. "I daresay he might have reason, but we must not comment. It would be rude."

John winced.

Peter did not want to offend his friend, but on the other hand, his first priority must now be his family—Arial and his sisters. "Barlowe, please show Miss and Mrs. Weatherall to the sitting room downstairs and arrange for refreshments." He managed a polite smile for the old harridan. "I am sure you will understand, Mrs. Weatherall. It is a private ceremony." She would probably make nasty remarks about her exile, but better that than insult his bride to her face.

Mrs. Weatherall puffed up her chest. "Well, I never."

Before she could let fly with whatever insults and demands were brewing, there was a stir on the landing above. Mrs. Weatherall looked up, her mouth dropping open. Miss Weatherall and John were likewise affected.

Peter turned to look. It was Arial, but not the Arial he had left this morning. Dressed in a golden gown with a matching half-mask, her hair dressed high upon her head, his mother's jewelry catching the light, she was a queen—no, a goddess—beautiful, mysterious, confident, alluring.

She descended the stairs, and he stretched out his hand to help her down the last few steps. "You look lovely tonight," he said.

She smiled. "You must also admire your sisters," she instructed him.

He tore his gaze away from hers. The girls were grinning at him, not at all offended that he had not even noticed them. Yes, and the governess and Arial's companion were also there, dressed in their very best. He offered compliments to all four of them.

Mrs. Weatherall was not prepared to be ignored. "Are you going to introduce your bride to us, Ransome?" she asked.

Arial raised an eyebrow. "This must be your friend John," she said to Peter. She smiled at the Weatheralls. "And you, I assume, are the captain's betrothed and her mother. My lord, will you present your friend and his guests?"

Peter gave a slight bow of agreement, secretly impressed at how she had so politely reminded Mrs. Weatherall that, as daughter of an earl, she was the one to whom etiquette gave the power to accept or refuse an introduction. "My lady, may I make known to you Mrs. Weatherall and her daughter Belinda. Also, my dear friend, Captain Forsythe, with whom I served in the army. As you so rightly assumed, the captain has the felicity of being engaged to marry Miss Weatherall."

Arial offered Mrs. Weatherall her hand and a gracious inclination of the head. Mrs. Weatherall bobbed a curtsey before she could stop herself, but made a recovery, dropping the hand and saying, "When I heard that my dear friend's son was being married, and with so much haste, I felt I must attend the ceremony so I could tell dear Lady Ransome what was toward."

Arial's voice was warm with humor when she replied, "Then you must be sure to report to Lady Ransome, or the dowager Lady Ransome, as she will be in a few minutes, that her stepson and I are married, and very happy to have his two beloved sisters with us to share our life."

She held out a hand to each girl. "May I present Miss Vivienne Ransome and Miss Rosalind Ransome?" The girls bobbed a polite curtsey. Mrs. Weatherall nodded, stiffly, averting her eyes from Rose and focusing on Viv. Miss Weatherall stared at Rose and turned to John with her mouth open, but Arial spoke before she did.

"And this is my dear friend, Miss Tulloch, and also Miss Pettigrew, who has just joined our household with the girls." She smiled warmly at the two she had named, ignoring Mrs. Weatherall's sniff and Miss Weatherall's sneer.

Again, Arial spoke before Miss Weatherall could turn her contempt into words. "But here we are, standing on the landing. Do step into the next room, please, ladies. The vicar has kindly made space for us in his evening, and we must not keep him waiting. Captain? If you would take your ladies in? And Peter, please escort Clara and Miss Pettigrew. My new sisters and I mean to make an entrance."

Peter followed orders, but murmured to her as he passed, "You are magnificent, my lady." She muttered something about fine feathers making fine birds, but he was not referring to her appearance, grand though it was.

No time now. Later he would tell her that he had been ready to leap to her defense against the obnoxious Weatheralls, until she proved she was fully capable of deflecting their barbs, and doing so with courtesy, grace, and good humor. *What a woman!*

Someone had seen to it that the drawing room was set up for the ceremony, with chairs set in three rows facing the large bay window, where the vicar stood holding a prayer book. Large vases, filled with roses, lilies, and greenery, flanked the bay. Mr. Richards had already taken a chair in the back row. John sat the

Weatherall ladies in the second. Peter conducted Miss Tulloch and Miss Pettigrew to the other two seats in that row, then took his place before the vicar, half turned to watch the door.

John came up beside him, assuring him of support with a single slap on the back.

As if that was the signal, Viv stepped through the door, her face solemn, her eyes glowing. She walked slowly and deliberately, pointing her toe with each step, making a procession of one as she crossed the room to the bay window. There, she stood to one side and turned towards the door.

Now Rose began her own walk across the room, walking with the same slow steps as her sister, looking up through her lashes at Viv and making straight for her. Side-by-side, the two sisters watched for the bride.

At last, Arial stood framed by the doorway. Peter, having been struck breathless by the sight of her on the stairs, was once more knocked back on his metaphorical heels. The gown hugged her curves, which were splendid. Her figure was the personification of a man's earthiest dreams.

And, at the same time, some of his loftiest imaginings. From the elaborate hairstyle held in place by his mother's tiara to the gold slippers that showed with each step beneath her lacy hem, she was too magnificent for a mere mortal male to conquer. *Goddess*, he thought again. It would be his part to surrender and worship. He could hardly wait.

Chapter Eight

THIS WAS AN evening of firsts for Arial. Dressing with the help of her new sisters. Examining her own reflection in the mirror and being pleased with what she saw. Making her appearance at the top of the stairs to see awe and admiration in the eyes of Peter and his friend, Captain Forsythe. And a darker emotion on the faces of the Weatherall ladies, but one she'd never expected to attract.

Perhaps it was bad of her, but their jealousy pleased rather than bothered her. If anyone had told her a week ago that she would look good enough to cause a petty-minded Society beauty to regard her with envy, she would not have believed them.

She smiled at them as she walked slowly past them on her way to where Peter stood before the vicar. They had come prepared to bestow pity, of course. How disappointed they must be.

With them behind her, she put them out of her mind. This was her evening, and she would not allow the Weatheralls to spoil it for her.

Her heart warmed and a lump came to her throat as Peter stepped to one side and held his hand out for her. His right hand. Her sighted side. She handed her wedding bouquet—made for her by her new sisters with herbs and flowers from the market—

to Rosalind and gave her left hand to Peter.

Another first. Her wedding. She had been damaged too young to have begun to dream of one and had been too realistic to allow such dreams to take root as she became a woman. Since Mr. Richards had proposed his scheme, she had been focused on selecting a candidate and on reaching an agreement that gave her the best chance of a reasonable life. The wedding had not been a consideration.

But here she was. Exchanging smiles with the most beautiful man she had ever seen, and about to join her life to his forever.

"Who giveth this woman to be married to this man?" asked the vicar.

"I give myself," Arial declared, and Peter's grip firmed as his smile widened.

Miss Weatherall whispered loudly, "Is that even legal?" and Captain Forsythe shushed her.

The vicar looked a little disconcerted for a moment, and then nodded, and moved on to the next part of the ceremony.

She had attended weddings in the village near Greenmount, and was familiar with the ceremony, but it was different as a bride. The admonitions, the solemn declarations, the vows, that moment when Peter placed his ring on her finger—every word resonated with some deep and previously unsuspected romanticism in her soul.

From this day forth, she and Peter were bound together, the bond between them as deep as the links of blood, no longer individuals from two different families but a couple in a family of their own. *In sickness or in health, for richer, for poorer*, they repeated after the vicar.

Arial's mind echoed the phrasing: *in happiness or in misery, in love or in hate.* She had seen both conditions in the families that lived near Greenmount. Marriage was for a lifetime. As she stood before the vicar, gazing at Peter with her hands in his, hope swelled. She had been prepared to accept a cold alliance, a marriage of convenience. With Peter, she could dream of so much more. Kindness, respect, even friendship. And perhaps children.

The vicar pronounced them husband and wife and called on them to sign the record of the marriage, then said, with a flourish, "Ladies and gentlemen, I give you Lord and Lady Ransome."

Peter tucked Arial's hand in his arm and turned them both, so they faced their witnesses. Clara was wiping her eyes with a handkerchief. Miss Pettigrew smiled as if she was personally responsible for the wedding, and proud to have pulled it off. Rose and Viv were so happy they bounced. And Mr. Richards, who truly was responsible for the wedding, beamed broadly.

Behind the small group of chairs, Nancy, Cook, Barlowe, Sergeant Miller, and the other servants stood silently, every one of them with smiles on their faces and several with tears in their eyes.

Then Captain Forsythe broke the spell of stillness in the room by grabbing Peter's free hand and shaking it. "Congratulations, Peter. I am so happy for you."

The two girls hurried forward to speak to Peter, and Captain Forsythe turned to Arial. "I've always thought Peter was a lucky devil, Lady Ransome, and winning you for a bride proves it."

Arial thanked him, though she was inclined to think the luck was on her side. She held out her arms to the girls and received an enthusiastic hug from Viv and a shy one from Rose. Then Clara took her turn, laughing and crying, and Miss Pettigrew with modest good wishes for the happy couple.

Barlowe must have chivvied his fellow servants from the room, for here they were returning bearing trays of food and drink.

"I WONDER HOW bad she really is under the mask," Miss Weatherall commented to John. Peter wondered if she truly thought she was whispering, or if she had pitched her voice to reach him, a few feet further away.

John, bless him, protested. "I wonder how that is any of our business, Belinda."

Miss Weatherall opened her blue eyes to their fullest extent and pouted. "I was only making a comment, Lord John. There is no need to leap for my throat."

Mrs. Weatherall made her own contribution to the conversation, abandoning the interrogation she had been attempting on poor Miss Tulloch. "We all know the poor viscount has not a feather to fly with." She giggled. "Had, I suppose I should say. I daresay one must have the utmost respect for a gentleman who marries a gargoyle for money, when he does it for his mother and sisters."

Miss Tulloch's mouth dropped open. Peter glanced around to see Arial deep in conversation with his sisters and Miss Pettigrew on the other side of the room. If she had heard, she showed no sign.

He caught back the hard words on his lips. These women would repeat their remarks to anyone who would listen no matter what he did. Any comment he made would be repeated, embroidered to their own design.

John was not so cautious. In a fierce whisper, he said, "Your remarks are intolerable. We are Lord and Lady Ransome's guests, and this is their wedding day. If you cannot keep from insulting them, then we had better leave."

Mrs. Weatherall managed to both glare at him and drop her mouth open in shock, at the same time.

"Really, John," Miss Weatherall retorted. "How can it be an insult if it is true? I only meant to point out what a hero your friend is, allowing himself to be sold to someone known to be horribly scarred."

Again, Peter stopped to think, though he was possessed by a fierce urge to protect Arial from any implication she had purchased herself a husband. Would he make things better or worse? But he could not let the repeated insults pass.

"She looks almost acceptable with the mask on," Miss Weatherall conceded. "How disappointed Lord Ransome will be when he sees her with it off!"

The rest of the room had fallen silent, and Miss Weatherall's voice was piercing.

Before Peter could tell Miss Weatherall, she was no longer welcome, Arial spoke. "I imagine many a husband must be disappointed when they discover that their wife has been hiding ugliness behind a mask. Fortunately, Lord Ransome has already seen me as I am." She smiled warmly at Peter and added, "I have always thought that ugliness of character, while easier to hide, at least temporarily, must be far more disappointing for a husband than a few physical scars. Far harder to live with, too."

For a moment, as Peter returned the smile and spoke directly to Arial, the rest of the room faded away. "My wife has a beauty that will not fade with age. She is a woman of character: brave, kind, and good. She is beloved of her servants and already a friend to my sisters."

It wasn't enough. How dare that witch call her a gargoyle? And for Arial to implicitly accept the insult! "She is also lovely in appearance," he added, "as every man here tonight can attest. I would be proud to take her anywhere on my arm."

He turned his attention to Miss Weatherall. "Before you say anything more, Miss Weatherall, you might wish to consider that she uses a mask to cover a few physical scars not for her own sake, but to protect the sensibilities of the small-minded."

NOT SINCE HER father had died had anyone stood up for Arial the way Peter did. And even her father had never claimed she was lovely. Pure flattery, of course. She looked well enough in this gown, with the pretty mask the girls had decorated, but she was not lovely.

Even without the lesser scars that traced a subtle pattern in a purplish red across her forehead and down her neck, she would not be considered pretty. She was too tall and her curves too generous. Her chin was square and her mouth over large.

And that did not begin to count the ugly, discolored, and broken knots beneath the mask and on one shoulder and arm under her gown. She had, or so they told her, been found with that arm over her chin and mouth, which had kept the worst burns to her cheek, eye, and forehead.

She appreciated the support Peter offered, whether his words were true or not.

Captain Forsythe was proving to be another champion. "Time for us to leave," he said, abruptly. "Come, ladies." It was the voice of an officer, accustomed to command, and the grim look he gave the Weatherall ladies had them scurrying out into the hall without another word.

Captain Forsythe bowed to Arial. "I am sorry I brought them, Lady Ransome. If I'd known…"

"Don't concern yourself, Captain. They are only saying what others will."

He didn't deny it. "But in your own house, at your wedding…" He grasped Peter's hand. "Congratulations, Peter. You have always been a lucky so-and-so." From beyond the room, Miss Weatherall's voice could be heard, complaining about being left in the hall. "I'd better get those two out of here."

After he took the Weatherall ladies away, the party broke up. Mr. Richards and the vicar took their leave, after expressing their pleasure at being of service, and wishing the bride and groom every blessing.

"Time for bed," Miss Pettigrew said to Viv and Rose.

"I shall come up and read you a story, shall I?" Clara suggested. The girls agreed, and they all took their leave.

"Once the girls are settled, I shall take Miss Pettigrew to my little sitting room for the evening," Clara whispered to Arial.

"You need not expect to see any of us again tonight."

Arial could feel the heat rising in her face. She knew in theory what would happen tonight, but theory was a long way from experience.

"I meant what I said, you know," Peter told her. "You are lovely. The dress. The mask. I was very proud to stand beside you tonight and take my vows."

"Thank you. Painting the mask was your sisters' idea. They did an excellent job, did they not?"

"They did. It is really pretty, and I'm glad you had something special for your wedding." He poured her a glass of wine, and one for himself.

She accepted the glass and felt a shiver all the way up her arm when her fingers touched his. "I never thought of decorating my mask. As soon as I saw their one in the mirror, I wondered why. The plain white draws attention. I've been told it makes people think of bone." She shuddered.

Peter sipped at his wine. "I don't know about that, but it isn't a pretty object in its own right. And why should you not wear pretty things?"

This was very true, and it put her in mind of something. "Thank you for your mother's jewels, Peter."

"Yours, now." His smile was tender. "They are Lady Ransome's jewels, and you are Lady Ransome."

She put a hand to her throat, over the necklace, overwhelmed by the thought.

Peter had some thanks of his own. "Thank you for my sisters' gowns, Arial, and for asking them to attend you. They were over the moon to be so favored."

"Not a favor. They are my sisters, now, too." She turned her glass in her hands, her eyes on that as one of Peter's statements echoed in her mind. "Peter, did you mean it when you said you would be proud to have me on your arm, looking the way I do?" She had never imagined going out in Society without a veil, but she had longed to do so. Perhaps she could be brave enough, if

Peter were with her.

He had been about to take another sip, but he put the glass down, his eyes wide in what looked like disbelief. "Are you joking? When you came down the stairs tonight, do you know the words that leapt to my mind? As you stood there in a gown that showed your magnificent curves, tall and graceful? Queen, I thought, and then, Goddess. You are glorious, my lady. When I said I was proud of you, I meant it."

His words warmed her and gave her courage. Did he mean them? She would soon find out.

"Then do you think we should remain in town for a short time? Perhaps… I have been thinking perhaps we should go out in Society. If you wouldn't hate it too much."

"Go out? You mean to soirées and dinners and balls and the like?" Peter frowned. He was surprised, and no wonder. She was surprised herself. She had been hiding away in the country for most of her life. But suddenly, she wanted more.

"I thought you wanted to avoid that kind of life," Peter said.

She could feel herself blush. "That is true. I did. I was afraid." As so often in her life, though, she needed to face her fears. Her cousin would never have been a threat if she had done so earlier, and now she had other people to consider, too. Peter. His sisters. Their future children.

"Peter, I may have lived in a country village and never come to town, but I know how people gossip. And I understand how cruel gossips can be. Do you believe that the two ladies who attended our wedding tonight will keep still tongues in their heads? Or that they won't repeat elsewhere what they said in our presence?"

ARIAL WAS RIGHT, of course. "Do we care what they say?" Peter asked, even as he choked back rage at the thought of the

Weatheralls spreading their poison.

"I tried to tell myself it didn't matter," Arial confessed, "but it isn't true. It needs to matter. If we do not counter the lies, they will become truth in the eyes of Society. That could affect your business dealings, your efforts to rehabilitate the reputation of your title. You told me you would like to take your seat in the House of Lords and see what can be done to help those who served in the wars. These lies could stand in your way. In a few years, your sisters will want to make their curtseys to Society. If our reputation is ruined, what will become of them? And what of our own children?"

Arial had been magnificent when the Weatherall women were trying and failing to cause pain. Now, less than half an hour later, she had assessed the risk of them continuing to stir trouble and come up with a plan. A plan that would mean facing her fears and putting herself in front of the sharks of Society. What an amazing woman she was!

"My sisters could make you a mask to match every outfit," he suggested.

"My thought, exactly. Rose, in particular, is very talented. If they would be happy to paint them, I would be delighted to wear them."

"Then we shall drop some cards off at the homes of a few important Society hostesses, so they can spread the word we are open to invitations. It will take a day or two to have the cards printed, I suppose. Richards will know how to get it done."

"And who those important hostesses are, I hope," Arial suggested. "I have no idea."

Conversation lapsed between them, as Arial gazed into her now empty glass. She had been sliding increasingly uncertain glances towards Peter and would not meet his eyes.

He could guess what was troubling her, and almost suggested that they each went up to their separate beds. His disappointment at the thought was beside the point. He had promised to cherish and protect her, and to his mind, that made her feelings more important than his.

He could think of two reasons to bed her tonight, quite apart from his own desire, but he couldn't tell how much his lust colored his thinking. What decision would be best for them both?

It wasn't up to him to decide, though, was it? That was his job as an army officer or a viscount, but not in this instance. He was a husband, and this decision affected them both. She was sitting on the left of the sofa, so her blind side was to the empty space. "Will you move over so I can sit beside you, Arial? We have a choice to make, you and I."

She lifted her gaze to him as she shifted. "What choice is that, Peter?"

He sat beside her and took her hands. She let them lie in his, a slight frown furrowing what he could see of her brow.

"I want to find out your thoughts on when we consummate our marriage. We have several factors we might care to consider."

Arial bit her lip and then licked it. For a moment, Peter couldn't tear his eyes away from her mouth and his simmering lust hit boiling point. She said something, and his brain struggled to process it. *Ah. That was it.*

"Do we not need to… will we be married without…"

Richards had been very clear. "Mr. Richards told me that, in English law, non-consummation is not grounds for annulment. Someone who wanted to challenge our marriage would have to prove I was impotent." He smiled at Arial, stroking her hands with his thumbs. "That won't be an issue for us, I can assure you."

"I see. We can wait, then?" She was still frowning. He could not tell whether she regarded the prospect of a delay with disappointment or relief.

"For a short while, at least. Just so we have time for something of a courtship." He shrugged. "I desire you and am willing as soon as you are ready. But I am a man. For women, or so I understand, desire has more of an emotional component, and we have known one another as adults for only one day."

Arial pursed her lips. "You want to wait?"

He still couldn't tell what she was thinking. Honesty was the best policy. "No. But this isn't about what I want. More than I want to take you to bed tonight, I want you to choose what you feel is best for you."

She nodded, thoughtfully. "I see. Thank you. You said several factors. What else should I know?"

"Two more matters. One is for you to consider. Will waiting make you more nervous or less? I can promise to do everything I can to make sure you enjoy the experience, but I understand that the first time can be awkward for a woman. I don't know what you know about what is involved?"

She grew to womanhood without a mother. Had anyone ever explained the basics of mating to her, or would that job fall to him?

"I am not entirely ignorant," she said. "I have seen animals and even interrupted a couple of servants on occasion. I also discovered an interesting book when cleaning my father's library after he died." She thought about that for a moment. "From the little I've seen, it seems very undignified."

"Dignity is not something you'll think about if I am halfway competent," Peter assured her, relieved he did not have to explain the process. "The other thing is your abhorrent cousin. Richards says we should not risk giving him grounds for claiming that our marriage is a sham."

Arial leapt to the correct conclusion. "Richards thinks we should consummate the marriage tonight."

Peter had thought of another option, though it would be torture. Still, he could do it for Arial. "We need him to believe we have done so, and we need to convince the servants of that fact. My sisters and Miss Tulloch, too. I know you trust them, but people can say things without meaning to, and if it came to questioning under oath, we want them to tell the truth as they see it. I believe I should spend at least tonight in your rooms. Not necessarily in your bed. Do you have a sitting room or a dressing room? I can sleep on the floor if there isn't a cot."

"I think I would like another glass of wine," Arial commented. "You have given me a lot to think about."

Peter picked up Arial's glass from the low table beside the sofa and fetched his own, then crossed the room to fill them. When he turned back towards her, she was standing. She held out her hand for her glass. "I will take it up to bed with me. Will you give me thirty minutes to change, Peter? And will you then come and knock on my door and join me in my bed? I want to be your wife in every way tonight."

"Are you certain?" Peter asked, ignoring the eager response from his body.

She smiled back at him and lifted her glass in a salute. "Absolutely certain. I did not let my fears keep me from coming to London, I do not intend to let them stop me from going out into Society, and I shall not let them keep me from finding out what all the fuss is about. You are right. Waiting will only make me more nervous. Let us begin our marriage tonight, Peter. We have the rest of our lives to get to know one another."

Peter clicked his glass against hers. "To finding out what all the fuss is about," he said.

Chapter Nine

ARIAL WAITED FOR Peter in her room. Thirty minutes, she had told him. To prepare herself.

Her maid had brushed her hair, turned down the bed, and unfastened Arial's gown. Arial had washed herself and changed into her night attire, including the soft mask she donned for sleeping. It was knitted in soft cotton, and covered her head, with a hole over her eye for her to see.

Where should she wait? Seated by the fire? Would he expect her to be already in bed, her robe off and the candles doused?

Would he want the candles lit? Surely not. He claimed to desire her and had admired her figure. But he had only seen her face and her hands. The rest of her was covered in clothing. He seemed unbothered by the less damaged side of her face, but he had not seen the marks left on her body where embers had burned through her clothing to consume her skin.

Well, there was nothing more than usual to see at the moment. Less, in fact. Even her shape was hidden by the abundant folds of her night rail, buttoned to the neck and at the wrists, with the voluminous robe over. And nothing showed of her face but her one eye.

What would Peter be wearing? The thought of his body made her uncomfortable in a not altogether unpleasant fashion—hot and breathless, with strange tremors in parts of her anatomy she seldom thought about.

Presumably, Arial could keep the nightgown on, even if she did leave one or two candles alight. She would certainly like to see her beautiful new husband!

So, this was desire. How awful if, when it came to the point, Peter was unable to go through with the consummation!

Before her agitation reached the point that she fled for refuge to Clara's sitting room, the knock on the door came, and Peter's voice. "May I enter, my lady?"

"Yes," she replied, her voice coming out in an embarrassing squeak. She swallowed and tried again. "Come in, my lord."

Peter's beauty intimidated her when he was clothed. He was even more beautiful in undress—in a robe that barely touched his knees and that opened at the top to show the nape of his neck and top of his chest.

Arial felt both decidedly overdressed and horribly exposed.

"Good evening, Lady Ransome," he said, with a formal bow that accorded poorly with his attire, but that allowed the robe to gape so she could see more of his chest. Was the robe all he wore? The thought took her breath away and she could do no more in response to his greeting than a shallow curtsey.

He took one of Arial's hands and led her to a set of chairs by the fireplace.

She said, "I thought we were going to…" She could not think of an appropriate word. She sat. She presumed Peter knew how to go about the matter and would follow his lead.

He pulled the other chair closer, hooking it with one foot, and sat without releasing her hand.

"I take it the stocking over your head is easier to sleep in than the rigid half mask that is your day wear." It was a statement, rather than a question, made in a calm and matter-of-fact tone. Meanwhile, as if possessed of a mind of its own, his thumb traced patterns on her hand in gentle, subtle touches that made her nerves quiver and yearn.

She managed to ignore the sensation enough to answer. "The day mask digs in."

Peter turned her hand over and began to stroke her palm with the same gentle pressure. "Do you think you could bear to wear the day mask while we engage in physical intimacy? I wish to kiss you, Arial, and to see what I can of your face, so I understand what pleases you and what doesn't."

"Oh." Arial considered that for a moment. "I'm sorry. I didn't realize. I shall change it." She made to get up, but Peter captured her other hand and began to stroke that, too.

"We have plenty of time," he said. "I hope one day you will feel comfortable enough to leave the mask off entirely when we are in bed together."

He didn't understand. "I wear a mask at night for my maid's comfort and now for yours, not for my own," she explained. "Also, if there is a fire or some other disaster and I have to flee my room, I do not want to upset people."

He rejected that argument with a soft smile and a shake of the head. "I am comfortable with seeing your face as it is, my wife. You were brave enough to show it to me before you would agree to our marriage, remember?"

"You were gentlemanly enough not to react, but I saw the horror in your eyes," she accused.

"You saw the pain I felt at what you have suffered," he corrected. "You do not need to be afraid to show yourself to me, Arial. Do you have scars on your body, too? Is that why you wear long sleeves in the evening and have your gowns made to button to your neck?"

She broke eye-contact, looking down at her lap, where his hands continued to play with hers. "I thought we were going to consummate our marriage." She screwed her eye shut, embarrassed at her petulant tone.

"We will, Lady Ransome," he assured her. "Never fear."

Honesty and frankness had served them well so far. She would be blunt. "I am afraid, Peter. Not of—" she hesitated for a moment, and then chose his term, "not of physical intimacy, precisely, but that you will find me loathsome if you see my body."

PETER'S HANDS TIGHTENED on Arial's. A world of disappointment and rejection colored that last sentence. He wanted to punish every ignorant fool who had ever made her feel ugly, starting with the Weatheralls and the unnamed suitor Miss Tulloch and Barlowe had both told him about—the one who ran from her presence to vomit into a plant pot in the front hall.

His heart clenched at the depth of her pain and her gallant determination not to show it. When he spoke, he had to stop, clear his throat, and try again. "I think I am both stronger and fonder of you than you think, but I will wait until you are ready, lady wife. Let's try this for tonight. You will put on your half mask and take off your robe but leave on the nightgown. And I will douse all but one of the candles. Will that be acceptable?"

She nodded and stood so he had to stand with her. "And you will tell me what I must do?" she asked, avoiding his eyes again. "I know very little, you see." She showed her courage again. "My father's book had illustrations, but I am sure some of those were unrealistic, and they don't explain—that is, they are not moving, so I do not know…"

She was stammering in her confusion, and he was certain her skin, if he could see it, would be bright scarlet.

He took pity on her. "I have no recent experience, but I was once a young and riotous officer with money in my pocket. I will be happy to teach you, Arial." The thought of teaching her was reviving his organ, which had retreated from full enthusiasm at the thought of her pain. "I will need you to tell me what touches please you and what causes discomfort. You will be able to stop me at any time, simply by asking."

He had another thought as she slipped her hands from his grasp and turned towards the dressing screen.

"Arial, let me know if there are any parts of your body you would rather I did not touch." He meant scars it would embarrass her to have him feel. He hoped she understood.

She stopped halfway to the screen, so all he could see was an amorphous shape, bundled in clothing from head to toe. "My right shoulder and upper back, and the top of my right arm. But why would you touch those? They are nowhere near... That is, the connection is made..."

She broke off and hurried to shelter. He hoped her fluster was at least partly due to incipient desire, prompted by thinking about their "connection." The images her reply had prompted had certainly had the desired effect on him.

He continued talking as he walked around the room, extinguishing the candles. "Touch is an important part of what we are about to do. We touch one another to increase our readiness for deeper intimacies."

"Like kissing," she said, her voice steady again. "I think kissing might be pleasant."

Kissing was pleasant with a temporary lover. Peter feared that kissing Arial was going to be so far beyond pleasant it would shatter his world and remake it. "Kissing can be very pleasant, as can other touches. You may touch any part of me that you like. Did you enjoy what I was doing to your hands? I would very much like to do the same to your breasts."

The noise from behind the screen was more intrigued than shocked, so he continued. "I would like to kiss them, too, and draw your nipples into my mouth. Then, if you like that, I shall kiss my way down your body to the center of your pleasure. Perhaps I shall stroke your inner thighs. The skin is very soft and sensitive there, and I think you will enjoy it."

He didn't know about Arial, but the naughty conversation was working on him.

She rounded the dressing screen then, and his generative

organ, already engorged, hardened still more. She had left the candle burning behind her, and the virginal white nightgown, though it still flowed around her like a tent, was rendered almost transparent by the light.

He took a step towards her, holding out his hands to take hers. Up close, he could see that she was flushed, her eye wide. He saw some trepidation in its depths, but also desire.

He bent his head and his lips touched hers.

She smelt of cloves and something floral. *Not roses or lavender—jasmine.* That was it. Her lips were as plump and soft to the touch as they had looked. He had time for that assessment before she began to return the kiss, then his every thought fractured, and it took all his determination not to fall on her like a ravening beast.

His cheek kept bumping the edge of the mask, impeding his movements and reminding him he needed to go slowly. Not that Arial was objecting to his hand on her breast while the other anchored her against him. Far from it. She pressed into his hand, and lower, too, tipping to grind her groin against him, her body understanding what her innocent mind had not yet grasped.

He broke away for long enough to ask, "Am I going too fast?" He was gratified at her dazed expression and slow response.

She shook her head. "I like it." And she tilted up her face, her mouth reaching for his kiss.

As he lowered his lips to hers, he suggested, "This time, will you open your mouth?"

Which she did, probably to ask another question, but before she could, his lips touched hers, his tongue already reaching to trace them. It was a long kiss, and even more fevered than the first. He explored her lips, her tongue, and her mouth. When she tentatively followed the retreat of his tongue with her own, he allowed her to explore in her turn, trembling with the effort it took not to take the kiss back over.

It did not help to give his mind another direction when he swapped hands, for her other breast responded as sweetly as the first, the nipple tightening and hardening under his ministrations. When she began to touch him in her turn, sliding her hands under his robe to explore his chest, he almost lost his control again.

He was desperate for more. He began to back her towards the bed without breaking the kiss until they reached that destination, and she turned her head as he began to lift her.

The single candle had performed the office she desired. As she lay back against the sheets, the stark white mask hid the worst damage on her face, and the dim light disguised the rest, so the visible part of her face appeared unblemished. Beautiful, too: her eye heavy lidded with desire, her lips swollen with his kisses.

He knelt beside her and bent for another kiss, then traced a row of kisses down the line of her jaw, stopping to nibble her earlobe and swipe up behind it with his tongue.

His progress down her neck was halted by the lace that trimmed the top of her night rail. He skipped over it and continued to kiss his way down towards her breasts, hoping enough sensation transmitted through the light cotton to give her pleasure.

Certainly, his attentions to her breasts had pleased her, for as his mouth reached a nipple, she lifted that side—an unspoken plea.

PETER'S MINISTRATIONS WERE certainly not making Arial more comfortable. Far from it, and yet the increasing discomfort was somehow wonderful, hinting at an even more marvelous destination. Her body had responded when he spoke about what he wanted to do with her breasts. Her body clearly knew something she didn't. She could never have imagined that her nipples were somehow directly connected to the place Peter called *the center of her pleasure.*

He spoke of kissing his way to it. As he began to do so, she regretted not removing the nightgown. What he was doing felt wonderful. What would it feel like against bare skin?

His hands quested ahead of his mouth. His thumb brushed over the place to which all these new sensations seemed to be directed. The bolt of pleasure was like nothing she had ever experienced. She pressed up, anxious to experience it again.

He responded by repeating the action, and then his mouth replaced his thumb, and Arial arched so far into the feeling that her buttocks came right off the bed.

When he lifted his mouth, she whimpered. It was only then that she realized his hand was on her knee.

"May I lift your nightgown out of the way? I want to touch your garden of delights."

"Are you sure?" Arial asked.

He sat back on his heels. She could not be sure, in the dim light, but she thought that was consternation on his face. "Do you not like what I have been doing?"

"Very much! But I thought—I want you to like doing this with me, too, if that is possible."

He gave a laugh that was close to a groan, and she could feel herself flush. He thought she was ridiculous.

But no. He untied the tie of his robe and shrugged it back off his shoulders. "I like it, Arial. I like it very much. Look." He gestured to his male organ, huge and upright. "You have done this. Making love to you has made me hard enough to hammer nails."

Fascinated, she reached for it, then snatched her hand away when he moaned at her touch. "I'm sorry. I did not mean to hurt you."

"Touch it, please," he begged. "It is the kindest hurt in the world, and only you can make it better."

She did as he asked, wondering at the soft, warm skin over the hard interior.

He allowed her gentle explorations for a minute, and then

took her hand and guided it to grasp the thing—as well as she could. Though her fingers were long, they did not quite touch her thumb. He showed her how to move her hand up and down, which made his whole body shudder as he groaned again.

"As firm as you like. You will not hurt it. Ah, that is wonderful. May I lift your hem, and return the favor?"

Absorbed in the feel of him, and in the wonder of his reactions, she did not answer until he said her name. "Arial?"

"Yes," she said. She had time for a fleeting concern about how high he might raise the night rail, and then his fingers were brushing her inner thighs, so that she squirmed to bring them closer to where she suddenly yearned to feel them.

He must have known. Suddenly, his thumb was back on that tiny nub of sensation, and one finger slipped into another place she had barely been aware of. An entry to her body that she knew from washing and from her monthly courses, but had never realized could feel so plump, so warm, so slick, so utterly entrancing.

"You are wet for me," Peter said. This must be a good thing, for he sounded delighted.

The second finger joined the first, sliding in and out of her, each thrust a cascade of pleasure. "This is where I shall put my cock," Peter said.

Arial's hands stilled.

One part of her mind, ever curious, noted the word. She had heard it before, overhearing the chatter of the maids, but had not realized it referred to a man's male part. Logical. It reared up, proud as a cock's neck, and very like in both shape and feel to such a neck when separated from the beast and ready for the cook. Firm but yielding flesh over the solid base, although Peter's was both thicker and longer than such a neck.

And, too, cocks—the poultry kind—were notoriously so focused on servicing their hens that housewives had to regularly culled their flocks of surplus males, so the poor hens had time to eat and sleep.

But she was allowing her mind to blather to distract her from her main concern.

Now Peter stopped. "Arial? What is the matter?"

She blurted the truth. "It is so big. Will it not hurt?"

He lay back down beside her and slid his arm underneath her to pull her close beside him. He did not, thank goodness, stop his ministrations with his other hand. "Can you feel how soft and wet you have become? That is your body preparing to receive mine. You and I were made to fit together. It can hurt when a man forces himself on a woman—but I would never do that. I have heard, too, there may be pain with a woman's first time. Just when I enter the first time, Arial. After that, there will be only pleasure."

He pressed a kiss to the corner of her eye.

Arial and pain were old acquaintances. She could cope with one time.

Peter had not finished. "I am hoping to give you so much pleasure that you will be eager for our next time, knowing the pain is behind you. Will you trust me, dear wife?"

"I am in your hands," she reminded him, and reached again for his cock.

He held his hips out of her reach. "Later," he said. "Any more, and I shall spend before I can enter you."

Arial had no idea what he meant, but as he wriggled down on the bed and put his mouth to the nub he had been working with his thumb, she decided it was a question for later. She had more important things to think about.

Chapter Ten

P ETER WAS RIGHT. It hurt, though not much more than a pinch, and the pleasure before and after more than made up for it. And the next twice didn't hurt at all, once in the darkest part of the night and once in the morning, when they lazed in bed sharing histories and opinions well past the time that Arial was normally up for breakfast.

Arial was definitely going to like this part of being married.

The rumbles of hunger eventually drove them out of bed. "We could send Nancy for sustenance, and stay here," Peter suggested. Arial was tempted. Peter grimaced. "I suppose not. If we stay, I will want to have you again, and you must be sore. Besides, I need to arrange for those visiting cards, and you must have things to do, too."

Arial had to admit she was a little tender down below. In need of a good wash, too, though Peter had insisted on gently washing her after each round of intimacies.

"Shall we come with you when you go to see Mr. Richards," she suggested, "and perhaps afterwards take the girls for an ice at Gunther's? Or perhaps tea at Fournier's." She had read about both fashionable activities and had always wondered what they were like.

"Good idea," Peter agreed. "First, though, we could do with a bath. And perhaps a snack while we wait for it to be filled, just so I don't die of starvation before breakfast. I expended a lot of energy last night." He dug his fingers into her side in a swift tickle and added, "and this morning."

"I shall ring for Nancy," Arial agreed. "You can have your snack here with me while we wait for our baths to be filled. I would love a cup of tea."

Peter looked puzzled and then disappointed.

Surely, he did not expect the pair of them to bathe together? "Peter, no one ever sees me in my bath. Not even Nancy."

He recovered his poise. "Yes, of course. Then send for Nancy, and we shall have a cup of tea together."

She let the matter drop.

They sat down with a pot of tea and fresh crumpets with Cook's gooseberry jam, discussing their plans for the day.

The girls would have another holiday. Last night, Arial had asked Miss Pettigrew to write a list of all the things the girls and Miss Pettigrew needed. After breakfast, Arial would lead an expedition to begin making those purchases, while Peter spoke to Mr. Richards about visiting cards and Society hostesses. He would also ask Mr. Richards to look into a townhouse for the dowager Lady Ransome and her daughters.

They agreed that Peter would purchase the townhouse and retain ownership of it, but would provide it rent-free to the dowager, along with a small allowance. "I need to make it very clear that nothing more will be forthcoming," Peter said. "I would not put it past her to gamble away the lot and then tell the whole of Society that her penury is my fault."

"You owe her nothing, Peter." From what Arial had heard about the woman, she was lucky Peter did not put her out in the street. In fact, he had suggested doing so, but Arial had pointed out that Society's sympathies would be with the widow if he did not make reasonable provision for her.

"Your father provided a perfectly adequate allowance, and anything more is out of the goodness of your heart," she pointed out. "If she is nasty, we will just withdraw all support. Or provide her with townhouse in Australia." And make sure that Society knew the dreadful woman deserved it.

"Hardly fair on Australia," Peter grumbled.

On one of her trips conducting the footmen who were filling Arial's bath, Nancy brought in the newspaper. Mr. Richards, with his usual efficiency, had managed to get the notice of their marriage to the press in time for this morning's printing. Peter looked for it and read it to her.

"Viscount Ransome of Three Oaks Manor in Suffolk is honored to announce his marriage to Lady Arial Bledisloe daughter of the Earl of Stancroft (deceased). The private wedding was held in London and attended by close family and invited guests."

Somehow the public notice made it all the more real. What would people think? What would Josiah say? She smiled at Peter. None of that mattered. They were married, and it was wonderful.

"Your bath is ready, my lady," Nancy announced. "So is yours, my lord."

Regardless of the watching maid and footmen, Peter leaned over the little table to give Arial a kiss. "Then I shall leave you to it, Lady Ransome, and see you at breakfast."

IN HIS BATH, Peter contemplated his own disappointment that he'd been exiled to another bedroom. He should be grateful that, after their first joining, she had removed the mask in the dark and gone to sleep in his arms. She had trusted him that much, and when she woke in the night and reached for him, he had had the joy of kissing her without any obstruction in the way. Which had led to round two.

In the morning, he woke to hear her behind the dressing screen, and when she returned to bed, the half mask was back in place. He expected too much, too soon. She had trusted him enough to give him her body. It would take time before she could bear to be naked with him.

The small bit of distance was to his benefit, too. This marriage was a civil arrangement. He did not intend to spoil it by becoming besotted with his bride.

He was already serving his breakfast when Arial arrived in the dining room. He had not been joking about his hunger. Despite the crumpets, he was ravenous.

And not just for food, he decided, when she entered the room and his male organ stood to instant attention. It seemed he could not get enough of his wife. It was probably just that he hadn't been with a woman for a long time, though that thought seemed so disloyal that he quelched it immediately.

Whatever the reason for his sudden surfeit of lust, he had to content himself with a peck on the cheek and a cheeky comment whispered in her ear so the attending footman could not hear it.

Her blush would have to be satisfaction enough for the moment, especially as Miss Tulloch took that moment to join them.

The girls had already eaten but came hurrying down from the schoolroom when they heard the newlyweds were up and dressed. They were delighted with the day's plans but took exception to Arial's plain mask.

"But the one you made for my wedding will not go with this gown," she protested. It was some tailored confection in a dark maroon, almost the color of a good port. Peter had signed for payment of enough dressmaker bills for his stepmother and stepsisters to know that daytime costumes could fit into categories of day dress, walking dress, and afternoon dress, but which this was he had no idea. It was charming, anyway.

Rose agreed. "Not at all, but we can do something quickly with pastels. I think some of the ones that old artist gave me are the right colors. Come on, Viv." The girls hurried out, but Peter signaled Miss Pettigrew to stay.

"What old artist, Miss Pettigrew? And how did he come to be giving gifts to my sister?" When he used that tone with his men, they had known to be fast and honest in their reply, for Captain Ransome had sensed danger, and would not tolerate prevarication.

Miss Pettigrew eyes opened wide in alarm, and she gulped. "It was innocent, my lord, truly. He said she reminded him of his granddaughter, and she was never out of my sight, only her skills are beyond mine."

Peter had been too abrupt. Beside him, Arial put a hand on his arm. "Lord Ransome is not blaming you for anything, Miss Pettigrew. I take it she met an artist who was painting in the vicinity, and he was kind enough to give her lessons?"

"He came to paint Lady Ransome, my lady," Miss Pettigrew explained. "Last year, this was. He gave Miss Rosalind one lesson, but then Lady Ransome found out and forbade any more. When he left, he gave me a box of pastels for her. Just stubs and broken pieces, but he said she had great talent, and must continue with her art. And he gave me a list of exercises for her to do."

"That was a great kindness," Arial said. "We will need to see about an art tutor, and you must tell us if either of the young ladies need special tuition in anything else, mustn't she, my lord? I wish to assure you, on behalf of myself and the viscount, that you have the position of governess for as long as you wish to retain it."

Miss Pettigrew's position was one of the matters they had discussed this morning, lying in one another's arms. Called into the conversation, he managed to reassure Miss Pettigrew of his respect for her and his gratitude for her care of both girls. "I will always be in your debt for rescuing Rose and bringing both girls to me here in London." He slid a sly sideways look at Arial and brought color to her cheeks by saying, "I daresay that, by the time my sisters leave the schoolroom, we will have begun filling it again."

The governess, pink and flustered at her employers' compliments, stammered thanks then excused herself to see to her charges.

Miss Tulloch was attempting to look delighted, but her eyes showed anxiety. Best let her know what they had decided about her, too. "Miss Tulloch, Lady Ransome and I have discussed your future with us also, now that Lady Ransome no longer requires a companion to give her respectability."

"Of course, my lord," the lady replied with an outward appearance of calm. "I had expected you would ask me to leave."

Arial put her hand on Miss Tulloch's arm. "That is not at all what we are asking, Clara, though if it is what you wish, we can assure you of a pension in thanks for all your years of service. I do not speak of your friendship, which has been beyond price to me, and for which I can only give my love."

Miss Tulloch's eyes filled. "I love you, too, Arial. Lady Ransome, I mean. I wish you and the viscount very happy, and I do not wish to leave you. But you have a governess and have just promised her a permanent role."

"My wife and I need a secretary," Peter told her. "Someone who knows the ins and outs of Society and who can track of our correspondence and our activities. Arial says you would be perfect for the position. Is there any chance you would consider it?"

Arial took up the plea. "I know it is unusual for a woman to be secretary to a man, but we do not think we need one each, and you know how I hate having new people close to me." She chuckled and smiled at her new husband. "Except you, Peter. And your sisters. And Miss Pettigrew."

Miss Tulloch was nodding. "I could do that. Are you sure? Am I dreaming? Oh, Arial, ever since you told me your plan, I have been trying not to worry about having to find a new position. Of course, I will stay, Lord Ransome."

Peter was pleased. Another matter settled to the satisfaction of all. "Will you do me the honor of calling me Peter? And allowing me to call you Clara? You have above all been Arial's friend, and I hope you will be mine, also."

So far, this marriage of convenience was exceeding his expectations in every way.

THE MASK THE two girls presented just after breakfast was perfect for Arial's ensemble, with the shades of the gown and the trim perfectly matched, and the flowers of the embroidery reproduced around the lower edge. She hurried up to her room to change the blank one for the pretty new confection.

Nancy was delighted. "The little ladies are very talented, my lady. I wonder that we never thought of matching the mask to your gown, but I could never have done it so well, and that is a fact."

She brought out the bonnet in the same fabric as the gown, its only trim a concealing veil. "It seems a pity to cover the mask up," she commented.

"Do we have some of the left-over ribbon used for trim?" Arial asked. The dressmaker often put a couple of yards of trim and a width of material in a packet with the gown, to enable any later repairs.

"We do, my lady." And Nancy found it and quickly unpicked the veil, then pinned loops of ribbon around the brim, finishing with a bow on each side.

Arial went out to face the world feeling more confident than she had in years.

The ladies' first stop would be a shop Miss Pettigrew knew where they might be able to buy the girls a good second-hand coat each just until the new ones were made. After that, they were off to be fitted for shoes, and then to call at the dressmaker's again. They dropped Peter off outside of Mr. Richards's office, his first point of business. "We will meet in one and a half hours at Fournier's," they agreed.

This first outing in London felt enormously challenging. Arial had to compose her face into a calm mask as unrevealing as the one she wore before they dismissed the carriage and set out to walk on their errands. Her instinctive reaction to staring had always been to shrink in on herself and hurry through whatever her business might be as quickly as possible so she could leave. It had become more tolerable in the village over the years, as people grew used to her.

Sure enough, she attracted both stares and comments. The colored mask, a pretty accessory in itself, prompted amazement and curiosity rather than horror. The errands, and the girls' delight in buying pretty things engaged her attention. By the time they reached the dressmaker's, Arial had almost dismissed her fears.

Until she saw was Miss Weatherall, sitting in the shop's waiting area gossiping with another fashionable young lady. From the way Miss Weatherall blushed and stopped talking, Arial guessed the topic of the gossip. The friend's eyes widened like saucers.

Then the dressmaker hurried up to greet Clara and Miss Pettigrew. When Clara presented her to Arial, the woman looked her over with a professional eye, and nodded thoughtfully. "Lady Ransome, it is great pleasure to meet you. Am I to have the privilege of designing a gown for you?"

"I understand you made the lovely garments my sisters wore for my wedding," Arial told her. "I have come to increase the order that Miss Pettigrew and Miss Tulloch made yesterday. My sisters need more of everything, for we are to stay in town, and the wardrobe for the country will not be adequate to their needs."

That was music to the dressmaker's ears. She called for refreshments and pattern books and fabrics.

Arial excused herself for a moment and crossed to where Miss Weatherall sat. "Miss Weatherall, I trust this morning sees you well?"

Miss Weatherall looked as if she had been sucking lemons. "It does, Lady Arial," she said, her voice clipped. She lifted her chin, as if in challenge.

"Lady Ransome," Arial reminded her. What a foolish woman,

to be so petty in public as to ignore Arial's new title. And how foolish Arial had been to let the likes of the Weatheralls prevent her from living her life to the full. Surely Miss Weatherall realized that, if Arial chose to cut her, Society would side with the earl's daughter, and not with the commoner?

The other woman whispered a demand for an introduction and Miss Weatherall had to comply. Her obvious consternation was a small but decided revenge for Arial.

A few moments later, an aide brought out the package the pair must have been waiting for, for they left the shop. Miss Weatherall commented as she went, obviously desiring Arial to overhear her, "I wonder that she can bear to be out in public."

The friend replied, "I don't know. The mask is rather fetching. Pretty and mysterious. She might set a new fashion."

Arial doubted it, but it was a nice thought.

In the end, she insisted on buying more gowns for Clara as well. "If you are to be our secretary, you will probably be going out with us," she said.

Miss Pettigrew also needed new clothes, for she had left most of what she owned behind in the country. "I can send for them," Miss Pettigrew suggested. Peter had expressed the opinion that the dowager Lady Ransome was likely to have destroyed everything. He and Arial were determined the governess should not lose because of her championship of his sisters.

The dressmaker was inclined to take exception at being asked to dress a governess. However, she found new enthusiasm for the task when her new and exceedingly wealthy client made it clear that otherwise, she would not be ordering anything for herself, and would furthermore be cancelling the orders made today. In the end, they left the dressmaker's shop a little late, and exceedingly pleased with themselves.

Peter was already waiting at Fournier's. So, it seemed, was half the polite world—taking tea and staring at Arial. Well, she had not cut and run at the staring and comments in the street or Miss Weatherall's nastiness. She would see this through, too.

Luckily, the girls were full of their doings, so Arial did not have to speak until she had recovered her equanimity.

Peter had found time to wander past Tattersalls, where a stableman had let him look at some of the horses being offered at the next auction. When the girls were busy with delectable little cakes and a hot chocolate each, Peter suggested, "I have been thinking we might wish to add a riding horse to the stables for each of us, and perhaps ponies for the girls so they can take lessons."

"And a piano, for the same reason," Arial suggested.

That was as far as they got, since the girls overheard the mention of ponies and wanted to go and buy a pair immediately.

"Ladies leave the purchase of horses to gentlemen," their governess informed them. "I am sure your brother can be trusted. He was, after all, a cavalry officer." The girls accepted the argument, but that did not stop them from chattering about ponies for the remainder of their outing.

Vivienne wanted a white pony. No, a black one. Or perhaps one that was white and brown, with a dark mane and tail. Rose agreed that all of these colors were nice, but she had once seen a bay pony with a cream mane and tail so long they dragged on the ground, and if Peter would buy her one exactly the same, she would never ask for anything else as long as she lived.

The discussion continued during their walk in Hyde Park, with the specifications becoming more and more detailed. Finally, Peter assured the girls that, while he would certainly look for ponies such as those they described, he'd be shopping for horses that matched each of his sister's personalities. "Both of them will be sweet and full of fun," he promised, and the girls were satisfied. He was a very patient man, Arial mused. It was too late to guard her heart, when his every word and action were so endearing.

The little family did not meet anyone they knew, but even so, they were the object of so much attention that Arial wondered if the Weatheralls' tongues had been flapping at both ends. She told herself once again that it didn't bother her; indeed, the attention seemed to be fascinated rather than horrified, and was far less intimidating than she'd expected.

She thought her companions oblivious to the rude staring until Peter whispered in her ear, asking her how she was bearing up. Rose slipped a hand into the crook of her elbow. Viv responded with a cold stare of her own to one particularly rude gentleman who had put his glass up to his eye in order to have a better look. "My governess always tells me it is rude to stare," she commented, loudly.

Miss Pettigrew, instead of correcting the girl, replied equally loudly, "Quite right," and sent the gentleman a glare of her own.

Arial appreciated their support but begged them to stop. "It is better just to ignore people," she told them.

"Yes," said Miss Pettigrew, her indignation making her voice loud enough to carry. "Let us show we are better bred than they are."

It did rather take the shine off the afternoon, but Arial supposed she was going to have to get used to it. She was determined not to allow her insecurities and fears to keep her from sharing the sights of London with the two girls and her new husband.

They were on their way out of the park when a fashionable barouche pulled up in front of them, and the occupant called out, "Arial!"

It was Margaret Denning, Countess Charmain, a neighbor from home. Like Arial, she was both an orphan and the daughter of an earl. Unlike Arial, hers was one of those rare titles passed down in the female line. Even more than Arial's wealth, Margaret's ability to pass a title to her son attracted suitors, most of them (according to Margaret) impossible.

Still, she claimed to enjoy the social round that her mother's sister, who lived with her, insisted upon.

"Lady Ransome, I suppose I should say. This must be your husband. I saw the notice in the newspaper and couldn't be more pleased. Will you not introduce me?" She gazed at Peter's sisters with open curiosity.

"Lady Charmain, may I present my husband, Viscount Ransome, and his sisters, Vivienne and Rosalind Ransome. My sisters now," she added, gleefully.

"Good for you," said Lady Charmain. "A husband and two sisters in one fell swoop. Very efficient. You must excuse me, Lord Ransome. I find that being blunt saves a lot of misunderstanding."

Peter bowed. "A friend of my wife's is a friend of mine," he said.

"Nicely spoken," she approved. "I have yet to make up my mind about you, Lord Ransome. But if you are good to my friend, I shall love you like a sister."

Well. That was being blunt with a vengeance.

"I'm on notice then," said Peter, and sent Arial that special smile that made her warm in her private places.

Chapter Eleven

RICHARDS WAS VERY efficient. The visiting cards arrived the next day. Arial and Peter decided they would spend a morning at home, make some afternoon calls, then Peter would go on to Tattersalls while Clara and Arial investigated pianos and music teachers.

After another blissful night with Arial in his arms, Peter was sitting in the drawing room with the newspaper, Arial across from him making some sort of a list. He could not remember when he last felt so contented.

Then someone banged on the front door. "Who could it be?" he commented. "John, perhaps? It is too early for callers."

The voice imperiously demanding entrance dispelled that notion. Peter's contentment fractured. He knew that voice. "I will not stand on ceremony," it declaimed. "After all, we are family."

The nerve of the woman.

The speaker sailed into the drawing room, already complaining. "Beau! How could even you leave me to learn of your marriage through someone else's letter?" Her daughters trailed in her wake.

Peter's training as a gentleman brought him to his feet. Manners applied even to harridans such as the dowager Lady Ransome.

"I have never been more astonished than when Mary-Louise Weatherall wrote to tell me she had been at your wedding. And when she told me the name of your bride! An earl's daughter, to be sure, but one nobody knows, and only a distant relative to the current earl. Still, she is rich, so that is a benefit, to be sure. You will now be able—"

"Hush your tongue, Madam." The abrupt command stopped the she-devil in mid-flow.

Peter turned to Arial, almost too angry to speak. But when his eyes met her laughing one, he suddenly saw how ridiculous his stepmother was. His equanimity restored, he said, "Lady Ransome, may I have your leave to present to you my father's widow, the Dowager Lady Ransome. Also, her two daughters, Miss Turner," he nodded towards Pauline, "and Miss Laura Turner."

"Good day," Arial responded, inclining her head graciously, very much the earl's daughter.

The Turner sisters bobbed a curtsy in response to Arial's tone, but the widow was made of sterner stuff. She acknowledged Arial with nothing more than "Harrumph."

Then she gave Arial her shoulder and started in on Peter again. "I demand you dismiss your coachman. I wanted to be here in London long before this. However, he insisted on stopping for the night. Absolutely refused my command to keep traveling and pulled into an inn where he told them to stable the horses. You must write to the innkeeper and complain. Am I nobody, to have my wishes ignored? Furthermore, the room was most uncomfortable."

Peter idly wondered how she had afforded a room, let alone the changes of horses needed between Three Oaks and London. Clearly, her claims that she had spent the whole of her allowance (on absolute essentials, apparently) were as fictional as her supposed affection for Peter.

"I will congratulate John Coachman on refusing to risk the horses, and incidentally your necks, driving in the dark. I expect my servants to follow my orders even where they conflict with yours, Madam."

She glared at him, and Peter waited for the next onslaught. However, Pauline tugged on her mother's arm. Her whisper was nonetheless loud enough to hear. "Careful. Remember what we talked about."

The widow took a deep breath and visibly composed herself before pasting on a shark's imitation of a smile—all teeth and no kindness. "There, but I should not scold. You have done what I told you, Beau, and taken yourself a wealthy bride. Now we are rich again, we have come up to London to enjoy the Season." She turned her attention to Arial. "Have rooms prepared for us, daughter-in-law. Mine must be on the quiet side, away from the street. I am a martyr to sleeplessness. We will need a room each, and one for our baggage. Or perhaps a dressing room? Do you have one with a dressing room? My girls will need a maid each. Peter made us manage with only my dresser between the three of us, but that will never do now we are rich again."

While Peter stood gaping at this latest insolence, Arial smiled gently. "I fear you are under a misapprehension, Lady Ransome. I know it is vulgar to talk about money, but I think we might be forgiven in this one instance when it would be best for all of us to understand what the financial situation is. It is true that I was a wealthy bride. Thanks to the marriage settlements, I am now a wealthy wife. Peter has also benefited, not least because his estates are now—or soon will be—unencumbered. We have discussed what we might do about his poor relations and other family connections such as yourself."

The dowager Lady Ransome interrupted at that point. "I am hardly a connection. I am his father's widow. I stand in place of a mother to him. My daughters are his sisters."

Peter decided it was time to assert himself. "Sit down, Lady Ransome, and do not speak until Arial and I have finished what we have to say. If you cannot keep quiet and listen, I will have the footmen put you and your daughters on the street."

The widow purpled and opened her mouth. Arial spoke before she could release whatever invective and accusations she had on her tongue. "If you listen, we will tell what we are prepared to offer to your advantage. Today. On this one occasion. Or you can protest and be ejected. For your daughters' sake, I suggest you listen."

Laura and Pauline, one on each side, guided their mother toward a sofa, begging her, "Mother, please, Mother." The old harpy subsided to a seat, a daughter on either side.

Arial nodded to Peter, who had remained standing. He looked down on the trio, his face grave. "It is my view, which my wife shares and with which my solicitor concurs, that I owe you, Madam, nothing beyond the allowance left to you by my father. Indeed, Mr. Richards notes that the dower fund my father set up for you, the interest on which should have formed your allowance, has long since been ransacked. He gives as his opinion that I owe you nothing more than the interest on what remains of that fund."

The widow had paled. "But I was promised!"

Peter kept talking as if she had said nothing. "As for Laura and Pauline, their support is the obligation of their father's family. My father made no provision, except to state an amount for their dowries. Again, those funds are gone." He looked at each of the sisters in turn. "I have no legal obligation, and no ties of blood or affection."

Arial silenced the sisters' outcry. "However…"

Into the sudden quiet, Peter continued. "My wife and I propose to reinstate those dowries. We also propose to continue the allowance that my father specified for his widow. Further, as long as either Laura or Pauline continues to live with their mother, we will pay double the allowance."

The dowager's eyes sharpened. "You mean, for as long as Laura, Pauline, or Vivienne lives with me."

"Vivienne will be living with me." Peter's statement allowed for no misinterpretation, but his stepmother began to argue, claiming that she could not let her darling little girl leave her side. Peter had no sympathy. Since Vivienne's birth, she cheerfully left her daughter in the country for months at a time while she enjoyed an active social round. Even when they were in the same house, she barely set eyes on her child. The butler paid Vivienne more attention than her own mother did.

Arial spoke again. "Lord Ransome is Vivienne's guardian. You would be wise to accept that. Carry on, Peter. Tell them what else we are offering."

Peter nodded. "In addition, Laura and Pauline, your respective dowries will become yours absolutely if, at the age of twenty-five, you are still unwed." Pauline sat up straighter, her eyes widened.

"We will also purchase a townhouse here in London. My wife will be the owner of record, but the three of you may live there rent-free until Lady Ransome remarries or dies, whichever comes first."

"I want to select my own house," the widow declaimed.

"That may be acceptable," Arial replied. "It would have to be at or under the amount we are prepared to spend, and we would need to ensure that it is physically sound and does not have other faults that would make it unsuitable. Alternatively, we can commission an agent to work to a list of your requirements, as well as our own, and you may select from the houses that the agent finds."

Peter took his turn. "I should make it clear that the offer comes with conditions. First, you will agree that we have no further obligations of any kind to the three of you. You will further agree that you will not seek to have my guardianship and custody of Vivienne overturned, either through legal means or by applying social pressure. Finally, none of you will criticize myself or my wife in any way. If you breach any of these conditions, the agreement is void. The dowries will be forfeit. The allowance will end. You will need to find new accommodation."

The look on the faces of his nemesis and her offspring as they digested the deal put before them was almost satisfaction enough to make up for paying them off.

Laura took out a handkerchief—a dainty square that was more lace than fabric—and dabbed at her eyes. Peter easily ignored the blatant bid for sympathy, thinking of long ago when the three furies had driven him from his home, and of more recent years, when they had made Rose's life miserable. The spendthrift ways of all three had contributed to bankrupting the estate. His stepmother's treatment of Rose, on its own, meant she didn't deserve a tenth of the consideration he and Arial were giving.

"If it were up to me," he said, "I would have cut you off without a penny. You can thank my wife for convincing me to provide what I have offered." She had practical arguments for the decision.

Arial had convinced him that Society's fickle sympathies would be with the widow and her daughters if he had followed his first impulse. He had to think of Arial's reputation and of later establishing Viv and Rose in Society.

Arial spoke next. "This offer is nonnegotiable, ladies. Mr. Richards will have it written out for you as a contract by the end of today. You will have two days to consider it and consult a solicitor of your own, should you choose to do so. At the end of that time, we will consider that you have rejected the offer, and that we have no further obligation to any of you."

ARIAL WAS PLEASED she and Peter had both been home when Peter's stepmother and stepsisters came to call. It was good that they could present a united front. Good, too, to have the initial confrontation over. It would not be the last, she was sure. They may have made it a condition that the three women would not criticize Peter or Arial, but vipers such as these would find a way to spread their poison without technically breaching the condition.

When it became clear to the widow that all of her grumbling would not change any of the terms of the proposed agreement, she asked to be shown to her room.

Arial's response drew another avalanche of carping and complaint. "It is a small house," Arial kept repeating, "and all of the rooms are taken." It was true. It was also true that she did not wish to offer guest space to a woman who had shown herself to be Peter's enemy.

At last, Lady Ransome wound down to the plaintive question, "But where are we to stay?"

Peter and Arial had not discussed this, not imagining the women would have the cheek to commandeer Peter's carriage, driver, and team, and come hurrying up to London. Arial met Peter's eyes; her brow lifted in a question.

He justified her confidence and rose to the occasion. "My thought, Arial, is that we send Barlowe to obtain rooms in a reputable hotel. One that caters to ladies. Barlowe will know just the thing."

"An excellent suggestion," Arial agreed. With an eye to cutting off any arguments, she added, "That said, it would probably be less costly to send them back to Sussex immediately. Surely, they could make Three Oaks before dark? But certainly, it will be more efficient for her ladyship, at least, to be in town to see the properties that Richards finds. I suppose, the Misses Turner could return to Sussex?"

To Arial's secret satisfaction, her ploy worked. The two sisters began pleading with their mother to stop being a crosspatch. "We don't want to stay with Beau, anyway, Mama," Laura insisted. "I daresay Lady Caliban—Lady Ransome, I mean—does not go out in Society."

"Nor will we," retorted Pauline. "We don't have anything fit to wear, and no money to pay the dressmaker. We are not likely to get money either, Laura, if you call Lady Ransome horrid names."

Arial thought it best to pretend she wasn't listening. Her good manners overcoming her good sense, she sent for refreshments.

When the servants brought the trays, Clara joined them. She had heard they had visitors and wanted to know if she was needed. The dowager, with a new audience, played for sympathy again. She addressed Peter. "Am I, then, to be kept from even seeing my darling Vivienne? Surely, Beau, a mother has some rights." She took a deep breath and looked at the ceiling, placing her hand on her chest. Letting the breath out with a deep sigh she observed, "None of you know the depths of a mother's heart, and the pain of losing a child."

Again, Arial and Peter communicated without words. Peter stood. "We do not intend to prevent you from visiting Vivienne, Madam. She will live with us. I will leave it to her to decide whether or not she wishes to go out with you, should you request it and should it fit in with our plans. I will go up now and ask her to come down and say hello."

Arial served tea and invited the others to help themselves from the plates of savories and cakes. The two sisters did so, while Lady Ransome favored Clara with some highly improbable tales that proved beyond doubt that Viv adored her mother and would be devastated to be parted from her.

Viv entered the room hand in hand with her brother and bobbed a curtsy to her mother from across the room. Lady Ransome held out her arms. "Come to me, you darling child. How I have yearned to behold you again."

Viv looked up at Peter. "Do I have to?" Even at the thought, the child's shoulders were hunching over, her neck shrinking— everything about her screamed resistance. When Arial was a child, she had hated being forced to allow loathed relatives to hug and kiss her. Josiah's mother had been one of the worst. She would pinch Arial's cheek, comment on her plain face and large body, and commiserate with Arial's mother that Arial had not been born a boy, since prettiness was not important for a boy.

Arial opened her mouth to defend Viv, but Peter spoke first. "Not if you do not wish to."

Lady Ransome wailed and patted a lace-trimmed handkerchief under each dry eye. "Sharper than a serpent's tooth is a thankless child," she misquoted.

"You have a new dress," Laura sneered.

Pauline's tone was pleasant. "It suits you, Viv."

Viv looked startled. "Thank you, Pauline."

"I spoke to Barlowe," Peter said in an aside to Arial. "He thinks Grillions will be just the thing and has sent one of the footmen with a note to make the arrangements."

Arial nodded her understanding. "Vivienne," she said, "your mother has nothing to eat. Will you fix a plate for her, please?"

Viv did so, ignored by Lady Ransome, who was busy telling Clara of all the occasions on which she, as a mother, had sacrificed herself for the sake of her youngest child.

Arial was pleased to note that Viv's only reaction was a contemptuous curl of the lip.

She brought the plate to her mother, who frowned at it. "What is this you have brought me. Hold it still."

Viv obeyed, the shrinking from earlier even more evident. Peter and Arial both stood and took a step forward to intervene should Lady Ransome attempt to hit the girl. Instead, she began moving things around the plate, putting the occasional small tidbit into her mouth and rejecting the rest. "I do not eat salmon pastries. And these are plum. Why did you not get me some of the cherry tarts, like Laura has? I wanted the cherry tarts. Not this cheese; it is too smelly. The bread is not the finest white flour. Arial, child, your chef is cheating you, buying a cheaper grade of bread flour fit only for servants. I would never allow such a thing to be served in any house of mine."

Peter, like the campaign officer he was, had already reacted before Arial fully realized what was happening. He put another plate on Lady Ransome's side table, murmuring, "For the items you do not want." At the same time, lifted the plate Viv held from the child's hands and put that next to the other. He drew her by the shoulder out of her mother's reach, and back to a chair near his own.

Lady Ransome was deep in a lecture about proper household management and did not appear to take any notice.

Viv soon asked to be allowed to return to the schoolroom. Peter and Arial gave their permission. Lady Ransome waved her off without ceasing her harangue.

As Arial told Peter after the three visitors left, she thought she should have taken notes, and made a point of doing the opposite of every piece of advice. "Except," she added, "in my household, we mostly do the opposite anyway."

From the time Viv left until the visit ended was a very long twenty minutes. At last, Barlowe entered to say that the arrangements at Grillions had been made, and that Arial's carriage was outside, already loaded with the luggage of Lady Ransome and her two daughters.

"That is over then," Peter said as they watched the ladies go.

Arial was developing the greatest of respect for Peter, but in this instance, he was underestimating the ingenuity of the truly venomous. *No*, she thought, *it is just beginning*.

Chapter Twelve

AFTER PETER'S STEPMOTHER and her daughters left, the afternoon proceeded as planned. Richards had sent Peter a list of names and addresses—people of consequence in Society who could ease the way of a pair of newcomers.

Peter conducted Arial from the house with a rare mix of excitement, and anxiety, and also with a touch of what honesty forced him to acknowledge was resentment. What would she think of his surprise? He had gone out and spent what he could not help but think of as her money without letting her know. Would she think he had overstepped the boundaries of their polite agreement?

Arial's reaction to the pretty little curricle was all he could have wished. She clasped his arm tighter and beamed at him. "Is it ours?" She let her eye track over the pair of greys that he had purchased with the rig. "Are *they* ours? They are so pretty!"

The grooms had curried the new arrivals to a fine gleam and polished the brass on the harness. Peter had to agree they did look pretty.

"I know we discussed a larger vehicle for trips with the girls, and I will see about that this afternoon. However, my first thought was for something for the two of us to go visiting or for a drive in the park. Or, if either of us have an errand on our own.

With the two vehicles, as well as our traveling coaches, various members of the family can go in different directions without any of us being subjected to smelly hired rides."

Arial had darted forward to become acquainted with the greys. "What a wonderful idea. But how did you find the perfect vehicle so quickly?"

Peter's chest swelled at her admiration, which was quite undeserved, for it had been mere chance. "My errands yesterday took less time than I expected, so I stopped by to see John—just so he would not think I was cutting the acquaintance after Miss Weatherall's behavior. He had a friend with him, and when I mentioned I was looking for a town rig, he said he was selling one. I took a look. It was not what we had in mind, but I thought it was just what we needed."

Arial nodded. "You are quite right."

Peter assisted her to mount, and then rounded the curricle to take his own seat. He took up the reins and gave the groom who was holding the heads of the team the nod to step away. "Apparently, it is not high enough to be fashionable, and greys are not as popular as chestnut or bays," he admitted. The groom clambered up behind, and Peter set the team moving.

"Those high perch phaetons are ridiculous," Arial declared, stoutly. "I love our new curricle, and greys are my favorite color. Why do they call them grey when they are more like milk?"

"They have dark skin and eyes," Peter explained, "so were probably not white when they were born, but their coat has turned white with age. Their age was another complaint of the former owner. They probably have another ten working years in them, but he was keen to have a pair of flighty young things. For myself, driving around town with a precious passenger, I prefer a couple of mature and sensible horses who know their business."

He and Arial were in perfect accord when they reached the first address on the list. The groom jumped down to take the team, and Peter hurried around to help Arial. Inside, they informed the butler they were merely leaving their card, placed it on the silver salver he offered, and left again.

They spent the next two hours repeating the process at house after house.

The only exception was the call on Lady Charmain. She must have heard their voices in the hall, for she hurried out and insisted on them joining her. Miss Denning, the countess's aunt, greeted Arial with delight. "My dear Lady Ransome. I saw your marriage notice! I had no idea you planned to wed but I could not be more pleased. This must be your husband!"

Peter bowed over her hand. "I have that honor."

Miss Denning insisted on Arial sitting next to her while Lady Charmain introduced the gentleman callers—three of them, two Peter would designate as young pups, and a man he thought to be in his late thirties or early forties. The pups looked discomfited by his arrival with Arial. The older man looked furious. But, when they realize Peter and Arial were married, their expressions relaxed, and they all pressed their congratulations upon him.

Miss Denning was asking Arial for details of how she came to know Peter. Peter found himself talking to the gentlemen while their hostess made fresh tea for the new arrivals. It was as he thought. All three were suitors for Lady Charmain's hand. The older man, a Mr. Snowden, must be the preferred candidate, for he treated the two pups with casual contempt and spoke of the countess as if he already possessed her.

Peter could not warm to the man.

Lady Charmain reentered the room, clapped her hands, and announced, "Gentlemen, it was very kind of you to call. I know you will understand that I would now like to be private with my friend and her husband."

The two pups made their farewells, one pressing a sheet of paper into Lady Charmain's hand. He was blushing as he said, "A little something I wrote for you, my lady."

She glanced at the paper and said, "A poem? How kind."

Snowden showed no signs of leaving, though he remained standing since Lady Charmain did.

When he saw the exasperated look in the countess's eyes, Peter decided to help. He held out his hand to Snowden. "Pleased to meet you, Mr. Snowden. My lady and I are fixed in town at the moment, so perhaps we shall meet again."

Snowden took his hand reluctantly but gave a short bark of laughter. "Lady Charmain, I had supposed you meant those two boys. Surely you did not intend to eject me?"

"That is a somewhat harsh interpretation," said Lady Charmain. "However, I was including you when I requested the gentlemen to end their call."

Peter had not thought Miss Denning was listening, engrossed as she was in interrogating Arial. She proved herself capable of paying attention to two conversations at once. "You have been here three quarters of an hour, Snowden. Over long for an afternoon call. Bad form to argue about it."

Snowden went white about the mouth and his nostrils flared, but his voice was perfectly even, if cold, when he said, "Then I will bid you good day, and do myself the honor of calling on you again." His bow was nearly shallow enough to be an insult. Peter's instinctive dislike for the man deepened.

After that, they had a delightful call. Apparently, Arial had told Miss Denning she and Peter had been friends as children, and she was convinced they had been childhood sweethearts. Peter had no objection to that story spreading around town. Both Miss Denning and Lady Charmain—or Margaret, as she insisted he call her—praised Arial's mask.

"So much more appealing than the plain white ones," Margaret commented with the bluntness that appeared to characterize both women.

Arial gave the credit to Vivienne and Rosalind, and Margaret told Miss Denning how pretty the girls were, and how well-mannered. Indeed, when they left after half an hour, the polite time for an afternoon call, they were buoyed by the success of what must be regarded as their very first social engagement.

"We must remember though, Peter," Arial warned, "Margaret was already my friend."

"We will make more friends," Peter promised, hoping it was a promise he could redeem.

⫸⫷

ARIAL WAS DELIGHTED when Peter agreed the girls could have at least one meal a day with them—downstairs with the adults rather than in the nursery.

"My mother always used to say," Arial said to Miss Pettigrew, "that the best way to learn good social manners is to observe them in adults."

"That's right!" Peter recalled. "She said you and I were old enough to join the adults! I remember that."

The following morning was the first breakfast under the new regime, and the girls were on their best behavior, determined not to lose the privilege. They even refrained from complaining when Peter's answer to their questions about their ponies was that they must be patient.

It was fun. Nice, too, to see them return upstairs to begin lessons, and to be left alone with Peter, who had a stack of mail to go through. He passed Arial some that proved to be invitations.

Arial leafed through them, torn between delight and trepidation. "Some of these are from people we have not even visited," she exclaimed. "Who is the Marchioness of Deerhaven? She says she has only just learned that we are in Town and newly wed."

"John must have mentioned it to her," Peter said. "She is married to his brother."

Arial raised both brows. She had known Forsythe was the Deerhaven family name, but had assumed John was, if a relation at all, one from a remote branch of the family tree.

"It is for tea tonight," Arial said. "I suppose we could go."

"I imagine people are curious," Peter said. "Newlyweds," he added.

Arial very much doubted that was the reason. "Kind of you, Peter. In truth, they want to see the gargoyle with the mask and the man who looks like a fairy prince."

Peter looked horrified. "Please do not describe yourself that way, Arial. If anyone else called you a gargoyle, I would call them out. And as for calling me a fairy prince! It makes me sound like fop and a bounder." His voice vibrated with exasperation.

She had put her cup down and was staring at him in surprise. "But Peter, I am horribly scarred. And you are one of the most beautiful men—no, *the* most beautiful man I have ever met." She hoped her sincerity was obvious to him. This was what she really thought.

He blinked a couple of times, and the anger in his eyes faded. He put his hand on hers and his voice was gentle as he said, "People judge us both by our looks. I don't like it, Arial. The way we look is not the sum of us. I don't see ugliness when I look at you. I see kindness and intelligence. I see the lips that kiss me so sweetly. I see the body that was made to respond to mine." He leaned across the corner of the table to place a kiss on the corner of her mouth.

"And if all you see of me is an outer shell I did nothing to deserve… I would be very disappointed, lady wife."

She turned her hand over to grasp his. "I see courage and honor and the capacity for great love. Your point is valid, husband of mine. Between us, the way we look is not important. However, we have agreed to go out in Society, and they judge by outward appearance. Please, Peter, don't go to war on those who comment on my looks. We must be prepared to meet many fools who see the glitter and the gloss and think it is the only thing of importance. Please, let us just ignore them."

Peter considered her plea, thin-lipped and stern. "I understand the point you are making, Arial. But I do not know if I can remain silent if anybody insults my wife."

"I am not asking you to ignore them, though I intend to do precisely that. Just refrain from calling them out. Please? For my sake and that of your sisters?"

A quick quirk of his lips assured her that his good sense had conquered his ire. "I can do that. I will keep in mind that I am not of high enough rank to get away with killing someone without having to flee overseas. Though if it came to that, you and my sisters could come with me." He grinned to show he was joking and changed the subject.

Chapter Thirteen

Peter's resolution was put to the test sooner than Arial expected. They were going through the invitations and discussing each one when someone set up a banging on the front door.

Arial's first thought was that Peter's stepmother was back with another litany of complaints. Then Barlowe opened the door, and the visitor began shouting before he was across the threshold. Arial flinched. She could feel herself shrinking in her chair. *Don't be ridiculous. You are married now. Josiah has no power over you.*

"What has your master done with my unfortunate cousin," Josiah shouted at poor Barlowe. "There are laws in this country against fortune hunters who inveigle wealthy halfwits into marriage. I warn you, the only way to save yourself is to abandon your master and turn witness for me."

Peter gave Arial's shoulder a quick squeeze of reassurance. He opened the door and leaned over the stairs to call down to the front hall. "Let him come up, Barlowe. On his own. Those other gentlemen can wait in the street."

Other gentlemen? Who had Josiah brought with him?

Peter added, "And close the front door, please. I imagine the neighbors have heard more than enough. If you have a moment, can you send someone with that message I mentioned earlier?"

Arial frowned at the last sentence, which seemed out of place. She took a deep breath. Peter knew what he was doing. Peter would not let Josiah hurt her. Her heart raced and her hands were clammy as the man's approach was heralded by continued threats against Peter. It was clear he assumed Peter had sent his unwanted wife away as soon as the money was in his hands.

Peter will protect me became a constant chant and allowed her to face the villain with an assumption of calm when Peter stepped out of the doorway to let him into the room.

Josiah stopped in his tracks when he saw her. "You are here. I thought…"

"We heard what you thought," Peter pointed out. "It is true, as my nurse used to say, we see in others a reflection of ourselves."

Josiah turned on him, setting his shoulders and clenching his fists. "Now see here—"

Peter was a good six inches taller and at least as broad, but without any fat. He greeted Josiah's attempt at intimidation with one lifted eyebrow, then interrupted the man to ask Arial. "The Earl of Stancroft, I presume?"

"Yes," Arial agreed.

Peter turned back to Josiah. "Leave our house, Stancroft. You're not welcome here."

"Now see here," Josiah hissed. "I have a warrant giving me guardianship of my cousin. You have no right to keep her from me. I have constables in the street to help me enforce the warrant."

That eyebrow went up again. "Show me this warrant."

It was a bark of command, and Josiah responded by pulling a folded sheaf of papers from inside his coat. Peter flattened them and read the top one, and then the next, and the one after.

For a wonder, Josiah waited. When Peter finished the fourth and last page, and handed the papers back to Josiah, Josiah smirked. "See? Hand her over, and there will not need to be any violence."

"I would like to avoid violence," Peter said, meditatively. "My wife has asked me not to call anyone out. Mind you, dearest Lady Ransome, you did not express an opinion about fisticuffs. Would you be offended if I punched your cousin?"

Josiah put his fists up in front of his face and backed away. "I will have you up for assault, as well as taking advantage of my poor deluded cousin."

There was a commotion downstairs, and another out in the street. Peter grinned. "Good man, Barlowe. Our reinforcements have arrived, my love." His grin broadened as he took in Josiah, his fists still protecting his nose, sweat popping out on his brow.

"We won't even bother having your warrant quashed, Stancroft. It is not valid. The name on it is Lady Arial Bledisloe. That lady no longer exists. Your cousin—I beg your pardon, my lady—your *second* cousin is Lady Ransome, my viscountess and my wife. I suggest you take yourself and your accomplices away before I have you arrested for disturbing the peace and being a public nuisance."

Even then, Josiah would not leave. Not until Barlowe showed John Forsythe into the room.

"Hello, Lady Ransome. Lovely morning. We've disbursed the men outside, Peter. They were under the impression that the lady had been gulled into a false marriage. Also, that she was deranged, and incapable of making a reasoned decision. I told them I was a witness myself and sent them to the vicar and Richards for a second and third opinion."

Josiah burst out, "She is deranged! Everyone knows that her own appearance drove her out of her mind. Even her own father couldn't bear to look at her."

Perhaps he had more to say, but he did not have time. Peter's fist hit his face. Arial heard something in his nose crunch. He fell over backwards like a tree cut off at the roots, turning a side table into kindling with his weight and narrowly missing the door jamb with his head.

"Nice jab," John commented.

Peter bowed to Arial. "I apologize for hitting someone in your drawing room, my lady. It needed to be done."

To herself, Arial could admit it was very satisfying. Perhaps she could tell Peter that, when they were alone. Not in front of Barlowe or John, or the two burly men that John beckoned into the room.

"This is the Earl of Stancroft, men. I imagine his equipage is the one waiting on the corner. Put him in it, will you? Tell them to take him home. Then return here for further orders."

The men carried Josiah out. He was stirring, and groaning. On the whole, Arial was glad he was not worse hurt. Injuring an earl might have repercussions they did not want to deal with.

"Thank you for coming so quickly, John," Peter said. "I was afraid Barlowe's messenger might find you out."

John grimaced. "It was the least I could do. I am afraid his appearance today is down to Mrs. Weatherall. She is friends with Lady Stancroft and wrote her a letter. I found out by chance when I arrived early for an engagement with Belinda and overheard the two of them talking. Of course, I guessed he would come here, so I made my apologies and sent for the men. We were just leaving my building when your messenger arrived."

He cast Arial a helpless look. "I am so sorry I brought this trouble upon you."

"You could not have known that Mrs. Weatherall would be so determined to make mischief," Arial pointed out. "Nor are you responsible for her actions. I join my thanks to Peter's. Your arrival was timely, indeed. This is obviously something the two of you planned. Who were those men?"

"Soldiers we knew from the army," Peter explained. "John has been helping them to find work and accommodation while he waits for another post."

"I'd like you to employ the two that took Stancroft away," John said. "They need work, and you need guards. Peter told me, Lady Ransome, that the men you already have are keen to head back to your village."

"Yes, and where were they?" Peter wondered.

Barlowe wasn't sure, but when he went to inquire, he came back with Sergeant Miller, who was very apologetic about having been out when the villainous earl arrived. "I gave the men the morning off, my lord," he said. "I, er, just stepped out for a moment. I should not have done so, but I never thought of anything happening this early."

The sergeant agreed that the two men from Sir Thomas were keen to go home but asked if he could stay on. "I want to protect her ladyship, and I can see that the job isn't done," he said.

So, Peter accepted the services of John's ex-soldiers to bolster their strength. "I'm sure Josiah will not win in the end, but I'm equally sure that he has not given up."

"I think we have something else to thank you for, Captain Forsythe." She picked up the invitation.

"Oh, yes. I did happen to mention my old comrade's new bride to my sister-in-law. Will I have the pleasure of seeing you tonight, then?"

Arial nodded. At least one other person they knew would be there. Or perhaps two. "Will we also have the felicity of seeing Miss Weatherall?" she asked.

John replied in the affirmative, but he did not look happy about it.

Poor man. Arial revised her opinion that the Weatheralls would break off the betrothal if someone better-connected showed an interest. Poor John was heir apparent to a marquess, since Lord and Lady Deerhaven had no sons. A parvenu like Belinda Weatherall was unlikely to find someone better connected than that.

Chapter Fourteen

London, March 1817

"THREE WEEKS OF dinners, soirées, balls, musicales. Afternoon calls and drives in Hyde Park." Peter grimaced. "I think it's been necessary—I think it has worked. But I hate that establishing Arial's sanity and her right to her own choice of husband means impressing people for whose opinion I don't give two farthings."

He was having lunch with John at John's club. Peter, too, had joined Westruthers, figuring he needed a refuge for occasions like today, when the female component of his family had gone out without him.

"Cordelia seems to have taken your wife in great affection," John commented.

That was true. Lady Deerhaven and Arial had liked one another from the first, and Lady Deerhaven's sponsorship had opened many doors for the Ransomes. "Arial and my sisters are visiting her at the moment. The girls have become great friends with your older nieces."

"What of the evil cousin?" John asked.

"He seems to have given up, at least for the moment." Peter shrugged. Stancroft's next ploy, after the failed attempt to burst into Peter and Arial's townhouse with constables, had been to lay an information with the local magistrates, alleging that Arial was feebleminded, and that Peter was holding her against her will.

Accusations made by an earl could not be ignored. Accusations made against a viscount concerning his viscountess could not be actioned without further investigation. Three magistrates questioned Arial, Peter, the household servants, Richards, John, and the vicar who performed the wedding. They then told Stancroft that his cousin was well and of sound mind and had married Peter of her own free will.

Arial was relieved. Peter did not trust Stancroft's silence.

"Most of the gossip now is just sour-minded, and people take it as such," John offered. "A few people tried to make a thing of her masks, but Cordelia told everyone she knew that they were marvelous." He raised his voice in a very inaccurate imitation of his sister-in-law.

"So pretty, and practical, too. She was badly injured in a fire when she was a child, you know. Poor darling. Her mother and brother died, and she was not expected to survive. She is a real lady, to cover her scars for the sake of the weak-minded, do you not think? I have always said that character matters more than looks, but I must say, with those lovely masks and her wonderful carriage, she is a beautiful sight to behold, is she not?"

Peter grinned. "That's what she said, is it? And no one will gainsay the Marchioness of Deerhaven. Not that she's wrong, John." To him, Arial was beautiful inside and out. He had become well enough acquainted with every part of her, except for the side of her face she kept covered and scars on her shoulder she still would not show him. Therefore, he was the only person with a right to an opinion.

He supposed she was not the kind of ethereal sprite or cuddly little doll that Society currently seemed to prefer, but neither type had ever made his mouth water. Nor other juices rise.

She was a wonderful companion, an excellent partner who

matched and inspired him, and a delight in bed. Sometimes, he could even imagine she had married him for himself, and not for his protection.

"You have that fatuous smile on your face again," John observed. His smile was weak. "I am delighted for you, my friend."

Peter just wished that he could see a like happiness in John's future. But unless Miss Weatherall abandoned him, that was unlikely—and it seemed John was coming to realize that fact.

Peter cast about for a change of subject, but had no time to introduce it, for a complete stranger walked up to the table where they were sitting, dropped to his knees, and said to Peter, "I know you will want to call me out, Lord Ransome, or horsewhip me, more likely. And I don't blame you. I didn't mean to do it. I don't know how it happened. But I am so sorry. I cannot express how sorry I am."

Peter was fairly certain he had seen the man before, but he couldn't put a name to the face. "I'm sorry? What is it that you've done? And who are you?"

"His name is Mandeville," John said. "He is one of Belinda's court."

Ah, yes. Peter had seen him at various entertainments, following the lady like a puppy along with half a dozen other gallants.

"You had better take a seat, Mandeville, and tell me why you have come."

Mandeville did as he was told, looking even more like a puppy, and one in expectation of a sound kick. "Buck is going to kill me. Uncle only lost all our money. I've destroyed our reputation, or I will have if people find out it was me. I will do anything to make it up to Lady Ransome, my lord."

Peter, who had been watching the performance with some amusement, stiffened. "You had better start at the beginning."

It was worse than Peter could have imagined. This idiot had been one of Arial's suitors. Like the others, he had given his solemn word not to speak of her husband hunt or of anything that Richards or Arial herself disclosed.

"I drank too much," Mandeville admitted. "I saw you and her out and about, so happy. Everyone was talking about how rich you are now—how you've paid off your mortgages and bought a townhouse for your mother." Peter clenched his fist. He hated any reference to Arial's wealth. Mandeville made him sound like a damned fortune hunter.

But Mandeville had not finished. "And Lady Ransome—I never knew she could look like that. Like a queen. Everyone admires her. I thought, that could have been me."

Maudlin and drunk, he had poured out the story of his interview with Arial to one person. He would not name the person, but his furtive glances at John were a strong hint.

"I told her it was in confidence," he said. "She would not have talked to anyone else, would she? Not when I told her it was a secret."

Mandeville's behavior seemed an overreaction. Until he laid a flyer on the table—one of those scurrilous cartoons that the printers pasted in their windows and sold as news.

The figures were a caricature of a plump woman from the side, a half mask in the hand away from the viewpoint, and a skinny man who was in the act of losing his lunch into a flowerpot.

The caption said, in large letters, "Lady Beast's Husband Hunt," and underneath, "A certain masked lady purchased herself a husband—once she found someone brave enough to embrace what lies beneath the mask."

The speech bubble above the woman read, "But sir, will you not come and embrace all my lovely money?" The man had a speech bubble, too. "The horrific sight of Lady Beast's scars offends my stomach. No amount of gold can entice me to wed her."

John glared at Mandeville. "You bastard."

Mandeville gave a sob.

Peter's surge of rage was not helpful. He needed to clear his mind and think about what was best for Arial.

"Am I right in thinking that the most damaging part of this is the suggestion that my lady wife purchased herself a husband?" Peter asked John. "As this worm says, people have seen how lovely Arial is, and Mandeville's reaction to a few scars is on him."

Mandeville shrank a little more at the contempt in Peter's voice.

John nodded, thoughtfully. "We need Cordelia," he said. He stood and gestured to Mandeville. "Bring the worm."

Chapter Fifteen

AT THE DEERHAVEN townhouse, the three men were directed out into the garden. Arial, Clara and Miss Pettigrew were in the garden with Lady Deerhaven, watching a flock of girls at play.

Five of them—Viv and Rose among them—were sitting on the grass chattering like starlings while they wove flowers into garlands. Two very little girls were playing with a pair of kittens. Another two, slightly older, were floating paper boats in the fountain under the supervision of a pair of nursemaids.

"Here come my brother-in-law and your husband," Lady Deerhaven declared. "And young Mandeville, Breckham's brother. Do you know Mandeville, Lady Ransome? Miss Tulloch?"

Arial paled, and Peter moved to take her hand, and tuck it into his arm.

"Cordelia, we have need of your expertise," John told the marchioness. "Can you spare some time to give Lord and Lady Ransome some advice on some news Mandeville has just brought us?"

Lady Deerhaven's brows climbed towards her hairline. "Is there a problem? Yes. I see that there is. Come along, then. We shall go to the library. I believe Deerhaven is there. Would you object to involving him, Lord Ransome?"

"Not at all. His advice would be welcome." In the few weeks since Lady Deerhaven had taken Arial under her wing, Peter had come to admire the marquess's bluff good sense and his affectionate respect for his wife.

"I will stay with Miss Pettigrew and watch the children," Clara offered. Lady Deerhaven led the rest of them inside.

Peter would have spared Arial the cartoon if he hadn't been certain that someone else would show it to her if he didn't. Her reaction was not what he expected. "Poor Mr. Mandeville. You must be so embarrassed."

Mandeville was pathetically grateful for her forbearance and apologized repeatedly until Lady Deerhaven interrupted. "Yes, yes, Mr. Mandeville. It is done now, and it is to be hoped you have learned from the experience, and in future will keep your mouth shut when you have promised to do so."

He subsided into a wilted silence.

Lady Deerhaven had more to say. "For the most part, my dear Lady Ransome, this is easily managed. You were forced to consider an arranged marriage to protect yourself from that villain Stancroft, is that not correct?"

"It is," Arial agreed.

Lady Deerhaven beamed. "Your solicitor presented you with a carefully vetted list, but nobody suited. Then your childhood sweetheart came along, and you were wed."

She dusted her hands, though Peter doubted the marchioness had ever touched anything dirty in her life.

Lord Deerhaven beamed at his wife. "Well done, Cordelia. Stancroft becomes the villain, Mandeville the idiot, and the two of you the romance. Everyone will sympathize with you, I can assure you."

"But if I admit it was me, everyone will know that it is I who spoke of the matter," Mandeville objected.

Both Lord and Lady Deerhaven subjected him to a withering glance, lifting their eyebrows in unison. He subsided again.

The marchioness cast an imperious glance around. "Anything

else?"

"No, Lady Deerhaven," Arial told her. "We will do as you say."

Lord Deerhaven added, "John, you may tell me that the baggage who has her claws into you had nothing to do with this reaching the caricaturist, but I shall not believe you. I shall not interfere if you mean to keep her, but if you want to be rid of her, then you could do worse than to discuss the matter with my lady wife, for she knows exactly how to deal with designing hellcats like that."

"I say," say Mandeville, "I cannot believe that the divine Miss Weatherall meant to cause any mischief. She spoke out of turn. Might have happened to anyone."

John looked at him thoughtfully, then spoke to Lady Deerhaven. "Perhaps we might have that discussion now, Cordelia, if it suits you."

Deerhaven ushered the rest of them out of the library. "Mandeville," he said, "a word, if you please."

Mandeville managed a nervous bow. "My lord."

"This entire conversation was confidential, man. I trust you now understand what that means. You do not breathe a word of it. Not to anyone. Not in your cups, not when stone cold sober, not under any circumstances." He paused to study the man, his brows slightly furrowed, then pressed his lips together and nodded.

"In fact, given that almost all of Society is going to be laughing at you by this evening, once that scurrilous bit of trash has made the rounds, a repairing lease in the country would be just the thing."

"You mean…" Mandeville paled still further, which Peter would not have thought possible. Any moment, the man was going to pass out at their feet. "But do I need to tell people it was me. Lady Ransome—the mask, and… well… But—You won't tell people, will you?" He looked at each of them.

Peter thought he probably looked as inflexible as the marquis.

"If people do not guess, Mr. Mandeville, you may depend upon it that Miss Weatherall will tell them." If Society laughed, so be it. Peter certainly had no sympathy for the man.

But Arial was made of kinder stuff. "You are concerned about disappointing your brother. Is that it?"

Mandeville nodded, gratefully.

"You will have to tell him what has happened, of course, but tell him, too, that you are going to stay in Town and take responsibility for your mistake. You can make recompense to me, Mr. Mandeville, by being brave enough to admit to anyone who asks you what you have told us. That you were disappointed at not winning my hand, got drunk, and told someone in confidence of my attempts to arrange my own marriage. And that you are ashamed of your breach of confidence."

"And your weak stomach," Peter muttered, adding in a louder voice. "I don't think he can be trusted, Arial."

"I do," Arial said. "Mr. Mandeville is very sorry, and he has learned his lesson. He was brave enough to come directly to you with the flyer, Peter."

"I can do it," Mandeville insisted. "I will do it. Thank you, Lady Ransome. I am so sorry for... I'll do it. Thank you. Thank you." He took his hat and gloves from the butler who had materialized to hand them to him, and allowed himself to be conducted from the house, still repeating his thanks.

"I need a drink after that," Deerhaven announced. "Anything, Ransome? Lady Ransome?"

Arial excused herself to return to the garden and the girls. Lady Deerhaven joined them there a short while later. "Your husband and his friend have gone to see the printer of that objectionable piece. Deerhaven has gone too. It will probably do no good, but it makes the men feel useful."

At that point, one of the littlest girls tried to climb into the fountain after a boat and burst into tears when restrained by a nursemaid. Lady Deerhaven hurried over to take the child from her servant and soothe her with a mixture of cuddles and to scolds.

For a time, Arial was able to put the nastiness to one side and enjoy helping the garland makers to form and don crowns of flowers.

She was then co-opted as part of the audience for a presentation the girls had apparently created between them while making the garlands. The eldest Deerhaven daughter introduced herself as the Princess Cassandra, cursed with never being believed. She then declaimed the tragic story of four other princesses from history, while the girl representing that princess mimed the actions beside her.

The littlest girl wriggled into her nursemaid's arms then went to sleep. The child on Lady Deerhaven's knee watched every move, as rapt as the erstwhile boat mistresses. The servants sighed and cheered in all the right places. And everyone clapped enthusiastically at the end of each story, and at the end, when all five princesses curtseyed, their faces flushed with success.

"Bedtime for the little ones," Lady Deerhaven proclaimed, "and milk and cake for everyone else. Come and give Mama a kiss, my darlings, and off you go. Lady Ransome, do say you will allow your darling sisters to stay a little longer and join my daughters for a snack?"

Arial was happy to agree, and Viv and Rose strolled off with their new friends, hand in hand in a long chain of five girls, still wearing their flower crowns.

Lady Deerhaven took Clara and Arial inside with her. "We, too, need refreshments, do we not?"

Her servants clearly understood their mistress, for tea and cake waited in a pretty little sitting room.

"May I ask what was troubling Lord Ransome?" Clara asked, once they were seated.

Arial gave her a quick summary as Lady Deerhaven prepared them each a cup of tea.

Clara shook her head. "Why would a person wish to be so mean? I cannot see how Miss Weatherall is advantaged by making that disgraceful story public."

"It is much to her disadvantage, I assure you," Lady Deerhaven declared, with some satisfaction. "My husband's brother has become disenchanted with the young woman. However, as a gentleman he could not break the betrothal, and saw no choice but to wait for Miss Weatherall to do the right thing."

She nodded, decisively. "I have made several suggestions. For example, I do not suppose for one moment that Miss Weatherall has considered what a marriage to a career army officer might involve, especially to a husband who has no reason to treat his wife with more than common decency."

Her smile was akin to that of a cat with exclusive access to its own cream pot. "She has an eye on the marquisate, of course, though dear John would be horrified should he be forced to take on the title. However, Deerhaven and I have at least ten more breeding years yet, and I do not mind telling you that in a few months from now we hope to relieve our brother's mind."

She had no more to say on the topic, instead turning the conversation to Arial's need to continue to go about in Society as she had been doing. "The more people see you are every inch a lady, and your husband is devoted to you, the more they will be offended on your behalf at that scurrilous flyer. And the less they will be inclined to believe defamatory comments and insinuations from your despicable relatives."

Arial had to agree, but she was not looking forward to the next few weeks.

As Lady Deerhaven predicted, Peter and his friends had no success with the printer, who claimed he had not named anybody, and, therefore, no harm was done. Peter was annoyed about that but delighted that John planned to disentangle himself from Miss Weatherall.

"Lady Deerhaven suggested that he adamantly refuses to house Mrs. Weatherall or make any financial contribution to her upkeep," he told Arial. "And John is to play the stern tyrant from now on, demanding that his betrothed banishes her court. He will make it clear to her that, given her behavior, he will not trust her. He will give her the choice of coming with him on campaign or living quietly in the country on a small allowance while John is overseas. Deerhaven is helping John draw up marriage settlements to that effect."

"My goodness," Arial said. "I should think that will do it."

Peter agreed. "And if that is not enough, Deerhaven commented that his youngest daughter is nearly three years old. He hinted that he hoped for many more children and said that they would be cutting the Season short this year, for Lady Deerhaven always requires a lot of sleep when she is increasing."

"Miss Weatherall will not at all like being married to a second son with no expectations and being kept on a limited budget."

"One can only hope," said Peter. "Do we have to go to this ball, tonight, dear wife? In fact, can we not just go home to Three Oaks? I know Lady Deerhaven thinks to turn Society's mind in our favor. But if Society has a mind, it is small and mean. I am tired of small and mean."

"I don't want to run away, Peter. We can send our apologies for tonight, if you wish, but all our reasons for going out in Society still apply, if not more so. We may not like many of the people we meet, but their opinions will affect your sisters and our children, if not the causes that you and I support."

Peter sighed. "I'll go to the ball," he agreed, "if you really want to."

Arial did not particularly want to. She would really prefer to stay home and have an early night. But the girls were excited about the new mask they had made to match the gown that had been delivered yesterday. Besides, she hated to let small-minded gossips and nasty critics think that they had won.

"Then I had better go up and begin to prepare," she said.

Chapter Sixteen

T HE BALL WAS not as bad as Peter feared. Some women snickered behind their fans. A few conversations stopped when he and Arial walked by. A few would-be wits made sly allusions to the French tale, *La Belle et la Bête*, or the opera based on that story.

On the other hand, several people came up and introduced themselves. One of them put into words what the others were delicately dancing around. "I have seen the caricatures, Lady Arial, and they have made me all the more determined to meet you and to offer you my support."

The lady was a widow, a Mrs. Paddimore, and a friend of Lady Deerhaven. She stayed to talk for several minutes, finding common ground with Arial in their joint enthusiasm for a series of books by a pair of Englishmen who had, for the last decade, been entertaining the United Kingdom with their journeys in different parts of the world.

As had become usual when there was dancing, Arial soon accepted several invitations to dance. Peter wanted to refuse them all, afraid of what might be said to her when he wasn't at her side.

Also, if he was to be honest with himself, because he preferred to keep all her dances to himself. She showed to advantage on the dance floor, though she had confided in Peter that all her experience until her marriage had been confined to dancing with Clara.

He had, as usual, solicited the first dance of the evening, and the supper dance. But when the music began for the second set, a contre-dance, he had to release her to go off with Lord Hershaw, a prominent Corinthian whom Peter might have liked if the man had not been so obviously an admirer of Peter's wife.

Presumably, Hershaw said nothing out of place, for Arial was smiling when her second partner of the evening took over for the next dance in the set. Again, nothing went wrong that Peter could see. Arial returned to Peter's side slightly flushed from the exercise but smiling.

She was engaged for the next set, too, and this one was clearly not as innocuous. Watchful from the sidelines as she and her partner stood together waiting for their turn to take up the pattern of the dance, Peter saw her stiffen at something the man said.

In the next moment, she pasted a smile back onto her face, saying something in reply.

The man stiffened in his turn, then bowed so slightly that the courtesy was itself an insult and offered his elbow. Arial ignored it, turning away and setting off around the edge of the dance floor toward Peter. As he strode to meet her, Peter saw Stancroft and his wife pushing their way to the front of the spectators so Arial had to pass them. They hissed something as she came level with them.

A few steps later, she placed her hand in his, her color high and her eye glittering.

Peter looked over her shoulder for her dance partner. He was nowhere to be seen. Probably as well. Punching him would relieve Peter's feelings and enliven the evening but was unlikely to quell the rumors.

He tucked Arial's hand onto his arm and escorted her out onto the terrace where they could talk. "What did he say?" he asked.

"Mr. Frankton? Or Josiah?"

"Yes." He lifted her hand to his lips. "I can see that Frankton upset you, and whatever Stancroft said, I'm sure it was poison."

"As to Josiah, it was nothing. Just spite. Marjorie commented that she was astounded I was brazen enough to show my face, and Josiah replied that I didn't. That I went everywhere masked, so I did not frighten children and spook horses." She shrugged. "Perfectly true about the children. I suspect horses are made of sterner stuff."

Peter thought a foul oath but kept it behind his teeth. He had not hit Josiah hard enough, but that could be amended. "And Frankton? It must have been bad for you to walk away from him in the middle of the set."

"I should not have done that. I made a scene and drew attention to myself."

"On the contrary. You were overcome by the heat and needed a moment outside. What did Frankton say, Arial?"

Arial looked down at their hands, still clasped between them. "Do you promise you will not call him out? Or make a scene?"

"I will not call him out, and nor will I make a scene. But I will make him regret the day he insulted my wife. He did, Lady Ransome, did he not?"

She looked up and met his gaze. "He asked me if, like the Loathly Lady of Arthurian legend, I turned into a beautiful succubus at night, and then proclaimed it apparently didn't matter to you, since my money was lovely enough. He said he had heard that you cover my head with a flour sack before lying with me. He offered himself as a substitute, since I apparently possessed—I cannot repeat the word, but it referred to what he sees as the important part of a female's body."

Peter passed straight through red-hot rage to stone cold wrath. *I will kill him. I will hunt him down and extract his balls through his nostrils. When I have finished with him, there will not be enough left to bury.*

"Peter, you're hurting me."

Peter became aware that Arial was trying to tug her hands free. He loosened his grip. "I am sorry," he said. "Are you all right?"

"Are *you* all right?" She put a hand up to cup his face. "I should not have told you. Peter, he only said what others are thinking." Arial cast a quick glance around to make sure they were alone on the terrace, then slipped her arms around his waist and rested her head against his chest. "I am all right. Their words cannot hurt me, Peter."

Peter moved farther into the shadow beside the door. Holding her in his arms quieted his battle rage like nothing else could. But it also fed the cold anger behind the rage. Whatever Arial said, she was wounded by the gossip. He saw it in her eye, felt it in the stiff way she held herself.

Frankton could not be allowed to get away with treating her so contemptuously.

As for the insult to him, it stung all the worse because it was partially true. He *had* married Arial for her money. He was ashamed that it was true, and it shamed him more because he had chosen it freely, and still resented it.

After a while, she sighed and lifted her head. "Thank you, I needed that. We had better go back in."

"Let us go home," Peter begged, but he was not surprised when Arial expressed a preference to stay. "The next set starts soon. My next partner will be looking for me."

"Who is it?" Peter asked and conceded that the man was decent enough. He hovered through that set, and only relaxed when Deerhaven took Arial onto the floor. The supper dance came next. Peter had half an hour to hunt for Frankton. But search as he might, the man was nowhere to be found.

It was probably just as well. Peter would not have been able to contain his wrath, and Arial would have been displeased. The man had only postponed his punishment. An example had to be made, so the whole world knew the dangers of insulting Lady Ransome.

Chapter Seventeen

T HE FOLLOWING DAY, Peter made certain that Arial was fully occupied dictating replies to correspondence from her investment managers. She was going to be busy all morning, she said, when he'd asked what she had planned for the day. He did not want her going anywhere without him, though he sensed she would take exception if he made that an order.

When she said she planned a couple of afternoon calls, he offered himself as escort, and was relieved when she agreed. Nonetheless, when he left home on his own errand, he worried that she might set out on an unplanned excursion and meet with further insult.

It irritated him that she would not be guided by him and retire to the country until all of this nonsense blew over. Why didn't she understand that he only wanted to protect her?

John was waiting for him at their club. "Are you going to call him out?"

"I promised Arial I would not do so. Did you find out where he spends his time?"

"My valet spoke to his, and I managed to talk to a couple of his friends," John said. "He is a late riser, so he will be at his townhouse, probably having breakfast, if you want to deal with the pond scum in private."

Privacy didn't suit Peter's plan at all. "I want somewhere with an audience of gentlemen, the more the better," he told John.

John rattled off the places that Frankton was likely to be during the remainder of the day.

"Tattersalls will suit," Peter said. "Just to be certain we have reputable witnesses, John, who do you know that might like to come and look at horses with us?"

They invited several other club members, and John decided to see if he could bring Deerhaven. "No one is more reputable than my brother the marquess."

They agreed to meet at Tattersalls an hour after midday, and Peter headed home to make sure Arial was still there and was safe.

He was at Tattersalls at the appointed hour and found a dozen men waiting for him—a mix of officers and peers, all men of honor.

"Here he comes," John warned.

Peter kept out of sight in the crowd, waiting for Frankton and a couple of his friends to pass them so there was no way the villain could exit the horse yard without going through Peter.

"Frankton!" he called.

Frankton turned in his tracks, paled, and then sneered. "Look, gentlemen," he said to his friends. "Lady Beast's lapdog."

Peter cast a glance at his friends and gestured towards Frankton. "Look. It is a worm, pretending to be a gentleman." He examined Frankton from head to toe and back again and curled his lip. "No. Worms are useful creatures. Let us say, rather, a cowardly cattle tick. And what do we do to cattle ticks, gentlemen?"

Frankton paled, then flushed. He puffed out his chest and demanded, "You shall meet me for that insult, Ransome."

Peter returned sneer for sneer, with interest. "I would not demean myself by meeting you, Frankton. You are not a gentleman."

"How dare you!" Frankton shrieked, putting up his fists and

beginning to dance from foot to foot.

Peter spoke over him to the men around him. "I ask you, gentlemen. What manner of man invites a lady to dance so that he can whisper unspeakably corrupt lewdness to her? If he does that to a married lady whose husband is a seasoned army officer, and well able to protect her, can he be trusted with any lady ever again?"

Frankton was sputtering, but Peter called out two of the men he knew by sight, because they had been escorting their sisters to some of the events Peter had attended with Arial. "Wilson? Becksnaith? Do not let him near your sisters. I won't repeat what he said to Lady Ransome, but if he can act with such disrespect to the daughter of an earl and the wife of a viscount... Well, I leave it your imagination how little respect he will show to ladies such as your sisters."

"No!" Frankton protested. "I wouldn't! Not a true lady! But Stancroft is her cousin, and he says she is a monster. And Ransome's own mother agrees! Ransome is the one showing disrespect, carting that hideous bitch into decent homes and pretending she is a lady."

He found himself dangling by his cravat from Peter's fist. Peter's voice was a low growl. "I strongly suggest you do not insult my wife again, Tick."

He shook the man once more for good measure and dropped him to cough and splutter his way to a full breath.

"Bad form, Frankton," Becksnaith said. "Come on, Wilson. The air stinks around here." They left, taking another couple of Frankton's erstwhile companions with them, so that only one remained.

Peter stirred Frankton with his foot. "You have been listening to the wrong people, Tick. Stancroft is a leech who resents his cousin because she was a better steward of the earldom than he will ever be. My stepmother... well, I will not sully my tongue with insults to a lady."

Frankton made to get up but froze when Peter stretched out

his hands as if yearning to strangle the man. Which was no more than the truth.

Deerhaven took a hand. "London has suddenly become unhealthy for you, Frankton. I recommend a long journey."

Peter agreed. "Starting by nightfall, after which I shall come looking for you with a horsewhip. Do I make myself clear?"

"Oh, I say," said Frankton's remaining supporter.

Deerhaven lifted his eyebrows and stared down his nose at the man. "Markham, is it not? Do you believe it is the act of a gentleman to accost a gently born lady and sully her ears with threats of corrupt intimate practices?"

"I didn't!" Frankton sobbed.

"Ransome's lady wife could not bring herself to repeat the words you used to make your threat," John told him, "But we got the sense of them. A bag, Frankton? A rope, too, I imagine, for I cannot envisage any female submitting to your vileness without being restrained."

Frankton whimpered as his last supporter turned away, having to push through the onlookers who had gathered from all four corners of the establishment.

One of them was Richard Tattersall, the second of the name and the third of the dynasty who had run the famous sales yard and subscription rooms since 1766. "If my lords have quite finished imparting a lesson to this scoundrel, I trust you will allow us to return to business," he said politely. "You may be sure that Mr. Frankton is no longer welcome in these premises."

"I will blackball him at my club," offered another gentleman.

"And I at mine."

Frankton picked himself up and ran from one person to another, babbling explanations and begging for a second chance. At a nod from John, two of the men who had come to support Peter picked the louse up by the elbows and carried him to the entryway, throwing him into the street.

"Now, gentlemen," said Deerhaven. "Were we going to look at some horses?"

Chapter Eighteen

ARIAL REALLY SHOULD have kept what Frankton said to herself. She had been in shock. No one had ever spoken so crudely to her. Or, if they had, it was before she had any experience to be able to understand what they were saying.

She heard about Peter's retribution not from him, but from Lady Deerhaven. "Deerhaven is very proud of himself. I just hope they have not drawn even more attention to these ridiculous flyers."

There was a second caricature out the day after the confrontation at Tattersalls. This one showed a man with his breeches down to his knees, his bare buttocks on display as he bent over a woman with her skirts up. Both figures wore sacks over their heads, and the caption read, "When I tup Lady Beast, I wear a bag in case hers falls off."

Peter kept that from Arial and was indignant when she marched into the room he was using as an office and slapped a copy in front of him. "Where did you get that? I gave instructions…"

She met his anger with her own. "To keep me in the dark? To treat me like an infant?"

He leaned forward over the desk. "Dammit, woman. To protect you!"

Arial swallowed her response and took a deep breath. Shouting back at him was not going to help. She forced her shoulders to relax as she let the breath out. "A partner. A friend. That is what you said you wanted, Peter. That's what I want to be. Someone on your side and at your side. Is that still true? Because when you go off and confront Frankton and do not tell me about it, when you try to hide this stupid image from me, it does not feel like it."

It was Peter's turn to swallow back whatever words had boiled onto his tongue. "I did say that didn't I? I apologize, Arial. I did not mean to insult you. I just don't want to see you hurt."

Arial slapped the piece of paper. "This nonsense does not hurt me. Having you keep me in the dark hurts me." Tears scalded her eye and she blinked furiously.

Peter rounded the desk and gathered her into his arms, and for a moment, she just wanted to lay her head on his shoulder and let the tears out. She resisted. "I am so angry, Peter. I seem to have brought you nothing but trouble."

"The trouble came with me," Peter insisted. "The pot is being stirred by my stepmother and my best friend's betrothed."

"And my loathsome cousin," she reminded him. "Perhaps I can concede that we both have unfortunate connections."

He chuckled, she smiled, and they kissed. Then Peter told her about his visits to Josiah and the dowager Lady Ransome, both of whom denied any connection to Frankton or the flyers. "And Frankton has left town. I have nothing to confront them with except his word, and I can't even produce him to confirm it."

Arial forbore to point out that running Frankton out of London was his idea. She was glad the man was gone. The people who talked behind her back were much easier to ignore.

Even after that discussion, she and Peter were still cautious around one another, each measuring their words and watching the other for a response. It did not help that Arial's female inconvenience arrived the next day, along with the usual cramps and headache.

"Peter," she told him, once she realized, "I will need to make my apologies for this afternoon's visit to the Tower. Will you be happy to escort the girls? If not, I am sure Sergeant Miller or one of Captain Forsythe's men will go along with the group."

"Are you unwell?" Peter asked.

"I am a little under the weather today," Arial admitted. "I am not ill, Peter. It is a regular inconvenience. I will be perfectly recovered in a day or so."

When Peter suggested that her symptoms were a response to the gossip, she realized he had no idea what she was hinting at. She struggled for the words to explain. "It is not that. I have my woman's inconvenience."

He still looked blank, so she tried again, her face heating. "It is the periodic bleeding to which women are subject. I have cramps in my belly, and plan to go to bed with a hot brick."

Now Peter flushed. "Oh. I didn't… That is, is there anything I can do for you? Should we have…? I mean, last night, was I too…?"

That he was as embarrassed as she was helped to steady her. "Last night was very pleasant." Last night, like every night in the past three weeks, had been magnificent, incredible, mind-blowing, but discussing things of the night in the broad light of day was making her very uncomfortable.

"I am like this every month. The discomfort will pass quite quickly. I will send a note to Lady Castleford begging off tonight's musicale—unless you wish to go without me?" At Peter's grimace, she nodded. "By tomorrow, I will manage my normal routine."

She needed to find a way to tell him how long before they could resume their nights together, which was even more embarrassing than the rest. Thankfully, he took the initiative. "When may we…"

"It varies. Perhaps five days?" Her face must be bright scarlet. "I will tell the housekeeper to make sure your bed has clean sheets."

Peter looked startled. "Clean sheets? Oh yes, of course." He dropped another kiss on the top of her head. "I hope you feel better soon."

Arial thanked him, and went up to her room, sending a footman for Nancy on her way. All the time she was sipping the peppermint tea her maid brought her, and afterwards as she lay in a curl under the covers, waiting for the heat from the wrapped brick to soothe her muscles, she wondered at that last exchange. What had surprised him about clean sheets for his bed? After all, he could not have expected to come to her own while she was indisposed. Could he?

PETER TOSSED AND turned for the second night in a row. It wasn't that the bed was uncomfortable. He had slept well enough his first night as Arial's guest. But ever since then, he had shared a bed with Arial. He missed her. He missed joining with her, but beyond that, he missed sharing a bed with her. He missed spooning himself around her, her fragrance in his nostrils, his torso pressed against her back, the bend of his knees echoing the bend of hers. He missed going to sleep with her in his arms and drifting upwards through sleep aware of her breathing softly beside him.

He should have asked if he could stay with her. But perhaps she didn't want him. Perhaps the presence that had become such a joy to him, even a necessity, was to her a disturbance. She was anxious to have a child. Perhaps she just tolerated his attentions in order to achieve that happy result. Though she certainly seemed enthusiastic enough at the time.

He had checked on her several times yesterday and today, but she assured him that all was proceeding as it should, and that she would soon be better. Clara said the same thing.

He sat up, got out of bed, and lit the candle. He would pour himself a drink and think about what he had learned today. There was new spate of flyers. The original printer was still reprinting the original caricature and the second one but had added a third.

"Lady or Fiend?" said the heading. The female figure underneath had a line drawn down the center of her body. On one side was a fashionably gowned and coiffed female. On the other a ghastly creature, naked, with six dugs, goats' legs and hoofs, a long serpent's tail ending in a narrow point, all topped by a horned skull.

Other printers had taken up the sensation of the moment, with variations on the theme that Peter's wife was hideous and had the behavior and appetites of a beast. Several showed the figure meant to be her naked but for the signature half mask, and in coitus in the position known as *doggy style*. The companion figure was not always human.

He was going to have to show Arial. If he did not, someone else would, and then she would be hurt he had kept the truth from her. Why could she not understand that it was killing him not being able to protect her from these malicious calumnies?

In the past few days, some of the invitations they had received had been rescinded without explanation. On the other hand, their company was being solicited by some of the worst notoriety hunters in Society. Peter wasn't sure which was more disagreeable.

From what his friends said—Peter had stayed home the last two nights while Arial was indisposed—public opinion was largely sympathetic. There were those who professed to be horrified by Arial's mask, now that they knew what was underneath, but many of them were friends of either Stancroft or the dowager Lady Ransome.

Peter could not prove it, but he was certain those two were stirring the pot. The Weatheralls were subdued, but John intended to make the break with them soon, and no doubt they would join the campaign against Peter and his wife once that happened.

It was dawn, and the house was beginning to stir. Peter was

clearly not going to go back to sleep. He might as well put on some clothes and go and read the steward's report that arrived late yesterday afternoon. Turning his mind to Three Oaks would be a welcome relief.

ARIAL CAME DOWN to breakfast and declared herself fully fit again. Peter didn't argue, though she was pale and had purple bruises under her eyes. He caught her up to date with the Three Oaks report, and she shared with him some of the correspondence that she and Clara had dealt with the previous afternoon.

When that conversation flagged, Arial had a request. "I hoped that today, it being fine, you might have time to take me driving in Hyde Park, Lord Ransome."

Hyde Park! Where every idle fribble, gossip monger, and counter coxcomb went on the strut to be admired? Peter could think of little that would please him less. "Are you sure? One cannot get the cattle up above a slow walk. I can think of better places for a nice drive."

Arial, though, wanted to see and be seen. "I have not been out for two days. I want people to know I'm not hiding. If you drive me around for half an hour or so, word will soon get to those who have not seen for themselves."

Peter would rather that they hid. Going back to Three Oaks was looking more and more appealing. However, he agreed to Arial's outing. First, though, he would have to show her the latest collection of flyers. He didn't imagine anyone would be crass enough to face her with them on their drive, but he didn't want to take the risk.

Arial raised her eyebrows at the pictures and blushed at the indecent ones. She was inclined, though, to be optimistic about their likely impact. "They have gone too far, Peter." She raised one of the worst and put it down again. "Our friends will be as indignant as you are, but even those who are mere acquaintances will recognize these as outrageous rubbish. The viciousness of the lies may work in our favor by garnering us the sympathy of Society's leaders. After all, if people can be made outcasts on the basis of provable fictions, nobody is safe."

Peter shook his head, doubtful. However, on the drive through Hyde Park and at the theater that evening, many people approached with invitations, compliments on Arial's gown or her mask, and even outright statements of support. Even one of the patronesses of hallowed Almack's sought them out to assure Arial that she would be sent tickets.

Then the Duchess of Winshire, one of society's most influential matrons, cast the weight of her reputation on their side. She had one of her stepsons escort her to the Ransomes' theater box, where she reminded Peter that she had known his mother. She further claimed to have kissed Arial when she was a baby. She took a seat next to Arial, in full view of the rest of the theater, chatting for several minutes.

When she stood to leave, she said, "You are doing the right thing, my dear Lady Ransome. Facing down these ridiculous calumnies is your best option. It is unpleasant, I know, and takes courage, but I and my friends have seen that you have plenty of courage and are of good character, besides."

She held out her hand to Peter. "You have found yourself a treasure, Lord Ransome. Young ladies who are beautiful on the outside are common enough in Society. Young ladies who are brave, wise, and honorable are much rarer—and my friend Cordelia Deerhaven assures me your wife is all three."

Peter bowed and mimed a kiss above the back of the duchess's hand. "I am fully sensible of how fortunate I am, Your Grace. My wife is a delight to my eyes as well as a true friend and partner."

"Good answer," the duchess replied. "Come along, Drew. Your father will wonder what is keeping us."

Chapter Nineteen

T HE DAY THEY went to Hyde Park and the theater proved to be the turning point. With people like Lady Deerhaven, the Almack patronesses, and the Duchess of Winshire showing their favor, the snide remarks, rescinded invitations, and public snubs ceased.

Undoubtedly, some people still chose to believe that Arial had purchased a husband because she could not get one by any other means, and that Peter had been greedy enough for her fortune he had been willing to take her along with it. That was close enough to the truth—if you left out the mitigating circumstances—to sting Arial's pride a little. The growing affection between Arial and her husband, which the same people regarded as a public display with no substance, soothed the sting.

The Stancrofts had tried to reignite the public outrage against Arial, but their remarks had so incensed those who followed the lead of Society's grand ladies, that they had retreated to their country estate.

As one of Arial's new friends, Regina Paddimore, said, "Good riddance."

The dowager Lady Ransome and the Turner sisters had been circumspect through the whole nasty business. If they had contributed to the gossip, they had been careful to do so away from the public eye, and those they confided in had been unusually silent about their sources.

As for the Weatheralls, Miss Weatherall had agreed to break her betrothal at the end of the Season. John—Arial and her husband's closest friend were on first name terms in private conversation—treated the Weatheralls with stiff courtesy in public, and his betrothed responded by flirting madly with her court. Arial assumed she hoped to find a replacement before the end of the betrothal. She doubted the split would come as a surprise to anyone.

Arial could admit to being selfishly glad it had lasted this long. According to Peter, John had told the two women he would publicly jilt Belinda if he found out either one had been speaking against Peter or his wife.

The end of May saw the couple still in London. Deerhaven had persuaded Peter to take an interest in the responses of the government to the disorder in the provinces. Peter sympathized with the need to address dangerous working conditions, and the economic hardship suffered by so many people throughout the country.

Deerhaven was a Foxite Whig, a member of the main Whig opposition. Peter was uneasy about some of the things espoused by the Whigs, but he agreed with their stand against the suspension of *habeas corpus*, and he had a deep sympathy for those labelled as seditious merely because they marched for reform.

He allowed Deerhaven to propose his name for several committees in the House of Lords.

While he was finding satisfaction in helping to run the country, Arial had cemented friendships with several ladies whose passion for helping people to a better life sparked her own philanthropic urges. She helped Lady Charmain raise money for a medical clinic in the slums. She, Mrs. Paddimore, and several other ladies made baby clothes for poverty-stricken mothers in expectation of a blessed event. She even taught for an hour twice a week at a ragged school, finding that the little ones learning their letters first demanded an explanation of her mask and the tracery of scars, and then ignored them.

She missed Viv and Rose. The two girls had returned to Three Oaks with Miss Pettigrew. Peter had made the decision after several incidents in which children repeated the insults they had heard from adults, sending Viv into a fighting fury and reducing Rose to tears.

They had gone willingly when they found that the promised ponies had been found, purchased, and transported to Three Oaks, and were ready to meet their new owners. They wrote several times a week, and Arial wrote back. Peter twice rode down to visit and to attend to estate business, but both times, she had commitments that prevented her from traveling with him.

Arial and Peter had settled into a routine that she found vaguely disappointing. The nights were still bliss. But the promise of those first few weeks of their marriage had never quite been fulfilled. Peter was always willing, when he was available, to be her escort. He always treated her with courtesy and respect. But their commitments took them in different directions, and they seldom spoke of anything more gripping than the weather, what joint invitations they might accept and snippets of news from the girls.

Arial could barely wait for Parliament to go into recess. In four more weeks, they would be on their way to Three Oaks. Perhaps, in the more casual atmosphere of the country, she and Peter could recapture some of the closeness that she missed.

Breakfast was her favorite meal. Peter was often at Parliament at dinnertime, and frequently ate lunch at his club. Or Peter was at home, and Arial was out and about. Even when they were both at home at the same time, Clara was always with them. In the morning, Clara usually took a tray in her room, and Peter and Arial breakfasted alone together.

They would tell each other their plans for the day, perhaps arrange a place and time to meet if they were going to the same event and discuss anything in the early morning mail that was interesting enough to interrupt breakfast for.

The interruption to breakfast on the second Monday in June came not through the mail but in a letter hand delivered to Barlowe. "A groom from Three Oaks arrived with this a few minutes ago, my Lord. He has ridden through the night. I hope it is not bad news, sir?"

From Peter's worried frown as he scanned the single page, it was bad news indeed. Arial reached out to put a hand on his arm, hoping to comfort him. He briefly covered his hand with his own. "Viv and Rose both have measles," he said. "Miss Pettigrew thinks I should come."

Arial stood. "I will order our baggage packed."

Peter caught her hand, and she turned to look at him. "Arial, have you had measles?"

Arial frowned. "Not that I can remember. Nancy might know." Nancy had been her mother's maid before the fire, so she had known Arial a long time.

"I remember I had it when I was nine. You and your family were staying, and they wouldn't let you visit me," Peter said. "Check with Nancy, but if you have not had the disease, you had better stay here in London or go to Greenmount. I don't want to risk you, Arial. Measles is dangerous enough for children, but it is worse for adults."

Nancy confirmed that Arial had never had the illness, and she reluctantly agreed to remain behind. Peter set Barlowe to packing his bag while he called Sergeant Miller in to remind him of his responsibilities. Miller had been missing several times when wanted—making up to a young woman, Barlowe said. Peter told the man to attend to his duty and leave flirting until his day off.

Later that morning, Arial waved Peter off from the front step. She had filled several baskets with treats and little gifts and foods that might attempt reluctant appetites. Another had medicines—a bottle of lemon and honey cordial for sore throats, a bottle of calendula ointment to soothe rashes.

It was all she could do, except wait and worry.

"Perhaps I should go home to Greenmount," Arial said to John when he called that afternoon. He had received a note from Peter and had come to offer himself as a replacement escort for any events she wished to attend while she remained in London.

"I can escort you to Greenmount, if you wish," John offered.

Clara narrowed her eyes as she looked up at the ceiling. "What would we need to cancel?" It was a rhetorical question. Clara had proven herself a superb secretary, the memory and eye for detail that had been an asset to her as governess and then companion coming into their own in her new role.

"The most important thing is our dinner party to solicit donations for retraining ex-soldiers," she concluded.

Arial grimaced. The cause was important to Peter and John. They both employed as many ex-soldiers as they could, and John had also sent many to work for Deerhaven. Such men had often joined the army with no skills or trade beyond that of laborer. Others could no longer return to their former work because of the injuries they had suffered. Training them in a new skill gave them back their pride and allowed them a future. The charity Arial and her friends were helping to set up aimed to extend that work beyond the small number that Peter and John had been able to help directly.

"The dinner party is in six days," she acknowledged. "We must stay for that. John, do you think Deerhaven would host in Peter's place?"

John shook his head. "My brother is taking Cordelia home. Her doctor and the midwife think she might be having twins. If so, they are likely to arrive early, and Deerhaven doesn't want his wife confined on the road, or here in London just as the hot weather starts. He is just tidying up a few loose ends, and they leave the day after tomorrow."

Arial made a mental note that she must call on Lady Deerhaven with her best wishes. She was not surprised at John's news. Last time she had seen the marchioness, Lady Deerhaven had looked huge, even in the fashionable gown designed by an expert modiste to disguise her condition.

"Perhaps you could do it, Captain Forsythe," Clara suggested.

It would be unusual for a bachelor to host a party where the hostess was a married woman, but everyone knew that Peter and John were the best of friends, and that the dinner was to raise money for their project. "Yes, John, would you?"

John did not answer immediately, doubtless having the same hesitations as Arial, but after a moment he agreed.

"What else?" Arial asked Clara. "Can we leave London after the dinner party?"

Clara lifted a hand and began checking events off on her fingers.

Several were before the dinner party, and Arial let John know the ones to which she needed an escort. A few days later was a garden party she thought she should attend. It would be her friend Regina Paddimore's first entertainment since she came out of her blacks, and Regina had been preparing for it for months. "Planning it has been the most fun I've had all year," she had told her friends. "I must admit to being anxious, though." A garden party. Arial could manage that.

"Clara, we will cancel anything else after the garden party," Arial said. "Please give me a list of the hostesses to whom I should write a personal note."

"Then," John said, "I will hold myself ready to escort you to Greenmount late next week."

"Ten days," Arial agreed, "Unless the girls are well enough for me to go to Three Oaks."

IN THE EARLY hours of the next morning, Arial lay awake thinking about her marriage. She found it hard to sleep without Peter beside her. It had been so from the first. When he took a quick trip to Three Oaks. When he retreated to his own room during her monthly inconvenience. She would toss and turn, unable to get comfortable, her mind wandering restlessly from one topic to another.

She had not expected to miss him so on that first night they spent apart. Almost, she had begged him to stay with her the following night. She talked herself out of it. She would be wise not to forget that theirs was a marriage of convenience. Peter's physical desire for her, and hers for him, was a bonus. She could not ask him to sleep next to her, primed for action, as it were, when she was not available to give him relief.

It crossed her mind several times to ask him how he felt about sleeping in her bed without marital congress. She could not form the words. She was too afraid he would reject her—or worse, agree politely, and force himself into something that he disliked.

Her marriage had turned out exactly as she feared. She had fallen in love with her beautiful, kind, clever husband. That was not part of the bargain, and she could never let him know.

AT THREE OAKS, Miss Pettigrew had confined the girls to the schoolroom floor, and banned any maids or footman who had not had the measles. Viv was rather grumpy about not being allowed out of bed. She was also running a fever, covered in an extremely itchy rash, and bothered by a persistent cough. Still, Peter thought that the time to worry about her would be when she stopped complaining.

He was already worried about Rose. Her fever was higher, her rash was worse, she complained that the light hurt her eyes, and she lay listless between bouts of coughing that racked the body that was still too thin despite several months of adequate food.

Miss Pettigrew offered the opinion that she had put her energy into growing several inches once she was properly fed and had little left to fight the illness.

Having checked on the girls, Peter went to wash and change, and found his housekeeper had celebrated the removal of his stepmother by having all of his things moved into the master suite, which Flora Ransome had claimed as her own when his father died. The room had been redecorated the way she liked it. The servants had taken down her fussy floral drapes and replaced them the plain deep blue curtains he remembered from his childhood, but the pink and gilt of the wallpaper and the white paint over the oak paneling still offended his eye.

He did not demand to be moved to another bedroom. He did not want to upset his housekeeper, understanding her need to make a grand gesture after her earlier vacillating. She had drawn him aside to assure him of her loyalty. His stepmother had warned her and Edwards the butler that she would still be here and still in charge after Peter had returned to the army, and they had believed her. "But now you are married, my lord, and she will never be mistress here again," the housekeeper proclaimed, with great delight.

Perhaps that was why a number of servants had followed the dowager to London. It left the house short-staffed, but Arial would soon put that right, and meanwhile, they would not be entertaining.

Peter gave orders for one of the bedrooms on the schoolroom floor to be prepared for him so he could be close to his sisters, and thereby avoided suffering Lady Ransome's décor while not hurting the housekeeper's feelings.

He settled in to help. Miss Pettigrew and one of the maids managed their intimate care, but Peter could lift them so their sheets could be changed. He could read to them and tell them stories. He could hold their hands when the urge to scratch became overwhelming and the soothing ointments that Cook made were no longer sufficient to stop the itch.

He could sit up with them through the night. It was not as if he could sleep when Arial was so far away. He missed her during the day, storing up thoughts to share with her, imagining her going through her routine and wishing he was there. At night, he yearned for her. Not just for her lovemaking, though he longed for that with a deep ache.

Rather, every one of his senses reached out to find her in the dark and woke him in protest at the vacancy in her place. The touch of her, within reach of his hand through the night. The sound of the little noises she made in her sleep. The smell of her—her soap, her perfume, the musk from their lovemaking, all mingled into something uniquely Arial. The taste of her, lingering in his mouth after he had kissed her and pleasured her. The sight of her in the early dawn or when the moon was full, all relaxed in sleep, her shape under the mask and her night rail even more familiar to him than his own.

Even after months of marriage, he had still not seen her un-clothed. He had still not persuaded her to sleep, or even to share marital intimacies, without the mask or in the light. He understood her reasons. It didn't stop her rejection from hurting. For if she truly loved him, surely, she would trust him?

Love. He grimaced in the dark. He could not blame her for not loving him when love had never been part of the bargain—when it was not something he had even wanted. He wanted it now. He loved his wife. He was not always comfortable with her. Little things irritated: her refusal to leave London and its insults, her insistence that the money she had brought into the marriage was his to do with as he liked, her self-possession when he wanted her to need him as much as he needed her.

He loved her anyway and wanted her with every particle of his being.

At least, if he sat with his sisters, he had something useful to do to distract him from daydreaming about his wife, naked and spread before him.

Three Oaks itself also kept him awake. He slept poorly, waking at the least sound, convincing himself with difficulty that he was alone, and no longer at war. One night, he was so certain there was an intruder in his room he got up and searched everywhere, even opening the door and looking down the empty passage. He had trouble going back to sleep, so certain he was that someone had left the room when he sat up in bed and called out.

Peter preferred being on the schoolroom floor with his sisters where his memories were mostly pleasant. His nanny, and later his tutor, before he went away to school. His mother, and occasionally his father. And sometimes the child Arial and Miss Tulloch—Clara, as she was to him now.

In more recent memory, before he left for the army, it had been a place of refuge—for the new Lady Ransome had little interest in the daughter she gave his father and even less in the daughter he had demanded house room for. Only Pauline occasionally ventured up to the nursery. Otherwise, Peter was free of them all up here.

His father's study was tolerable. Peter had made it his own when he came back here to live. The desk was not new, but nor was it the one that his father's new wife had installed to go with the new fashionable decor. He had recovered this one from the attics, along with several other pieces of furniture he remembered from his childhood, and a couple of rugs that help to change the appearance of the room.

Even so, the memory of his father lived in this room—his father as he was after the fire. Harried, drunk, and grumpy. That mood got worse when his father married the former Mrs. Turner, and brought her home as his viscountess, together with her two daughters. After that, the viscount was seldom home, and when he was, he and Peter clashed on every topic.

The rest of the house was full of ghosts. Many of the rooms echoed with Peter's old arguments with his father. Others with the carping and snide remarks of the Turner sisters, and the new viscountess's constant criticisms and demands.

Even without them, the disapproving presence of Edwards continued to invoke their memories. As soon as the crisis with the girls ended, Edwards had to go. He was surly. He obeyed orders as slowly as possible. His petty rebellions infected the rest of his staff, so that the footmen's work was slovenly and often only half done.

Peter had slipped on a soapy mess at the top of the stairs early one morning as he made his way from the girls' room to his own. It must have been there since his bathwater had been removed the night before, but no one had cleaned it up until after Peter had nearly fallen down the stairs.

Things had to change, and he would begin by dismissing Edwards. Once he could bring Arial home, he would beg her to redecorate throughout. Perhaps she could turn this old pile back into the family home he remembered from when his mother was alive.

How he missed her!

Chapter Twenty

June, 1817

IN THE EARLY hours of one morning, Arial sat looking out into the garden, a tapestry of shadowy shapes in the light of the half moon. She was sipping a glass of cordial and thinking about Peter's latest letter.

He had been gone five days and had written to her twice. A brief note when he first arrived to tell her that Viv seemed to be weathering the illness well, but that he was worried about Rose. Today's letter reported no change. Viv continued to be a little under the weather, and grumpy because she was not permitted to visit her pony. Rose was still running a high fever, was racked with coughs, and seem to be having trouble breathing.

Arial wished she could fly the miles to be with them all. If she did, she would only be adding to Peter's worries. All she could do was send up some fervent prayers.

It was too dark to reread the words at the bottom of the letter. Nor did she need to. They were engraved on her heart, and she only wished she knew exactly what they meant.

I miss you. Missed her as in her skills would be useful to him? Surely, he could not possibly mean that he felt incomplete without her, as she did without him.

Perhaps he just meant that his body craved hers. Hers certainly craved his. It was odd to realize they had only been married for a little over four months. In that time, they had enjoyed marital intimacy almost every night, frequently several times a night. Idly, she set her mind to calculating how many nights they had been married, and how many of those they had shared a bed.

They were married early in February, and it was now June. One hundred and twenty-two nights, then. This was the fifth night of the current separation. Two nights from the other two trips. And she had had her courses twice since their wedding.

Wait a minute. That cannot be right. She thought back over what they had been doing, the engagements she had cancelled on her worst days, what was happening in London at the time of each brief withdrawal. *Only twice.* The first time had been at the beginning of March. The second was the day after Palm Sunday. She had had her first cramps at Evensong the night before.

There had been two more full moons since, the latest a week ago.

She was with child. She cupped her free hand gently around her belly. *Hello, little one.* A kernel of acceptance opened, grew, and blossomed. Suddenly, the tenderness in her breasts made sense. And her sudden repugnance for smells that had never before offended her.

Apart from those, she didn't feel any different. If only Lady Deerhaven was here to talk to. Margaret and Clara were both unwed. So was Nancy. And Regina and her husband had never had children.

She should write to Peter. Or perhaps not. She would rather tell him in person. She continued to sit, her hand possessively over the child cradled within, her mind far away in the future.

JOHN ARRIVED AS she and Clara were having breakfast, so excited about the news that had been waiting for him when he got home the previous evening that he could not wait for a more civilized hour. He was at Barlowe's elbow before he could be announced, already talking as he walked into the room. "Good morning, Arial. Cordelia has given birth to twin sons. My brother says that they are very small, but perfect."

"Set another place, please Barlowe. Sit down and have some breakfast, John. How wonderful for Lord and Lady Deerhaven. Is she well?"

"It was quick and easy, my brother says, as these things go." He took the plate Barlowe offered and filled it with such a mountain of selections from the sideboard that Arial suffered a pang of longing for Peter, who also filled his plate high in the morning.

John took a seat and a sip of the coffee Barlowe poured for him before tucking into the food. While he ate, Arial and Clara peppered him with questions, most of which he laughingly disclaimed any answer to.

"Cordelia and Deerhaven have asked me to be godfather to the little sprouts," John told them. "They want me at Deerhaven Court for the christening. I'll be here for your dinner party tomorrow night, Arial, but I'll have to go home to Deercroft Hall the next day. If you will give me leave, that is. I know I promised to escort you to Greenmount."

Arial told him not to give it another thought. After all, she had Clara for company, and all her servants, including Sergeant Miller and the tough ex-soldiers that John and Peter had selected for her protection.

She was in no danger from the ordinary perils of the road, and marrying Peter had, as planned, made any attack prompted by Josiah's greed futile.

She would be perfectly fine.

Word of Deerhaven's twins was all over town. "I daresay you may expect to be jilted soon, Captain Forsyth," said Regina Paddimore, when she met John, with Arial and Clara, in the reception line for a ball that evening.

Regina was right. Not half an hour later, Belinda Weatherall stormed up to John where he stood with Arial and several other of their friends.

"You cad!" Her voice was a near shout. She snatched his wineglass from his hand and slammed something into his palm. He picked it out and held it up—the betrothal ring he had given her.

"Our betrothal is off," Miss Weatherall announced. "You can give that to your paramour. Oh, but you cannot, can you? Her husband might ask questions." She shot Arial a venomous glance.

The accusation was so unexpected that John's response was a weak, "I say!"

Miss Weatherall had not finished. "As soon as Lord Ransome left town, you have been in and out of that woman's house at all hours of the day and night, and you cannot deny it. How dare you make promises to me and then take up with a female who is more beast than human. I am glad that I have seen you for what you are before it was too late."

She opened her mouth to say more, but John had had enough. "No more! The reason I told you months ago that I would not marry you was because I saw you for what you are. Only a wicked mind would see evil in the commitment I made to my friend to look after his wife while he was absent. I said I would allow you to jilt me. Thank you for finally doing so." He gave her a courteous bow, ironically deep and theatrical.

Arial was tempted to ask Miss Weatherall whether her decision was influenced by the birth of the new heir apparent to the Deerhaven marquisate and his younger brother. Cordelia's timing could not have been better. She caught the words back, and watched Miss Weatherall flounce away, probably to spread her own version of the broken betrothal to her friends and sycophants.

Those nearest them had hushed all the better to hear the altercation. Regina spoke into the silence. "When I said she would jilt you now you are no longer heir to the marquess, Captain Forsythe, I did not expect to be proven right quite so quickly." She chuckled. "And how like Miss Weatherall to make up another calumny when it was her earlier lies that led to you revising your opinion of her character. Does she think Society is made up of fools?"

She had pitched her voice to carry beyond their group.

Arial could admire her strategy but was not confident it would achieve Regina's aim. After all, in Arial's experience, Society contained a fair proportion of fools.

Miss Weatherall had stalked the length of the ballroom to join her mother. As people clustered in groups to share what had happened and their opinion about it, Arial lost sight of Mrs. Weatherall. She didn't see the moment when the two of them met.

However, she did see who stood with the matron. Josiah was back in town, with his wife on one arm and Mrs. Weatherall on the other. Peter's stepmother and his two stepsisters also stood with the group.

Arial turned to tell John what she had seen, but he was looking in the same direction. "I imagine they mean to cause trouble," he said. "I am not sorry now that I lost my temper and spoke in an ungentlemanly fashion to my former fiancée."

"It is to be hoped," said Regina, "that your words and mine will give the gossips some truth to chew on along with their nonsense."

THE NEXT DAY, the caricature campaign began again, with some of the old accusations and several new ones based on Miss

Weatherall's accusations. "For them to be out on the street by dawn," John commented, when he called that afternoon, "they must have been on the presses before we met Belinda last night. This was planned, Arial."

He wanted Arial to change her schedule so he could escort her to Greenhaven before traveling on to Deercroft, though the marquess's family seat was on quite the other side of London, not far away from Three Oaks Manor.

Perhaps I can go to Deercroft instead of Greenmount and be close to Peter. Arial dismissed the thought. She could not impose herself, uninvited, on the new parents. "I am in no danger, John. They are only words. Those horrible people want to make me suffer, and I will not let them."

And, she would not let John know that these particular words made her feel ill. Such venom. Such nasty minds. She wanted to tell Peter all about it. She restrained herself. He would want to be there to protect her and would worry about her when his focus should be on his sisters. She had no intention of easing her own mind at the expense of his.

She also didn't mention to John, or tell Peter in her letters, that Mr. Richards's chambers had been broken into. The solicitor arrived early that day to let her know. "They did not manage to break into the safe, Lady Ransome, but they did steal some documents from the shelves where we file draft copies before destruction. I regret to inform you that your wills, yours and Lord Ransome's, were among those stolen."

She and Peter had made some minor amendments several weeks ago, to add small legacies for their new causes. She made a mental note that the wills would have to be revised again, to include the new baby, while assuring Mr. Richards that she was unconcerned.

"What possible use are our wills to a burglar? I daresay they merely picked them up in a bundle of other things."

She thanked him for his visit, sent for Barlowe to show him out, and settled to making some last-minute alterations to the evening's seating plan.

She welcomed her guests that evening with some trepidation. During the event, everyone politely ignored the caricatures and the scurrilous ballad sheet that had come out that afternoon. The food was delicious, the company pleasant, the conversation intriguing.

They moved from the dining room through to the drawing room, where she had set up card tables. In the conservatory beyond, there was room for a small dance floor, and she had hired a pianist to play for those interested in a more active form of entertainment. She, Clara, and John circulated through the rooms soliciting support for the retraining of ex-soldiers and were happy at the end of the evening to have sufficient promises to cover their first year of operations.

"Peter will be thrilled," John said, as he took his leave. "I'll leave it to you, Arial, to write to him and tell him how well we've done."

"I will do that in the morning," Arial promised. "Travel safely tomorrow, John. And please give my congratulations to Lord and Lady Deerhaven."

"Safe travels to you, too, Arial. You and Clara look after yourselves. And watch out for that pit of vipers while you are still here in London."

He kissed her hand and allowed Barlowe to show him out.

✦

Chapter Twenty-One

THE SUCCESS OF the dinner party lulled Arial into believing the storm had passed. She was disabused of the notion the very next day, when she and Clara went to an afternoon musicale. It was back again, and worse than when she was on Peter's arm—the sudden buzz of conversation when she entered, the number of people who turned their back and pretended they did not see her, the nasty remarks as she passed, whispered just loud enough for her to hear.

Head high, she greeted her hostess and did her best to ignore those who were determined to show their contempt. She should not have come. None of her particular friends were present. Only her pride kept her there, and once the musical selections were over, she made her excuses, and left.

There were a group of people outside her front door when the carriage drew up. They crowded up behind her footman as he opened the carriage door and put down the steps. At the head of them was a man with an open journal and a pencil, who shouted at her, "Arthur Scammell from *The Teatime Tattler*, Lady Ransome. The people have some questions. How do you feel about the caricatures of you?"

The footman elbowed Mr. Scammell in the chest, so that he stumbled backwards. Barlowe must have been watching, for

John's two ex-soldiers and several other footmen hurried down the steps from the front door, linking arms into two rows to make a path for her to walk through.

Mr. Scammell had picked himself up, and was leaning between the footmen, moving from one shoulder to another, shouting questions. "What do you look like without the mask? Is it true you are having an affair with Captain Forsythe? Is it true that Lord Ransome found you in an asylum and married you for your money?"

He was on her blind side, so she could not see him without turning her head. Nor did she see the screeching woman who threw herself against the protective line and tried to snatch her mask. A gasp from Clara made her turn around just in time to see Clara hit the woman's hand with her reticule. Others were heckling and jeering, and a group of urchins threw rotten fruit with little accuracy and great delight.

She hurried up the steps with Clara and Nancy at her heels, stopped in the doorway to usher them inside, and turned to take a final look at the mob just in time to see an egg flying directly towards her face. Before she could duck, a silver salver appeared in front of her. The egg crashed against it, breaking with a crunching sound. Barlowe shook off the salver, scattering droplets of raw egg across those crowded closest.

Arial stepped back, and Barlowe shut the door on the faces of the crowd.

"The men?" she asked.

"One has gone for the constable, my lady. Two will stand guard outside the door. The rest have been told to go around the house and check for intruders in the garden and the mews before coming in through the kitchen."

She took a deep breath for calm and smiled at him. "Thank you, Barlowe. You seem to have everything under control."

"You need a nice cup of tea," Clara observed.

Arial needed her husband. And she needed this persecution to end.

Once again, Sergeant Miller had been absent for the invasion. "He has been sneaking off, again, though Lord Ransome warned him not to," Nancy said. "He is courting, my lady, and very secretive about it, too. But he says she is a lady!"

Arial did not go out the next day, but she did read *The Teatime Tattler*. To her surprise, Mr. Scammell had written rather a sympathetic article. He described her courage under fire and the loyalty of her servants. He described "the graceful and dignified form of Lady R., whom some believe to be the Lady Beast recently lampooned by less reputable purveyors of news than this fine magazine."

He went on to report interviews with what he called, "...several interested parties, some sympathetic and some hostile." One of these was, apparently, "...a lady of society discomfited when the gentleman she had claimed as her own discovered her deceitful and unkind nature by comparison with that of the new bride of his best friend. Instead of amending her fault, this lady chose to slander the bride." His description of an interview with "a cousin of the gentle lady" suggested—without exactly saying—that said cousin was a vicious liar, driven by greed and jealousy.

Regina, who had called to see how she was, said she had spoken to the man herself. "I thought someone should explain to the newspapers what is really going on." She smiled what Arial thought of as her *cream pot* smile. "I told him why Miss Weatherall really broke off the betrothal, and about Stancroft's attempts to get his hands on your money."

She chuckled. "He came back later to tell me that Miss Weatherall contradicted herself with every second sentence, and that Stancroft threatened him with a beating if he mentioned him in any way."

Arial was impressed. "Perhaps I should give him the interview he requested, as a reward for his bravery."

Regina doubted it was courage. "I am sure his editor is selling newspapers by taking a contrary position to the other printers.

After all, the others have long since parted with reality to find something new to say. Defending your reputation is good business."

"I am grateful, whatever their reasons," Arial insisted.

"Have you told Lord Ransome?" Regina asked.

Arial explained, "I don't want to worry him. His sisters are both very ill. It is a nuisance, Regina, that's all. My people make sure I am not at risk."

"You know your own business best," Regina said, sounding doubtful. "You are right that your Peter would ride *ventre a terre* up to Town if he knew of this latest bother. He loves you." She sighed. "I do envy that."

Arial could not accept Regina's conclusion. It was true that Peter was protective of her, lusted after her, and treated her with respect. But that was not love. Was it? She changed the subject. "Will you marry again?" Then, embarrassed at prying, she added. "I apologize. I should not have asked."

"We are friends, are we not? Friends can be honest with one another. If you trespass, I will let you know." Regina studied her teacup for a moment. "In answer to your question, I would like children. A husband is a prerequisite. But I am not yet so old and so desperate that I will take any of the suitors currently showing an interest."

She shot Arial a wry glance. "Not that most of them are interested in marriage, as such."

Arial did not know quite how to respond. She knew that widows had a certain license but had not considered they might feel as hunted by prospective lovers as men often felt by prospective brides.

Regina sighed again. "As a young girl, just out, I dreamed of meeting the perfect gentleman. Of falling in love and being loved in return."

She shook off the dismal mood with a laugh. "Well. At some point, I shall tell you the whole sorry tale of my ruin and Gideon Paddimore's rescue. I was content in my marriage, Arial. But I would have liked children, and I do hope for more than contentment if I marry again. I said I envy you, but you also give me hope."

Arial hated to disabuse Regina of the notion that she and Peter had a love match, so she said nothing.

Regina continued. "Yours was an arranged marriage, whatever the story you've told the gossips, and yet you and Peter are thoroughly in love, as is plain to everyone except the pair of you. You should tell him how you feel, Arial. Gideon always used to tell me that men are idiots about feelings and need our guidance in such matters."

"Should you not be home getting ready for the garden party tomorrow, Regina?"

Regina laughed. "I am to stop trespassing, in other words." She waved a languid hand. "As to the garden party, friends are more important. I do not have so many I can afford to neglect even one. Are you sure you are all right? I would not blame you, you know, if you chose not to attend tomorrow."

"Not at all," Arial insisted. "I am looking forward to it."

"Liar," Regina said. "You are far too clever not to feel some concern. And far too proud to take any notice of it. Still, I think I can promise that you need not fear thrown eggs, Arial."

ROSE'S FEVER REACHED higher than ever, and the village doctor told Peter that the crisis would come soon. From that moment, he did not leave her bedside except for the most urgent calls of nature. For more than twenty-four hours, he held her hand and talked to her, sponged her to bring down the fever, fed her sips of lemon and honey water, and then did it all again, over and over.

At last, the fever broke, and she fell into a deep sleep—lying so still after the days and nights of restless tossing Peter was afraid she had died. He touched her, and she was warm, but not hot. He put his face close to her mouth and could feel her breath on his cheek.

His head dropped a little more. He would rest, just for a moment.

When he woke, the sun was well up in the sky. His bones ached from his awkward hunch against the bed. Rose was still sleeping.

"She is on the mend, my lord." Miss Pettigrew and the maid were sitting on the other side of the bed. "Have a bath and go to bed yourself. We will watch her now."

A bath sounded wonderful, and a shave. "You will call me if there are any problems?" he asked. With that promise, he went off in search of a footman to order a bath. He nearly went to sleep in the water, and his hand shook when he attempted to shave so that, for once, he allowed one of the footmen to do it.

Edwards offered, but Peter had a more important task for him. "Fetch me something to eat, would you, Edwards? If that doesn't wake me up, I will go back to bed."

He put a banyan over his pantaloons and shirt and checked on Rose one more time. She was still sleeping, with Miss Pettigrew watching over her. He visited Viv in the bedroom she had been moved to as she recovered. She was sitting up in bed playing with a wooden puzzle. "Miss Pettigrew told me that Rose is getting better, and that you went to bed because you have been up for nearly two days." She put her head to one side. "I think you should go and sleep. You look very tired."

He was about to say he was not tired when the fiction was interrupted by an enormous yawn. He gave Viv a kiss on the cheek. "You are looking better, too. Barely any rash."

"My eyes are hardly sore at all," Viv insisted. "I am sure it wouldn't hurt me to read just a little."

"We will see what the doctor says." He gave her an affection-ate pat on the shoulder and returned to his room where his snack was waiting. The yawn came with him, and he took no more than a mouthful before crawling onto his bed and falling into a deep and dreamless sleep.

When he woke in the evening, the doctor had been and proclaimed Rose past the worst of it. The fever was gone. She was coughing less and could take a deep breath without it hurting. Even the rash was less itchy. She was definitely on the mend. She was also asleep, which Miss Pettigrew said was the best thing for her.

Viv had good news, too. She was allowed out of bed, just for an hour at a time to start. And tomorrow, she would be allowed to move back to her bed in the same room as Rose. "I am allowed to read again, too, Peter. The doctor looked at my eyes and says they are not red anymore. But we have to keep this room dark for Rose, so I will go into the schoolroom and read when she is sleeping. And if I am still improving in two days, I can visit Dancer, my pony! Oh, and Moonbeam, too, just until Rose is better."

Peter stayed with Viv for a while longer, chatting, but when her eyelids began to droop, he excused himself, and went in search of food, since he hadn't consumed his snack. Downstairs, he had a solitary dinner to eat, and then he settled himself at his desk to write a long and happy letter to Arial, telling her that both girls were recovering, and he would be coming for her soon.

Perhaps a week to ensure that neither of them suffered a relapse, and that they were not infectious?

He folded it, franked it, and was about to write the address on it when he had a sudden thought. He knew what date Arial was removing to Greenmount, but he wasn't at all sure what the date was today. At that moment, Edwards came in to ask if there was anything he needed. "A coffee, my lord? A tea? A brandy? And may I say, on behalf of the staff, how happy we all are that the little misses are recovering."

Peter thanked him, and then asked him what the date was. "In the last few days, I have quite lost track."

It turned out that today was the date of Mrs. Paddimore's garden party, and tomorrow Arial would be leaving early for

Greenmount. He'd better send the letter to Greenmount.

He addressed it and went up to bed, and then had to send for someone to dispose of two rats who had chosen to die in the corner. Tomorrow, he'd ask whether anyone had been laying poison for the vermin. He'd make it clear that poison should never be laid on the schoolroom floor. Preferably not in the house. He'd rather have a couple of ratting terriers up from the kennels to hunt them down through the walls, attics, and cellars.

Chapter Twenty-Two

"THIS HAS NOT been as bad as I expected," Arial said to Clara, as they strolled from the Pall Mall game to the archery. For her garden party, Regina had borrowed the use of the gardens on either side of her townhouse.

The long, narrow garden of her left-hand neighbor had been divided into three zones, with winding paths through flowers and shrubbery connecting them. Nearest to the house, people could play chess using giant pieces set on a board marked into the grass by coloring alternate squares. Next, a Pall Mall game wandered around and through the flower gardens. At the far end, a band played under their own marquee, with room for dancing on the lawn beyond the band.

The garden of the right-hand neighbor had been devoted mostly to archery, since it had a long straight lawn from one end to the other. Nearest to that house, Regina had caused a marquee to be erected, where card tables were set up, partially protected from the sun and the wind.

Refreshments were laid out on tables that spread across her own paved terrace. Next to them, more games had been set up. Bowls on a meticulously flattened and groomed lawn. A space for shuttlecock. Another for a succession of more childish games—blind man's bluff, tug-of-war, even three-legged races. The most unusual feature was at the foot of her garden, through an archway that divided a tall fence. What had been a normal kitchen garden had been laboriously turned into a maze. Regina's estate carpenters had come up to London to create a series of wooden walls and trellises. Her gardeners had begun preparing for the party early in the Spring, and now beans, pumpkins, sweet peas, and all kinds of seasonal climbers covered the walls, so that the delighted guests walked between—and even under—verdant leaves and lush blooms as they tried to find their way to the pretty fountain that Regina told everyone was at the center of the maze. "With several nice benches for wanderers to rest on."

The two women watched a fiercely fought contest between several acquaintances, before abandoning the archery to wander back through the gate in the wall to the next garden. "Perhaps it is all blowing over again," Clara said, hopefully.

"No one has said anything to me," Arial noted. And those who were the source of the attacks on her character and reputation had not been invited. Indeed, the one piece of gossip she had been told during the afternoon was that the Weatherall ladies had packed up and retired to the country after yesterday's *Teatime Tattler* article.

Peter's stepmother was continuing to avoid Arial, refusing to meet her eye and moving away quickly when they happened to be in the same vicinity. Arial suspected that it might be guilt. She had been passing on anything Peter said to her about Vivienne's illness and return to health. The dowager Lady Ransome had yet to acknowledge a single one of the notes, though Pauline Turner had approached Arial one evening to thank her for keeping them informed.

As for Josiah and Marjorie, Arial was going to Greenmount tomorrow, and then on to Three Oaks as soon as she could. She would not have to see her cousin and his wife before the next Season.

It was with a light heart that Arial waved Clara away when her companion-turned-secretary suggested a visit to the ladies' retiring room. "You go. I shall be fine. I think I shall take another look at the maze. Such a clever idea."

"Do not venture inside without a safe escort," Clara reminded her, momentarily reverting to governess. Arial agreed. With its high walls and leafy bowers, the maze was a perfect place for courting couples and those in less-sanctioned relationships to steal a kiss and perhaps a little more. Arial had always assumed that her ugliness kept her safe, but the loathsome Mr. Frankton had disabused her of that notion.

Still, she could look through the archway and admire those parts of the maze she could see. Perhaps Clara would be up to exploring it with her when she returned.

"It is safe, you know," Regina said, startling Arial for she had not heard her friend approach. "I have stationed footmen at regular intervals to rescue foolish maidens and people with a poor sense of direction." She gave a husky chuckle. "They have been given strict instructions not to see or interrupt anything that happens when both parties are adults enjoying themselves."

Arial immediately thought of Peter, and blushed.

From Regina's amused smile, she had made a good guess at the direction of Arial's thought, but she was polite enough not to voice it. "I am free for the next fifteen minutes, Arial. If you wish to explore the maze, I would love to be your companion. I will ask Harold over there to let Clara know where you have gone."

So, Arial stepped through the archway, and for several minutes she and Regina walked slowly and in silence, taking in the beauty around them and filling their senses. They chanced to be alone, though she could hear voices elsewhere in the maze—several children laughing and shrieking, quiet conversation, bursts of laughter. Then she heard her name on the other side of a trellis and came to a halt.

"Lady Ransome has been very much maligned," somebody said. A woman's voice. "I have met her, and she is a very pleasant and normal woman."

"But the mask!" protested another woman.

Regina opened her mouth, but Arial signaled to her to remain quiet.

The first speaker declared, "Everyone knows she was badly burned in a fire. I admire her courage in coming out into Society at all, let alone continuing after those horrible people defamed her. It is not as if she shows her scars. That might be a bit hard to take if they are as bad as people say. Although how people are to know is beyond me. Anyway, she wears those lovely masks, which almost make me wish that I had something to hide."

A man's voice, ardent with feigned passion, immediately said, "Only your radiant beauty, fairest of all."

Another man's voice. "But what about the rumors about her and Captain Forsythe? Perhaps you can put the other attacks on her virtue down to spite—and given the source, I tend to agree with you. But Forsythe broke off his engagement as soon as Ransome left London and has been in and out of the lady's house at every hour of the day and night."

The old saying was true: eavesdroppers hear no good of themselves. Or perhaps it was not true, for the first speaker scoffed. "Have you seen Lord and Lady Ransome together? If ever there was a love match, it is those two. That's one of the reasons I disbelieve those who say her scars are truly hideous, for no one can doubt that Lord Ransome worships the ground she walks on, and I daresay he has seen everything she has to show."

"You and I could have a love match," crooned the first man. "Let these two walk on and I will show you."

"Oh, do give it a rest, David," the first lady replied. "But David is right, you slow pokes. Kitty, surely you have rested long enough. Let us go and find the center."

Regina raised her eyebrows at the names. As the people on the other side of the trellis walked away, their friendly bickering trailing behind them, Arial said, "You know who they are, do you not?"

"Probably, but I'm not going to tell you, Arial. If you do meet them, you will find it easier to ignore their opinions if you don't know they have them."

Her smile was kind, if a little condescending. "You may only show half your face, my dear friend, but that half shows everything you are thinking."

❧

Chapter Twenty-Three

I N PETER'S DREAM, he was a boy again, and Three Oaks was burning. His sisters were inside. Even in the dream, he knew that the house that burnt was not Three Oaks, and that he had had no sisters when he was a boy. Still, the dream imperatives ruled, and he rushed into the house.

It was full of smoke and noise. The roar of the fire. Timbers creaking and crashing as they burned. He dropped to his stomach and wriggled across the floor. He was eerily alone. But his sisters were here, somewhere above stairs. He filled his lungs and charged up the main staircase then dropped to the floor again, under the worst of the smoke. He found his way to the schoolroom, the flames licking at his heels and cutting off their escape.

Inside, Viv and Rose were playing at tea parties. He rushed across the room to the windows and began to tug at the bars. The girls asked what he was doing. "We have to climb out the window to escape the fire," he told them, and then let out an agonized cry of warning when Rose ran to the door and opened it.

Instead of the wall of flame and heat he expected, there was nothing. Just the passage that led through the children's wing, with the nursery paintings on the wall, and a badly worn strip of carpet.

Viv and Rose watched him as he peered along the passage towards the stairs. No fire. He could not hear it, nor could he smell it.

"There was a fire," he insisted. "You were in danger. I came to rescue you."

The girls sat back in their little chairs. "We do not need rescuing," Rose assured him. "We are well."

Viv produced another cup and saucer, though he couldn't see where it came from. "Shall I pour you a cup of tea, Peter?"

Rose touched the cup and it disappeared again, followed by the saucer. "He does not have time for that, Viv. He has to save Arial."

"Oh, yes," Viv agreed. "Peter, the fire is in London." A frown marred her brow. "Or perhaps on the road from London?"

Rose shook her head. "It does not matter. Peter needs to go to London to find out. Arial is in danger. Hurry, Peter."

The scorch and thunder of the fire surged around him again, and he stood in its midst as the house crashed around him and Viv and Rose sat in a bubble of peace and harmony, playing at tea parties.

He woke with his heart pounding and his lungs screaming for air. Arial was in danger. He was on his feet and halfway across the room before his conscious brain tried to tell him that it was only a dream. Even so, he was more than half-inclined to ride immediately for London, just to be sure.

Both sisters were now well on the mend. He wasn't needed here, and he needed his wife. On the other hand, she was probably on the way to Greenmount, two days journey from London. And would she even want him? In London, there had been a distance between them, and he had to admit it was largely on his side. It was hard to be in love with someone who had married you as a convenience.

He had not made up his mind when both Viv and Rose told him that they had seen Arial in their dreams, in both cases in jeopardy and calling for Peter. In Viv's dream, she was drowning in the lake at Hyde Park, and Viv's sister Laura was in a boat, pushing her under with an oar. Rose dreamt that she was tied up in the Tower of London, and the executioner was on his way with an axe.

Peter could find common-sense explanations for all three dreams, but he put his doubts to one side. He was going to London.

When he declared his intentions to Edwards and asked for a message to be sent to the stables, he caught a flare of alarm in Edwards's eyes. "Are you sure that is wise, my lord? The young ladies…"

"Are on the mend," Peter said, firmly. "I want my curricle at the door in thirty minutes, Edwards."

The butler bowed and went off with the message. Peter returned upstairs to say goodbye to the girls. "I'll bring Arial back with me within the week," he promised.

The curricle was waiting at the front door. Edwards stood by the groom who held the horses. "Is all well, my lord?" Edwards asked.

"Certainly," Peter said, as he hoisted his bag into the vehicle. He leaped up, took the reins, and released the brake. Despite his confident words to Edwards, he had an indefinable sense of something wrong, and years of military experience warned him not to ignore it.

He gave the groom the nod to step away from the horses and encouraged them into a fast trot. He should be in London by mid-afternoon. If Arial had already left, he would continue north, and catch up with her at her preferred inn.

He pulled up at the gates to wait for them to be opened and heard hoof beats behind him.

The resident of the gate lodge, one of John's ex-soldiers, limped out of his front door tucking his shirt into his trousers. He tossed Peter a casual salute and hurried to the gates. The hoof beats had stopped.

Peter set the horses trotting, then pulled them up between

the gates. Again, he heard the hoof beats. Again, they stopped abruptly a couple of seconds after his own halt. He turned back in his seat to exchange greetings with the gatekeeper and ask how he was, and also to examine the carriageway behind him, and the home wood that stretched between him and the house on either side of the carriageway.

He saw nothing, and perhaps it was nothing. Just a groom exercising one of the horses and stopping coincidentally when Peter did. The instincts honed by his years at war were tingling, but the war was over. This was England, and he had not yet even left his own estate.

Waving goodbye to the gatekeeper, he turned the curricle into the lane, and headed for the highway to London.

Twice more, when he rounded a corner with enough cover in hedgerows or trees to hide him from any pursuer, he pulled up and listened. Both times, he could hear hoof beats. It was possible that one of his neighbors was riding this quiet lane rather than going cross-country, or a local farmer wealthy enough to own riding stock was heading in the same direction as Peter. Still, his instincts had the hair on the back of his neck standing on end and every nerve alert.

On his third stop, the tone of the hoof beats had changed. They were no longer falling on the hardpacked earth of the lane. He caught movement from the corner of an eye and turned to peer over a hedgerow. A horse had just leaped a stone wall on the other side of that field to disappear into a small covert. The rider was off on his own business.

Or perhaps not. There was a spot that would work for an ambush not far from where the lane emerged onto the road to London. The lane dipped into a depression within an unkempt wood. If the rider intended to attack Peter, that would be a good spot. On the other hand, if Peter got there first, he could hide and see what transpired.

It was a good team, and fresh. The lane was dry and baked hard by the summer sun. The curricle flew along it at a pace that would be dangerous if they met anyone coming the other way. Fortunately, they didn't.

Peter slowed the horses as they cantered into the hollow, gently applying the brake to reduce the momentum of the vehicle as the horses dropped to a fast walk and then a complete stop.

With a sharp crack, followed by a series of crashes and creaks, one side of the curricle suddenly dropped from beneath Peter. He fell, mostly onto the grass at the side of the lane and picked himself up to see that the wheel had collapsed. He fetched one of his pistols from its holster in the curricle and hurried to the heads of the horses. They were stamping and twitching and rolling their eyes as they tried to figure out what threat had made that noise behind them.

He did not have time to settle them, though, because there again were the hoof beats. *No. Two sets of hoof beats.* The one to the side of the road and slightly behind him ceased, to be succeeded by the sound of something large pressing through the undergrowth. The other was coming towards him along the lane from the direction of the road to London.

Leaving the horses, he leaped the ditch on the other side of the road, climbed the bank, and wriggled into the bushes. He turned and lay on his stomach to keep watch from behind screening weeds.

Beyond the curricle, at the top of the opposing, slightly lower, bank, the undergrowth waved vigorously and then stilled. From his vantage point, Peter could see a pair of hands part the grasses and a head peer down at the scene of the collapse. Then the figure stood to have a better view. It was the groom who had prepared the curricle. Peter had not yet learned his name. He was one of the new hires added to the staff since the infusion of Arial's money.

Any doubts about the man's intentions were put to rest by the rifle he carried, which he raised to his shoulder as the other rider Peter had heard rounded the corner of the lane, caught sight of the crashed curricle, and nudged his horse into a trot.

Peter recognized him as he dismounted—*John!*—fortunately on Peter's side of his horse. Whether the groom recognized him too, or whether he simply did not want witnesses, he sighted his rifle, leaning out over the bank, waiting for a clear shot. Peter shot him first. He aimed for the man's shoulder, and at less than ten yards, he couldn't miss.

John pulled a weapon from his saddle holster and dropped to roll into the ditch.

Peter called out, "It's me, John. Peter."

John rose out of the ditch, dusting himself off with his free hand, and looking around for the groom.

The groom lay dazed at the foot of the bank, the rifle just out of his reach. His fall had probably done him more immediate harm than the bullet. John reached him first and picked the weapon up.

"Were you planning to have a party without me, Peter?" he asked, flippantly.

"This man invited himself, too," Peter said, grimly. "He is one of my grooms, John, and if we look at the curricle wheel, I imagine we'll find it has been sabotaged."

The groom still had a pulse, but Peter's hand checking the back of his head came away covered in blood. "Help me to get the horses out of the traces and put him over the back of one. We'll take him to the constable in the village. I am glad to see you, John, but you nearly missed me. I am on my way to London."

"Are you going after Arial?" John asked.

And when Peter nodded, he added, "I'm glad. With these new caricatures and rumors, I can't be easy in my mind about her heading off to Greenmount on her own. That's what I came over to say. If you hadn't been able to leave the girls, I intended to go back to London myself."

Peter's mouth went dry, and his heart pounded. His muscles trembled with the effort to stay still and hear John's news. Arial needed him! He had to get to London! "New rumors?" he croaked. He tried to calm his breathing. He had to know what was happening so he could help her. "She hasn't mentioned them. Ride beside me, John and tell me what has been happening."

Chapter Twenty-Four

TWO CARRIAGES CONTAINING Arial's servants left London not long after dawn, accompanied by several outriders. They would stop at the inn where Arial had spent the night on the journey up and leave two maids and several footmen to wait there for Arial and Clara. Sergeant Miller was in charge of the party, and had instructions to commission rooms, stable space, and an evening meal. The rest of the servants would continue on to Greenmount, taking advantage of the long midsummer day.

Arial was leaving a small skeleton staff to close the townhouse. She and Peter had decided not to renew the lease for the next quarter, but instead to buy a townhouse of their own in time for the next Season. Quite apart from the social and cultural life of the capital, Peter's new interest in the work of the House of Lords justified having a London base.

Since Arial and Clara were only making half the trip that day, they departed London in the mid-morning, escorted by John's ex-soldiers. This trip was very different to the first. Armored behind one of her new pretty masks, Arial felt comfortable about taking refreshment at the various inns along the way when they stopped to change the horses. The journey was still somewhat tedious, and she was pleased when they turned into the stable yard to descend for their overnight stop.

There was Sergeant Miller, watching for them from by the stables.

He hurried to help her descend. "Your rooms are ready, my lady. You and Miss Tulloch have a room each with a shared sitting room. The maids will have pallets in the sitting room, and the men are set up with rooms above the stables. The kitchen has water on the heat for a bath for you. As soon as we saw your coach, I sent one of the men to order refreshments, and they should be delivered to your rooms shortly."

"Thank you, Sergeant. I was sure I could rely on you," Arial said.

He moved slightly, so he was out of her line of sight, but not before she caught a strange expression on his face, as if he had bitten into something sour.

"Before you go up, my lady," he said, "may I take a moment of your time? There was something I wanted to ask you."

Clara, who had begun to walk towards the door, stopped and turned back.

The sergeant looked askance and began to shuffle. Was that a blush? "Just the two of us, my lady, if you do not mind. It is a private matter."

Arial, intrigued, said to Clara, "Go on up, Clara. I will be there shortly." Whatever did Sergeant Miller want? Was it about his secret romance, perhaps?

"We could talk in the garden," the sergeant suggested.

Arial walked in the direction he indicated, waited for him to open the gate in a tall fence, and passed through.

The word *garden* was overstating the case. It was a tangle of shrubs around an open area behind the inn. A door probably let on to the kitchen. Several tidy sheds undoubtedly held firewood and other utilitarian supplies.

Sergeant Miller pointed to a bench seat along a little path. Beside it, stood the cloaked form of a lady. "If you would be so kind, my lady. The young lady has asked for a moment of your time."

Arial, making wild guesses as to whom it might be, walked to the indicated seat. In the next moment, a rag with a sickly smell was stuffed into her mouth and her head began to spin. As she fell into darkness, she heard Sergeant Miller protest, "You are not Miss Turner!" and Josiah's voice commanding, "Seize him."

Josiah's was the first voice she heard when she surfaced, too.

"Come on, Lady Beast. I know you are awake."

She felt a sharp pinch on her arm and could not suppress a squeak of pain as she tried—and failed—to move away from whatever injured her.

Her sight was clearing, though her head felt heavy, and her brain struggled as if through wads of cotton wool.

There he was. Her cousin Josiah, with a satisfied smirk on his face. She glared at him while she made sense of the constriction around her arms and on her ankles, and the cold breeze that blew on her face, her shoulders, and her knees. The glare was wasted, for he stared over her head.

She was sitting in a chair in her chemise. The smelly rag was no longer in her mouth, but her arms were bound to her torso with strips of cloth, and her ankles were also tied, presumably to the legs of the chair. Her mask was gone. She looked around the room. It contained four people besides Josiah, none of them Sergeant Miller, all of them avoiding Arial's eye.

Marjorie was there, a cloak the color of the one Arial had seen in the garden folded over her arm. *Why did Sergeant Miller think she was Miss Turner?* The other three looked like hired muscle, even the woman. It was to them Josiah said, "Wait outside."

"Are you certain, my lord?" said one of the men.

"She is hardly a danger to my wife and myself," Josiah scoffed. "Not bound as she is."

Marjorie added, "Lady Arial is a dear member of our family, despite her affliction. Please let us say our goodbyes."

They began to shuffle out. "Wait!" Arial said. "Whatever the earl is paying you, Lord Ransome and I will pay more."

The woman shook her head. "Poor lady." Her comment was

to one of the others, and Arial heard her add, as they all stepped outside and left her alone in the room with the Stancrofts, "She is so fortunate to have relatives who care."

"Let us get right to business," Josiah said. "Sign this, Arial, and I will let you go. Well, not go, exactly. But I will arrange for you to live in comfort. You will have to disappear of course, but that cannot be helped."

She glanced at the page he waved before her but didn't bother to read it. Her stomach lurched, and she avoided vomiting by sheer effort of will. "Let me go, Josiah. My husband will come for me, and if he finds you have kidnapped me, he will kill you."

Josiah laughed. "That is not going to be a problem. We forgot to tell her, Marjorie."

Marjorie crooned, "Poor Arial. You'll need to get out your blacks, darling cousin."

Arial's heart clenched, understanding their meaning before her dazed mind caught up. Peter! What had they done?

Majorie giggled. "Not that you will need your blacks, where you are going."

Arial shook her head, trying to clear it. No. Peter was safe at Three Oaks. They were lying.

"Now, Marjorie." Josiah's playful scold made little headway against the glee in his voice. "Arial can avoid the asylum if she will just sign the document."

He shook the paper. It had the numbering used in contracts and other legal documents. She must not sign! It was the only thing she was certain of, as her mind struggled to focus through the lingering effects of whatever they'd drugged her with, her fear for Peter, and her dread for herself and the baby.

Josiah slapped her face, the blow stinging and whipping her head to the side.

"Stupid bitch."

He strode towards the door. Marjorie put out a hand to stop him. "Josiah? We need her to sign that will!"

"She'll sign it." Josiah's voice was a threatening growl. "After a couple of nights in that place, she'll sign anything I put in front of her."

Marjorie looked doubtful. "I suppose."

Josiah pulled out a handkerchief, and after he whipped opened the door, he dabbed it to his cheeks, while saying to those in the other room, "Alas. I cannot get through to her. She refuses to believe she has no husband. Completely mad, poor woman. I'll have to let you take her away."

Arial opened her mouth to tell the people from the asylum, for that was who they must be, that Josiah had kidnapped her; that Peter would be coming for her. Before she could say a word, Marjorie slapped a cloth over her mouth, and the same sickly-sweet smell stole her senses.

BY THE TIME Peter arrived in London, it was early evening. He and John had taken the would-be murderer to the nearest magistrate, who had called a doctor for the still unconscious groom and taken their statements. Peter also told him about the night he had slipped on a patch of grease at the head of the stairs, the odd-tasting tea he had poured out because it was too bitter, the dead rats after he'd left a snack uneaten in his room, and the night when he'd been certain he'd had an intruder in his room. He could not imagine that a groom he'd never spoken to had a personal grudge against him, so he feared a wider plot.

At his request, the magistrate sent a groom to Three Oaks to enquire about his sisters' welfare. The groom returned with a message from Miss Tulloch saying both girls continued to improve and were anxiously waiting for him to fetch their new sister home. He also brought a message from Edwards, saying nothing appeared to be out of place in the house, but that he would be fully alert until Peter's return.

John sent a message, too, to his brother. "I've told Deerhaven

I'm going with you to make sure that Lady Arial is safe. If I'm not back in time, I can be made godfather by proxy. Deerhaven will understand."

He had come out for a morning ride, fortuitously for Peter, but insisted he didn't need to be any better-equipped for a trip that may extend to several nights. "I have clothes in my rooms in Town, and if we detour past Deercroft, we'll never make London by dark."

As it was, even without the interruption to deal with the assailant, Peter would not have arrived before his wife left. The knocker was off the door, but Barlowe opened when Peter hammered on the wood with his first. "My lord! We were not expecting you. My lady has already left for Greenmount."

She had been gone for hours, apparently.

"We'll stay overnight, and travel on to Greenmount at first light," Peter decided.

Barlowe arranged for beds to be made up, and even managed a tolerable dinner, though he apologized it was not the kind of meal he was used to serving his lord and lady.

John and Peter were sitting over their port when there was another hammering on the front door.

Several minutes later, Barlowe entered. "Miss Turner has called to see Lady Arial, my lord. She wonders if she might see you, instead."

Peter nodded. What did Pauline want with Arial? Something nasty, no doubt. He would give her a piece of his mind and turne her out.

But when Pauline entered the room, she hurled herself on to Peter and burst into tears.

At first, all he could gather through her sobs were the repeated words, "I thought you were dead. I thought you were dead. I am so glad you are not dead."

In the light of the incident on the road, not to mention the earlier accidents, her words were extremely sinister, even if her emotion was surprisingly flattering.

John thrust a glass of port into Peter's hands, and he settled Pauline on a chair and encouraged her to drink.

She took a couple of deep gulps, which seemed to calm her, even though tears continued to stream down her cheeks. "Where is Arial? The butler said she is not here."

"She has gone out of town," Peter explained, wary of giving any details. He had no reason to trust his stepsister beyond her seemingly genuine relief at seeing him alive.

Pauline clutched his arm. "You must go after her before Stancroft reaches her first."

"Stancroft cannot touch her. He has no rights, and she was well-guarded."

"You must listen to me," Pauline pleaded. "Peter, Stancroft thinks you are dead. Edwards wrote to my mother and told him that you did not drink his poison or fall into the trap at the top of the stairs, and you slept too lightly to smother in your bed. He was going to have you ambushed and shot, he said. You were planning to go into the village, and it would happen then. It was meant to be yesterday."

The men's eyes met over Pauline's head.

"It was Edwards, then," John said.

Peter nodded. "I had intended to go into the village yesterday, but I fell asleep instead. And then this morning I decided to come to London."

"That is good." Pauline gave a relieved sigh. "I have been so worried ever since I heard my mother and Stancroft talking. Ever since, I've been trying to get out of the house." She looked down at her hands and shifted uneasily. "Peter, I know I have not been nice to you, or to your wife, but I never meant either of you any harm. I just didn't want Mother to beat me." She burst into tears again.

Peter didn't know what to think. Pauline had aroused his sympathies, and she had certainly known about the ambush, but who was to say she wasn't part of whatever game his stepmother and Arial's cousin had concocted?

"Miss Turner," said John, "I think you had better start at the beginning. You say your mother and Stancroft have been plotting together. Start from there. What is their plan? What is their motive?"

His friend's calm tone seemed to help. Pauline took a deep breath. She shuddered a bit as she let it out, but the second one left her back in control of her feelings. "Mother wants control of Vivienne, and any money you leave her when you die. She managed to get hold of a copy of your will, and apparently Vivienne and Rose get quite a lot. Mother says she refuses to keep Rose, and, in any case, Vivienne will be Rose's only relative, so will inherit all of Rose's money. I have known Rose since she was a baby, Peter. I don't want her to die. I don't want you to die."

Though Pauline had addressed her answer to Peter, John continued the questioning. "You say Edwards agreed to kill Peter or have him killed. Why would Peter's own butler do that?"

Pauline's eyes widened in astonishment. "Because he is Mother's lover, of course. He has been for as long as I can remember. She wouldn't marry him, because he was a servant. But she had to marry someone when Vivienne was on the way, so they plotted to trap your father."

It was too much for Peter to take in. He would think about it later. About how Edwards treated Peter like an interloper. About his father's misery in his marriage. About Vivienne. Dear Merciful Heavens. Vivienne must never find out!

Put it to one side. He forced his emotions under control. Arial needed him.

"And Josiah?" he asked. "What does he hope to accomplish?"

She frowned. "He hates Arial. He wants her to make her will in his favor, leaving him all the property that she retained in your marriage settlement. He intends to put her into an asylum until she agrees. He believes you are dead, Peter."

Peter was on his feet. Her story was all too plausible. He would proceed with caution, lest she was lying, but he was going to find his wife.

John said, soothingly, "She has her guard, Peter. Sergeant Miller is in charge. He is a competent man, and Josiah will need an army to get past him."

Pauline was shaking her head. "You don't understand. They are using Sergeant Miller. Laura is using him. He is in love with her, and he thinks she wants a private meeting with Arial, away from our mother, to make peace. But it is a lie—I do not know quite how they plan to use him, but if Arial trusts him, I fear she will be much mistaken."

Peter met John's eyes again. "Are you with me?"

"Of course," John said. "Miss Turner, I take it you cannot go home."

Pauline shuddered. "Mother will kill me when she knows I have told you all this."

"Barlowe!" Peter shouted. The butler appeared within seconds. "Barlowe, Miss Turner will be staying. In fact, she is not to leave the house. Nor is she to have visitors. Assign her a maid who must be with her at all times. I do not trust you, Pauline. But if you are being honest with me, I owe you more than I can repay."

At that moment, the front door was assaulted with another barrage of thunderous knocking.

Peter wrenched it open himself. It was one of John's ex-soldiers. "My lord!" the man declared. "And Captain! Thank all the powers you are both here. Lady Arial has gone missing, and so has Sergeant Miller."

Chapter Twenty-Five

THE CARRIAGE—IT WAS more of a prison cell on wheels—stank of vomit. The smell made Arial nauseous again, but though her stomach heaved, there was nothing left in it to expel. Mrs. Parker, the hefty warden from the asylum, offered her another sip of weak tea. Arial nodded. It was only lukewarm by now, but it soothed the rasp in her throat.

"Not far now," Mrs. Parker said. "You'll be the better for being out of this contraption."

Whether the woman referred to the conveyance or to Arial's bindings, Arial was not certain.

She had refused to untie Arial but had otherwise been gruffly kind since Arial had woken once again, her head pounding and her stomach even more rebellious than when she first came round.

When the male warden who had been sharing space with them threatened to strike Arial for spattering his boots when she was sick, Mrs. Parker took him to task. "The poor lady cannot help it, can she? It's that foul ether. There was no need for it. I don't like this, George, and that's a fact."

Mrs. Parker had insisted that the driver stop so she could fetch a bucket of soapy water to clean Arial and roughly sluice out the cell. She had also fetched the tea. And when George had declared he would sit up with the driver and leave Mrs. Parker to cosset and to coddle the patient, she had said, "Good riddance," as soon as he closed and locked the door.

Since then, Arial had coaxed her name out of her, and learned a little about the elderly parents she supported with her wages at the asylum.

Arial thought telling Mrs. Parker why she was here might win the woman's support. "I have been kidnapped, Mrs. Parker. My cousin tried to convince a magistrate I was insane. He failed. So, he has gone behind the law. He is locking me up because he wants me to sign my will in his favor, and I refused. My husband, Viscount Ransome, will be looking for me."

She swallowed a lump in her throat. She had to believe that Josiah was lying about Peter. "My household and my solicitor, too."

"Well, dearie," the big woman said, "yon earl told us that's what you would say. Said you didn't have a husband. Said you didn't have any money. Said you were mad but very convincing."

"He lies," Arial insisted.

Mrs. Parker shrugged. "That's for the doctor to decide."

But when they arrived at the asylum, and Arial met the doctor, she knew she would not get a fair hearing from him. Unlike the two wardens, he would not look her in the face. He gave her one glance when she shuffled into his office, her gait limited by the bindings that linked her ankles and turned his eyes on Mrs. Parker. "Lock her up immediately, somewhere I don't have to look at her," he demanded.

"But, sir, I don't think she is insane. She says her cousin is after her money. Don't you want to talk to her?"

"Talk to her!" said the doctor. "I don't even want to look at her. She makes my stomach turn. She stinks, too. No wonder the poor earl was driven to having her confined for treatment."

The place was a large house, perhaps once someone's country seat, perhaps even a home where children once played, and families loved. Now, it resonated with misery, loneliness, and despair. Mrs. Parker and the grumpy George conducted Arial up the stairs, following another warden with a lamp. When her bindings made climbing the steps slow and awkward, her two wardens picked her up by an elbow on each side.

A scuffed door at the top let on to a long passage. The doors on each side had barred windows, through which leaked moans from one, high-pitched singing from another, cackling from a third, and so on down the passage. Latches, locks, and bolts, firmly fastened, kept each inhabitant within their room.

Halfway down the passage, a door stood open. Mrs. Parker nodded to it. "This will be yours, dearie."

It was small and drab. As she shuffled inside, Arial catalogued the contents. It did not take long. A bed and a chair, both bolted to the floor. A washstand, likewise. There was no bowl and jug. The bed had a sheet and blanket. The window had bars but no drapes. And that was it. Nothing else to see.

Arial turned to Mrs. Parker. "May I have a wash?"

George snorted. "Fancies herself, doesn't she? Ugly witch."

"I'll see what I can do, dearie. First, let's get those bindings off you."

Arial sat in the chair while Mrs. Parker undid the knots at her ankles and loosened the cloth bandages enough to slide them over Arial's feet. "If I let your arms free, dearie, will you sit still and be good?"

George snorted again. "Can't trust a madwoman."

Mrs. Parker ignored him. At Arial's nod, she began wrestling with the knots behind Arial's back. The man with the lamp said nothing.

As the bindings that held her arms to her torso loosened, Arial became aware again that she wore nothing but her shift, and the two men showed no signs of leaving. Indeed, they studied her body with interest.

"Pity about the scars," said the other warder. "Wonder how far down her body the ones on her shoulder go?"

George grunted. "The scars don't bother me none," he

claimed. "Bit of a surprise, at first. You don't have to look at them, do you?"

The other warder chortled. "Could use a flour sack!" he proposed.

George thought that was hilarious, and repeated the words, "Flour sack!"

Mrs. Parker tensed, her hands stilling on the last swathe of bandage.

The other warder felt it necessary to explain his joke. "Lovely curves she's got. I'd like a piece of that, if I didn't have to look at her face."

Mrs. Parker dropped the bandage and turned on the men. "You two stop ogling the poor lady and making disgusting remarks. You should be ashamed of yourselves. Arthur, what would your wife say if she heard you? And George? Your mother would clip you over the ear. And I will, too, if you don't go and make yourself useful. Get Lady Ransome a bucket of warm water. Warm, mind, and clean. And some of the nice soap."

"Here! What are you on about?" George demanded. "She ain't no Lady Ransome. Leastwise, that's what that there lord said."

Mrs. Parker advanced on the men, and although they were bigger and taller than her, they both backed away. "Go on. Hurry up with you. And don't barge in here when you get back. Put the bucket outside and call through the door."

Arthur scurried away. George grumbled some more, but he left.

"I'm sorry about that, dearie," Mrs. Parker said. "They're not bad men. Just stupid. Now, you are not to worry. This place is not as bad as some others. The doctor says the patients are to be treated as guests. Not that I would keep a guest in a room like this, but still."

"Will you help me?" Arial asked.

"As much as I can, my lady, but you can't expect me to risk my job, now, can you? I'm just going to get you a clean shift to put on after your wash. I'll lock the door while I'm gone and take the key with me, so you need not worry."

The warder's repeated advice not to worry was rather alarming. Arial was pleased to hear the tumblers fall into place as Mrs. Parker kept her word and locked the door.

Arial continued standing. She did not want to sit on the bed, or even the chair, until she was clean. She was still nauseous and dizzy from the remnants of whatever they had given her to make her unconscious. She wanted nothing more than to lie down, pull the blanket over her, and go to sleep.

No. That wasn't true. She wanted nothing more than to be safe and Peter's arms again. She began praying he was unharmed. The thought of a world without him was too dismal to contemplate.

She offered a few prayers for herself and for the baby. For Mrs. Parker was a questionable ally, and she had no others in this place.

PETER STOOD BACK as the king's men, the magistrates, hammered on the Earl of Stancroft's front door, and banged on it again when there was no immediate response. It was near dawn, the sky sporting ribbons of pink and color slowly seeping into the landscape below.

Three hours ago, Peter and John had reached the inn where Arial had stopped for the night, to find that the search for Peter's wife had been fruitless. No one had seen her taken. No one knew who took her.

Her own people suspected the Earl of Stancroft and his wife, who had left the inn shortly before Arial arrived. But the local constables dismissed their claims as nonsense, and had done nothing to pursue the couple, and the local magistrate had agreed with them.

The search he ordered had found Sergeant Miller, in a ditch a couple of miles out of town. His throat had been slit. "Did you not find it suspicious," Peter asked the magistrate, "that the last man seen with my wife was found dead on the road that leads to Stancroft's family seat?"

"Can't question an earl without better cause than that, my lord. What did we have to go on? He and his cousin don't like each other. He left the inn before she arrived. No evidence there."

If they had found Arial in Stancroft's carriage, no questioning would have been necessary, Peter thought. Despite his annoyance, he moved past the point. "We have a witness who heard him and another person planning my murder—which would have occurred if they hadn't been so clumsy—and the abduction and imprisonment of my wife. Is that sufficient cause?"

Which brought them here. Standing in the earl's forecourt, while the magistrates from three different parishes made a racket to be allowed in. One was the man investigating the kidnap. The jurisdiction of the other two straddled Stancroft's lands, and they had insisted on both being present. Perhaps, Peter reflected, to hold one another up, since all three of the men were wary about demanding answers from an earl.

A sleepy butler in a nightcap, his bandy calves showing under the hem of a clumsily tied overcoat, opened the door. He was crowded to one side by the magistrates and John and Peter, who started forward at the first sight of movement. The magistrates' constables, John's ex-soldiers, and the footmen and grooms Peter had brought with him all followed behind, joining the crowd in the earl's front hall.

"Now see here—" exclaimed the butler.

"We are here to see the Earl of Stancroft, in the name of the king," declared the oldest and most pompous of the magistrates— the one who had refused to question Stancroft without evidence.

The butler bowed to combined authority and force and scuttled up the staircase to awaken his master. The local magistrate led the rest of the crowd in his wake.

Peter held John back. "Let's go up last." It would be interesting to see Stancroft's reaction to Peter's continued existence.

It was even better than Peter hoped. Stancroft was sitting up in bed, thundering about the invasion of his house and an Englishman's inviolate rights when Peter made his way through the constables. Lady Stancroft stood in a doorway to one side of the bed, quivering with indignation. She saw Peter first. The blood drained out of her face, and she dropped in a faint.

"See what you have done?" Stancroft ranted. "My wife—" as he swept his gaze across his audience, he saw Peter. His mouth dropped open. He pointed, and stammered, "But you are dead. Flora had you killed."

It should have been easy after that. He had condemned himself out of his own mouth. But he and a subdued but obstinate Lady Stancroft denied kidnapping Arial and disavowed any knowledge of the plot against Peter.

The magistrates ordered them arrested, to be held in their own rooms. They questioned the servants, particularly the grooms and coachman. They searched the earl's study for incriminating papers. They stayed irritatingly close, so Peter couldn't follow his burning desire to beat Arial's location out of the Earl.

They did not stay close enough to Stancroft. Those deputed to guard the earl permitted him to go to his study and stood in the door watching him. When he pulled a dueling pistol from his desk drawer, they were too late to prevent him from pulling the trigger.

Lady Stancroft, informed of her husband's demise, went into strong hysterics. Peter despaired of finding anything that would lead him to his wife.

Then the butler asked Peter for a private word.

"Is it true, sir? Are you really Lady Arial's husband?"

Peter nodded, only half his mind on the conversation. If need be, he'd search every asylum within a day's ride, and then widen the search. He had heard terrible things about what went on in some of those places. He was terrified for Arial.

The butler was still talking. "Is it Lady Arial you are looking for, my Lord? I heard the magistrates say that Lady Arial has been taken, and they think the Earl did it."

The man looked worried. For Arial? Or for Stancroft? Peter's answer was short and to the point. "He took her. We have reason to believe he has her imprisoned in an asylum for the insane."

The butler's next words captured Peter's full attention. "Then I might know where she is, Lord Ransome."

The butler had taken a cup of tea out to the earl's coachman when the man had dropped Lord and Lady Stancroft off. The driver, the grooms who had traveled from London with the earl and countess, and their outriders had all been delighted to be rewarded with a one-week holiday.

"John Coachman was suspicious," the butler said. "The earl is not a generous man. He thought it was probably because of what they might have seen. But he was not going to look a gift horse in the mouth or interfere in the doings of the nobility. He went off to visit his daughter."

"What did he see?" Peter asked, every nerve thrumming to squeeze the butler to make the story run faster.

Not much, but enough. The earl had brought a couple of extra servants with him from London, "Big men, and rough, John Coachman said. Criminal types."

At the inn, Stancroft and his wife had met with another gentleman, who was also accompanied by several such types. "They arrived in a prison van and went off with his lordship around to the back of the inn."

Stancroft's usual servants were told to take the carriage back out onto the road, and to wait not far around the corner, just behind the inn. About half an hour later, the earl and countess came back alone, got into the carriage, and gave the order to continue on.

"You think they gave her to the men with the prison van—it would have been from an asylum." Peter made that statement.

He had no doubt of it.

The butler nodded. "Yes, my lord. John Coachman recognized the van's driver."

At last! "His name, man. We'll need to question him and find out where she was taken."

"Oh, I know that, my lord. That is what I have been trying to tell you." And he gave Peter the name of the doctor who employed the driver, and the address where he lived and ran a hospital for private patients whose families had committed them for the treatment of mental illness.

Within ten minutes, Peter and John led a small force, including one of the magistrates, away from Stancroft's house. Peter was muttering prayers under his breath that they were in time to save his wife from worse than unjust incarceration.

Chapter Twenty-Six

ARIAL LAY ON the bed listening to the sounds of the asylum. The creak of the warders' boots as they walked up and down the passage outside, occasionally banging the batons they carried on the bars of individual cells. Their ribald remarks, some of them addressed to Arial. The moans, shrieks, pleas, singing, shouting, and laughter of the other inmates. Apparently, the asylum never slept.

It was never dark, either. Lamps in the passage cast their light through the bars, so that, even if she had not heard them, Arial would have known the warders were passing because their shadows moved, dark and sinister, across her walls and ceiling.

The asylum had a smell, too. Carbolic soap and despair, with undertones of more noxious substances.

Her own wash had been made more pleasant by a kinder soap—something with floral tones. George and Arthur had objected to her "special treatment," but Mrs. Parker had ignored them. She had been apologetic when she helped Arial into a clean shift and then a garment that covered her from neck to ankle, and had extra-long sleeves, the ends of which could be tied together around Arial's waist, so that Arial was effectively bound inside her own shroud.

At least she was decently covered when the doctor came to

examine his newest patient.

If it was an examination, then she didn't pass. He dismissed every answer she gave to his questions. According to him, she had no husband. She was not a viscountess. Nor was she the daughter of an earl. Her cousin, or so said the doctor, was a kindly man doing his best to look after a deranged relative. When she would not agree with him, he insisted on taking that as proof of her insanity.

"But you are not to worry, Miss Bledisloe. I have had great success with delusions of your type. We shall start treatment in the morning, and in a month or so, you will not know yourself."

That was precisely what Arial feared.

After he'd gone, she asked Mrs. Parker about the treatment, but Mrs. Parker just repeated that she was not to worry. Then she left the cell, bolting it and locking it behind her.

Arial just hoped she had taken the key.

Perhaps she hadn't. At the sound of a key scraping in the lock, Arial sat upright, swinging her legs over the side of the bed to compensate for not being able to use her arms. Her heart pounding, she watched the door open. Bound as she was, she could not resist if one of the warders was intent on putting his disgusting suggestions into practice.

"It's me," Mrs. Parker whispered, and Arial slumped as she let out the breath she had been holding.

Mrs. Parker closed the door behind her and crossed the room in the patchy light. "You must be quiet," she said. "I'm here to help you. When those louts talked about flour sacks, I remembered the lady in the caricatures, the one *The Teatime Tattler* wrote about. You're her, aren't you? Lady R.?"

"Or Lady Beast, they called me, too."

"And your cousin is the evil Lord S. I've spoken to my parents, and they agree I have to get you out of here. Those on guard are having supper in the warders' room at the other end of the passage. It won't take them long, so we must hurry."

As she was speaking, she was undoing the knotted sleeves,

and unwinding them from around Arial's waist. She fumbled at the buttons behind Arial's neck, and in a moment, Arial was able to shrug out of the garment.

Mrs. Parker handed her a cloak. "Follow me," she whispered.

Arial thought of asking where to, but she could not be worse off, and Mrs. Parker was the only person in the place she partially trusted. Enveloped in the cloak, the hood pulled up over her head, she tiptoed behind the woman along the passage.

The worst part was passing the warders' room. Mrs. Parker went first, glancing inside as she passed the open door, then beckoning to Arial. Arial glanced inside, too. Five or six men and two women, passing a bottle between them as they exchanged raucous stories about tricks they had played and punishments they had given to the inmates.

At last, Arial and Mrs. Parker slipped through the door at the end of the passage and began to descend the stairs.

The light was poorer, here. Only one lamp was lit, and that a portable one on a table at the foot of the stairs next to the door that led to the doctor's office.

Feeling for each step, Arial followed Mrs. Parker down the stairs.

Arial was stepping off the bottom step and Mrs. Parker was almost at the front door, when the office door opened. The doctor stood in the doorway. Arial froze in place.

The doctor's eyes widened when he saw her, and he shouted, at the top of his voice, "Escape! A patient is escaping!" He glared at Mrs. Parker. "Parker, seize this woman."

Instead, Mrs. Parker tried to open the front door. It would not shift, and before she could pull the bolts and turn the key, it was too late.

The floor reverberated with the thud of boots as the warders upstairs responded to the doctor's shout. Arial darted towards Mrs. Parker and the doctor grabbed for her but caught her cloak. Arial reached Mrs. Parker's sheltering arm, and the two of them turned at bay as the doctor and his warders closed in on them.

PETER AND THOSE with him had ridden cross country—hair-raising in a night lit only by a half moon and a few stars. The magistrate said he knew the land well, and he set a cracking pace, cutting across the corner of fields, jumping hedgerows, splashing through streams—he clearly knew what might happen to an unprotected woman in one of those places.

Peter knew they couldn't go any faster without risking injury to men and horses, but still every mile seemed to take an hour, and the tightest discipline on his mind could not prevent it from rehearsing the horrors that Arial might be suffering at this very moment.

When at last they pulled up in front of the doctor's house, he checked his watch, and was surprised to see they'd done the whole trip in less than thirty minutes.

A constable was already dismounted and banging on the door, shouting, "Open in the name of the king!"

Despite the hour, the windows, including those near the front door, showed light. Peter, with John at his shoulder, joined the magistrate under the portico as the constable pounded on the door again.

The rumble of voices within was followed by the sound of bolts being drawn back. As soon as the door opened a crack, the constable shouldered it to open it, but the person on the other side resisted.

"Open for the king's man," shouted the constable, shoving harder. Peter and John loaned him their weight against the door, and all of a sudden, the person holding it closed stepped away, so that the constable fell inside, and Peter was only able to keep to his feet by leaping the man.

Behind, he could hear the others entering, but he had eyes for only one person.

There, dressed only in her shift, her arms held behind her

back by a brute twice her size, was Arial.

Her face lit up when she saw him. "Peter!"

The brute shook her. "Quiet, you," he growled.

Peter saw red. He had no memory of drawing his sword or of crossing the hall, but in seconds, the brute was backing away, whimpering, his hand to a cheek that dripped blood.

And Arial was back in Peter's arms where she belonged.

He held her close, kissing her hair, her forehead, her ear, anything he could reach while she was plastered to him, saying over and over, "You are alive. Josiah lied. I knew you would come if you could."

"Nothing and no one could keep me from you, my dearest love," he told her, and she stopped trying to burrow her face into his chest and looked up, her eye shining like a star.

He kissed her lips, and at last some of the tension that had driven him for hours slipped away.

He slowly became aware once more of his surroundings—of John, his own sword unsheathed, keeping everyone else at a distance while Arial and Peter had their reunion. Of the asylum's servants, all herded into a corner by the men who had come with Peter. Of the magistrate telling the doctor that Arial was, in truth, a viscountess and a married woman, and that the earl her cousin had shot himself to avoid arrest for murder and kidnapping.

"I am arresting you as an accessory to kidnapping, and I will be examining all of your records and talking to your patients to see how many other people have been unlawfully confined by you and their relatives," said the magistrate.

"What do we do with these?" the constable asked, indicated the cowed people in the corner.

"Peter," Arial murmured, "Mrs. Parker needs to come with us. She protected me from the other warders and was helping me to escape when the doctor caught us trying to leave."

"Mrs. Parker?" Peter called, and added to the men, "Let her through."

The woman won Peter's gratitude immediately by marching

up to the doctor and tugging a cloak from his hands, then coming to Arial and gently placing it around her shoulders to cover her from neck to toe. "There you are, my lady." She put her head on one side and examined Peter. "You would be Lord Ransome, then."

"I am," Peter acknowledged. "My lady tells me that we owe you a debt of gratitude."

The large, tough-looking woman blushed. "I only did what any decent woman would do, my lord. But if you could perhaps see fit to providing a reference? I won't be getting one here, that is for certain."

"Come with us, and we will make sure you do not suffer for your kindness," Peter said. "Magistrate, I need to find a place for my wife to rest. I will leave you to clean up here."

The magistrate nodded. "I will need to interview Lady Ransome, but it can wait until she has had an opportunity to sleep," he agreed.

"There's an inn in the village," Mrs. Parker suggested. "I can show you."

Peter took Arial up before him on his horse. John suggested that Mrs. Parker ride behind him, but she declared that she'd probably squash the horse and would certainly fall off. "It is only a ten-minute walk, my lords, my lady. I'll walk."

So, Peter and Arial rode, and John walked beside Mrs. Parker leading his horse. Now that Peter had Arial safe and, in his arms, fatigue was dragging at his limbs and weighing down his eyelids. No wonder, after two sleepless nights, a series of long rides, and hours of frantic worry.

Mrs. Parker woke the innkeeper and an ostler and arrange two rooms and stabling for the horses.

"And a room for yourself?" Arial asked, through a yawn. Arial must be nearly as tired as Peter, and John, too.

"My parents live just along the street," Mrs. Parker explained. "The innkeeper can tell you where. Send for me when you wake up, my lady, and I shall be your maid."

Arial let go of Peter for long enough to give the stalwart female a hug. "Thank you again, Mrs. Parker. I thank God for you."

Mrs. Parker proved that the first blush was not a fluke by coloring up again. "Go along with you and get some sleep, my lady," she said, the tone a loving scold. "A lady in your condition has to look after yourself."

It was good advice, and Peter wasted no time in availing himself of it. He would have liked a bath and Arial agreed it would be nice, but said, "We cannot ask the innkeeper to be hauling water at this hour, and besides," another large yawn, "I do not think I can stay awake any longer."

She was right on both counts. Peter turned back the covers. Arial let her cloak drop and crawled into bed. Peter stripped off his clothes and joined her, opening his arms to receive her as she snuggled up to him. He put his head on her hair, marveling at the feel of her so close to him without acres of night gown, with no mask as a barrier between them. On that thought, he slipped into a deep and dreamless sleep.

Chapter Twenty-Seven

ARIAL WOKE TO find Peter watching her. The room was flooded with light, and it gilded his hair, including his lashes, which, seen so close up and in the light, were ridiculously long and lush. The fair hairs on his chin, too. She had never seen him with prickles before, and she put a hand out to touch them, which made him smile. "I have not shaved since Three Oaks. I must look like a brute."

She had woken with his words echoing in her mind and they sprang from her lips without her conscious decision. "My dearest love?"

He did not understand that she was quoting him. "I hope so," he replied, "for I love you, Arial, with all my heart. When I thought I'd lost you, I did not want to live."

She returned the words to him. "I love you." She lifted her lips, and he saluted them with a gentle kiss that immediately turned hungry. Her own passion rose to meet his. She needed this. She needed him.

"Hurry," she told him.

"Never," he said. "I intend to enjoy every inch of my beloved wife, and I hope you will return the favor." He was kissing his way down her neck and pushing the shift down so he could reach her breast with his mouth, skin on skin.

Aaah. That felt marvelous. Arial tugged at the shift to give him better access and ended pulling her arm out of it.

"I have missed you so much," he mumbled, his mouth full.

"I missed you more," she challenged, caressing the hair on his nape with one hand while the other explored.

He kissed his way to the other breast, pushing the shift off that shoulder. Again, she wiggled her arm out so that her hand was free.

Heated moments later, it occurred to her that the scars on her shoulder she had hidden from him through their entire marriage were fully exposed, but by then his fingers were doing amazing things lower down her body, and she dismissed the thought. If he didn't care, why should she?

Her own hands were exploring—her eye too. Doing this in daylight had a great deal to recommend it.

And then she stopped thinking altogether, as she and Peter joined. They climbed together towards their peaks, so in tune, so intertwined, that everything except she and Peter ceased to exist. So close that she was him, and he was her. All was sensation. All pleasure so acute it was almost unbearable. Then suddenly they went over the top together and began the long blissful coast down the other side, still blind to everything but each other.

Arial had no idea how long it was before the weight on her shifted. She clutched Peter around his body to hold him in place.

"I am too heavy," he protested, but as he slid sideways, he wrapped his own arms around her and took her with him, offering his shoulder as his pillow.

The shift was gone, she realized. When did that happen? She let the thought go.

"I love you," she said again. It no longer hurt, now that she knew he loved her, too.

He said the words and kissed her hair. "I love you, beautiful wife."

She pulled away, her eye filling with tears. Was he mocking her? "You've seen me, Peter. I am not beautiful."

She would have left the bed, then, and wrapped herself in the cloak on the floor, in lieu of any other choices, but Peter rolled her onto her back and knelt astride across her hips.

"Let me go," she demanded.

"In a minute, if you still want to, but first you will give me the courtesy of a hearing." His face was stern. His clenched jaw showed anger, carefully held in check.

"I am not beautiful," Arial repeated defiantly.

"You are scarred," Peter corrected, "and your scars make me want to weep because they caused you pain and they still do. But you are not your scars, Arial. They are not what I see when I look at you."

He shaped his hands over her breasts, still so sensitive from his previous administrations. They trailed down her sides, and out around the flare of her hips. "I see this body, and it is magnificent. The body of a goddess, and with a goddess's power to enthrall. When you came into the room dressed for our wedding, I knew that I was born to worship you. These months, when we have loved one another in the dark, I have found it to be true. And now, when I see you naked in the light—Arial, you are all of my dreams come true."

He bent forward to trail his fingers over the broken side of her face. "This side is a sad ruin," he agreed, "but that is not why I pay it little attention." He brought his other hand down from her temple to her chin, and then another feather light-touch down her nose. "On this side, I see you as you are, the beautiful woman you are within. I see your strength, your kindness. I see a determined chin, and smile lines, just beginning, reminding me that my beloved has the courage to find humor in life, though, heaven knows, many in your shoes would have found only despair."

He smiled, then, and she realized that his anger had dissolved as he touched her, and so had hers. But he hadn't finished. "I see your eye and in it I see your soul." He was suddenly grave again. "Arial, I swear to you on my name and on my honor that I find you beautiful both within and without. I even, poor benighted fool that I am, love your scars, though for your sake I would wish them away, if I had that power. But they are part of the woman I love. Part of what made you the person you are."

He shifted off her, and his last remark was petulant. "And dammit, if I want to call my wife beautiful, I will."

Arial lay still, absorbing his words. He meant them! He had spoken with such passion, his face so earnest, that she could not doubt. Not anymore. She wanted to laugh and to weep both at the same time. Her heart was so full it ached. To Peter, if to no one else in the world, she was beautiful.

Peter broke the silence, "I apologize for my language, my lady."

He was sitting on the edge of the bed, now, gloriously handsome and naked.

Arial, completely melted by his passionate defense of her beauty, pulled herself together enough to get up on her knees at his back, and reach as far around him as she could.

"You make me so happy," she told him. "I'm sorry I doubted your word."

He turned enough to kiss her. "You are not in a hurry to get up are you, beautiful wife?"

"What did you have in mind?" she asked, and then looked down. Her eye widened. "Again? Already?"

"Or we could get up and find out what has been happening since we went to bed," he offered, without much enthusiasm.

"We can do that later," Arial suggested, falling backwards onto the bed and tugging him with her. "My husband, my love."

Chapter Twenty-Eight

"Your condition, Lady Ransome?" Peter asked his wife as they lay in bed after greeting the morning with another round of marital enthusiasm. Mrs. Parker's words had seeped into his mind and connected with some other interesting facts. She had not banished him to another bedroom for at least two months. Her breasts were rounder and even more sensitive than usual, and her belly, too, was larger than before.

Arial's contented smile and the hand she placed over said belly confirmed his suspicions. "Mrs. Parker has guessed I am with child, Peter. I have only just realized that in the last few days, and I have no idea how she knows."

Peter placed his own hand over hers. "A child." He had guessed as much, but Arial's confirmation sent a cascade of emotions through him. Joy. Love—for her and the babe. Pride. Fear, because childbirth was not without its risks.

How foolish he had been to let his niggling discomfort with spending the money she brought to the marriage keep him from admitting his love months ago. Thank God, he had found her in time! Now he could spend every day for the rest of their lives together telling her how vital she was to his wellbeing.

"Are you pleased?" Arial sounded anxious, and he hastened to reassure her.

"Thrilled beyond words, my love." And even more upset that Stancroft had put this dearest person in the world and her precious burden at risk. "Are you sure your ordeal... that is, should we consult a doctor?"

Her response reassured him. "I was not hurt, Peter. And today, now that we are together again, I feel marvelous. And hungry. I am very, very hungry. Do you suppose they have bacon?"

He vowed that his lady would have bacon if he had to ask at every cottage in the village. "Let's get up and find out, shall we?"

Extraordinary measures were not required. The inn happily provided their honored guests with bacon, sausages, eggs, toast, and several dishes in which baked vegetables featured prominently.

The magistrate arrived with his questions as the Ransomes, and John were sitting over a second cup of tea while the remnants of their meal were removed. "We have concerns about several of the other patients," he confided. "This is a da—a bothersome mess, begging your pardon, my lady. It will take some untangling. You're taking the Parker woman with you, I hear? We may want to talk to her again."

"Lady Ransome, shall we leave Mrs. Parker and her parents at Greenmount until the magistrate has finished his investigation?" Peter suggested.

"A good idea, my lord. If we are taking several of the household staff with us to Three Oaks Manor, we will be able to find positions at Greenmount for our new employees."

Peter had told Arial about the staffing situation at Three Oaks. Taking trusted servants from Greenmount was a brilliant idea. "So, there you are, sir," Peter said to the magistrate.

After that, they parted from John. Greenmount was only a two-hour carriage ride away from the inn where they'd stayed the night but would take John out of his way. If he made the long ride to London today, he was hopeful he could get back to Deercroft Hall the following day in time to see his godsons christened.

"John, you'll see to the arrest of my stepmother and her butler?" Peter asked, and John promised that he would.

Peter and Arial made an altogether more leisurely journey. They stayed the night at Greenmount so that Arial could consult with the village doctor, who already had her trust. "Lady Arial—I beg your pardon, my lord—Lady Ransome is very well, apart from a few minor bruises," he declared, setting Peter's mind at rest.

He advised Arial to eat heartily and rest when she felt like it and told Peter not to fuss. "I do not hold with these London doctors who turn breeding women into invalids," he said. "Lady Ransome can participate in all her normal activities for as long as she continues to enjoy them."

He gave Arial an avuncular pat on the arm. "When something is uncomfortable, my lady, stop doing it. Meanwhile, carry on. That includes long walks, horse riding, intimate activities, and any other exercise you are prone to enjoy."

Peter appreciated the man's bluntness, though Arial blushed.

They left Greenmount the following morning and stayed overnight at the inn from which Arial had been abducted. The innkeeper and his wife could not do enough for them, but they were not sorry to leave in the morning.

THE LONDON TOWNHOUSE looked almost bleak. Arial had sent a message from Greenmount saying she wanted the servants to leave when she and Peter did. The servants had sent off the furniture that hadn't been hired with the house, and anything else not required for the continued accommodation of Pauline Turner, the remaining staff, and Peter and Arial.

Pauline was waiting for them when they came in from the carriage. "Lady Ransome! I was so relieved to hear that you were unharmed."

Arial, taking in the woman's red-rimmed eyes and subdued posture, decided to take the statement at its face value. "I understand I have you to thank for that, Miss Turner. You told my husband where to look for me, and it is thanks to you that he found me so quickly."

After a few more stiff remarks, Pauline took a deep breath, as if nerving herself for something unpleasant.

"Peter, there is a letter from Miss Pettigrew. It is to tell you that Edwards tried to kidnap Vivienne, but the servants managed to stop him. Vivienne is safe, but Edwards got away."

"You opened my letter?" Peter's voice was indignant, but Arial put a hand on his arm.

"There is more you want to say, Pauline, is there not?"

Pauline turned to her, and the words tumbled out. "My mother has fled England with Edwards. They took Laura with them. I was afraid they had taken Vivienne, too, so I opened the letter to Peter from Miss Pettigrew."

She drew in a sobbing breath. "I know you do not trust me, Peter. But I love Vivienne. I love Rose, too. And for all that Mama thinks she owns Vivienne, and I think Edwards actually cares for her, those two girls belong together, and with you and Arial." She blushed. "That is, if you want Vivienne."

Peter's frown had turned bewildered. "Why would I not want Vivienne?"

Arial guessed what Pauline was trying to say. "Edwards is her father?"

Pauline nodded. "I thought you knew, Peter. Your father did. He figured it out when she was born too early to be his."

Peter shook his head. "I did not know until you told me yesterday. Was it only yesterday? Father would never criticize his countess to me. Instead, he drank himself into a stupor and ruined the estate because he'd made a mistake he couldn't fix."

"It doesn't matter," Arial pointed out. "You are putting the estate back on its feet again, and Vivienne is our sister in all the ways that matter."

He put his arm around her and kissed her forehead. "Wise wife. I have loved Vivienne since she was a baby, and the fact I didn't like her mother never made any difference to that love. So, the identity of the man who bred her is of no importance. My father gave her his name and his heart. And so do I."

Pauline was blinking hard. Arial held out her hand to her former enemy. "You, too, Pauline. You have a home with us for as long as you need one."

Peter kissed Arial's forehead again as Pauline lost her battle and burst into tears and hurried away with a handkerchief pressed to her face.

Arial let her go, though she would follow in a minute. She had cried alone too many times not to offer comfort if she could. First, though she wanted to embrace the greatest of her many blessings.

"I love you," she told him, as he hugged her back and returned the words.

If someone had told the Arial of just six months ago that the year would bring her a husband who loved her, sisters, and a place in Society, she would have thought them as crazy as Josiah called her.

Peter had seen the truth from the start. He had not agreed that her outward appearance defined who she was as a person. He had seen past it to the beauty within. He had given her the confidence to be herself, dropping the mask of reserve and caution that hid her far more than the physical mask she wore.

She was no longer Lady Beast, the daughter of an earl who hid her ugliness from the world. She was Lady Ransome, wife, lover, viscountess, sister, soon to be mother… With her beloved at her side, she hid from no one.

Epilogue

Bledisloe House, London, March 1818

"ARE YOU SURE you are not tired," Pauline asked Arial. "It was a long trip yesterday." She moved the parasol above Arial's head a fraction to the right, so that she remained in shadow as the sun shifted.

"I am enjoying sitting here on the terrace," Arial answered, "reading a book that Regina Paddimore recommended to me. Take a seat, Pauline, and have a cup of tea with me while we have a few moments of peace. John Henry will be awake at any minute, and then I shall need to go inside to feed him."

Pauline settled in the next chair, the mention of Arial's baby bringing on the besotted smile she'd worn in his presence since the day he was born.

"You have done wonders with the house," Arial told her. "You have a real gift."

Pauline, out from under the influence of her mother and sister, had proved to have impeccable taste, not just in fashion but in home décor. She had helped Arial to redecorate Three Oaks and had come on ahead to London when Peter and Arial's search for a townhouse had come to an unexpected conclusion.

The search for a Stancroft heir had been unsuccessful, and the earldom had been about to revert to the crown when someone—Arial suspected a certain marquess—suggested to the Prince Regent that he might win some public approbation by becoming part of the story of Lady Beast and her bridegroom.

Peter's rescue of his wife from the wicked machinations of his stepmother and her cousin had caught the popular imagination. Deerhaven, if it were he, engaged the ready sympathy of the prince for a lady in dire distress, and also pointed out that the estate was impoverished and would take more to put into a saleable condition than it was worth.

The upshot was that Peter was the new Earl of Stancroft, ostensibly as a reward for his services during the war, and the titular owner of the entailed property included Bledisloe House—rambling, run down, and in much need of refurbishment and redecoration.

Pauline beamed. "I'm glad you are pleased."

They were interrupted by a troop of schoolgirls, walking up through the garden under the supervision of Miss Pettigrew.

When Marjorie heard that Peter and Arial were now Lord and Lady Stancroft, she had taken to her bed, turned her face to the wall, and refused to have anything more to do with her daughters, who had betrayed her by being born girls.

She had been installed at Greenmount under the care of Mrs. Parker, and her three timid little girls had been added to Peter and Arial's growing family. With Viv as their leader and Rose to love them, they were coming out of their shells nicely.

And Miss Pettigrew now had a maid and an under governess to help her with her flock of charges.

The party stopped by the tea-sipping ladies, and Anne, the youngest of the Bledisloe sisters, climbed up onto Pauline's lap, while Viv and Rose leaned one each side of Arial's chair.

"We have been learning about garden creatures," Viv informed Arial.

"Did you know," Anne asked Pauline, "that one must be very gentle with a worm, because a squeeze might hurt him. One must put him down and let him burrow back into the ground."

Pauline had an arm around the four-year-old and was kissing her forehead. "I hope you were very gentle, Anne," she said.

"I was, after," Anne declared, which left Arial wondering about the fate of the first poor worm.

After a bit more sharing about garden creatures, Miss Pettigrew led the girls back upstairs to the schoolroom. Her voice carried back to Arial and Pauline as they walked into the house. "Milk and seedcake, after you wash your hands. Properly, Lady Anne. And then we shall write stories about what we found in the garden."

"You will make a wonderful mother, Pauline," Arial said.

"Unlikely, at my age and with my history," Pauline replied. "Who would have a harridan in her twenties with a criminal for a mother and no dowry? I know you want me to go out with you and Peter to the entertainments of the Season, but after how I behaved last year, I doubt I will even be invited."

Arial lifted a hand to count off her points. "You are not a harridan. I don't think you ever were, really. You behaved as your mother expected, and I don't blame you. You are twenty-three, which is still plenty young enough for those who hope for a wife with a little more sense than the average girl just out of the schoolroom. Your mother's behavior was criminal, but we did not prosecute, and nor did we noise her behavior around Society. Therefore, you are not the daughter of a criminal. And Peter reinstated your dowry at the beginning of last Season."

Pauline's eyes watered. "You and Peter have been too good to me."

Arial squeezed Pauline's hand. "You are our sister now, Pauline. Come out with us. I know Cordelia, Margaret, and Regina will invite you. And when others see how nice you are away from your mother and sister, you will be invited everywhere. I have every confidence you can find someone to love you as Peter loves me."

Just then, Peter come out of the house, John Henry in his

arms. "Why were the girls talking about drawing worms and spiders?" he asked. "I spied them on the stairs."

Arial and Pauline exchanged smiles. "They are studying garden animals," Arial explained, while Pauline rose and held out her arms for the baby.

He went to her willingly and held up his face for a kiss. He then, however, remembered the purpose of his visit to the garden, twisting in Pauline's arms so he could see his mother, and casting her a soul-filled look accompanied by a quivering lip.

"Lord Ransome has put in an urgent order for his comestibles," Peter commented.

The little boy, who had been landed with his father's former title, gave a couple of quick sniffs, preparatory to the full-blown roar of a tyrant denied immediate gratification.

"I will leave you to it," Pauline suggested, handing Henry over.

"I will take him upstairs," Arial declared. "Come along, Peter. We can chat while I'm feeding him."

"Good idea, wife. I have missed you this last fortnight while you were at Three Oaks, and I was in town." He followed her and the baby into the house, leaving Pauline to sit down again and take up her book.

"You didn't miss me last night," Arial suggested in a whisper, nudging him with a free elbow.

Peter slipped an arm around her waist and another around his son, stopping them for a hug at the bottom of the stairs. "I am already missing you again," he murmured into her hair. "And after you have satisfied the bottomless pit here," he leaned over further to kiss John Henry, "I trust you will feel able to accommodate my own appetite."

John Henry, who felt he had been patient for long enough, let out a whimper, and Arial led the way up the stairs. "Come along, then, my lord. I believe we have a busy morning ahead of us."

Even in today's more diverse culture, physical appearance makes a huge difference in people's lives. Being heavily overweight, disfigured (especially in the face), or otherwise not fitting social norms for appearance can count against a person in the job market, in romance, and in dozens of other ways.

The Regency era held that attractive people were more trustworthy, more capable, better adjusted, and more worthy in every way. Recent research suggests that things haven't changed. Across cultures, including our own, people judge others on the basis of their attractiveness, and the idea that "beautiful is good" seems to require a "disfigured is bad" corollary.

Then, as now, assistive technology focused on improving aesthetics as well as function. An example would be a wooden hand that mimicked a real one, where the disfigurement needed to be disguised or hidden in order not to provoke horror.

Could I write a heroine who evokes the typical horrified reaction to disfigurement that has been recorded through time, and who is, nonetheless, a sympathetic character that we want the hero to love? You be the judge.

I also want to say something about asylums for the mentally ill. In the eighteenth and nineteenth century, they existed to keep the inmates in custody. Some of them were huge affairs, run by charitable foundations, such as Bethlem Hospital in London, popularly known as Bedlam. Others, such as the one I invented for this story, were private establishments run for profit, often by someone who had set himself up as a doctor with few, if any, qualifications.

None of them were nice places. The keepers were guards—untrained in anything except restraining those who did not want to be there. Patients were often restrained. Treatments were barbaric: being bled, purged, blistered, beaten.

The system was ripe for abuse, and it was abused. Those with mental illness were undoubtedly not helped by being in such surroundings, but asylums also held those who were not insane. Even into the 20th century, deaf people and people with severe physical disabilities were committed to asylums because they could not talk.

Children and women were admitted to asylums on the word of the male head of their family—husband, father, brother, or even, in some cases, a male friend of the woman or the child's mother.

Epilepsy was reason enough to be committed until the 1950's. Depression after the loss of a loved one. Abusive language. Being overly religious. Even being overtired! Or, for that matter, for no reason at all except that their continued freedom was inconvenient to someone.

In one case, a man confined his wife after she objected to her niece, with whom her husband was having an affair, being named as mistress of the household. Her incarceration came to an end when she managed to persuade a boy working in the garden of the house next door to take a message—and her shoe (to identify her)—to friends who rescued her and hired a lawyer to defend her.

Like my Arial, she was one of the lucky ones.

ABOUT THE AUTHOR

Have you ever wanted something so much you were afraid to even try? That was Jude ten years ago.

For as long as she can remember, she's wanted to be a novelist. She even started dozens of stories, over the years.

But life kept getting in the way. A seriously ill child who required years of therapy; a rising mortgage that led to a full-time job; six children, her own chronic illness... the writing took a back seat.

As the years passed, the fear grew. If she didn't put her stories out there in the market, she wouldn't risk making a fool of herself. She could keep the dream alive if she never put it to the test.

Then her mother died. That great lady had waited her whole life to read a novel of Jude's, and now it would never happen.

So Jude faced her fear and changed it—told everyone she knew she was writing a novel. Now she'd make a fool of herself for certain if she didn't finish.

Her first book came out to excellent reviews in December 2014, and the rest is history. Many books, lots of positive reviews, and a few awards later, she feels foolish for not starting earlier.

Jude write historical fiction with a large helping of romance, a splash of Regency, and a twist of suspense. She then tries to figure out how to slot the story into a genre category. She's mad keen on history, enjoys what happens to people in the crucible of a passionate relationship, and loves to use a good mystery and some real danger as mechanisms to torture her characters.

Dip your toe into her world with one of her lunch-time reads collections or a novella, or dive into a novel. And let her know what you think.

Website and blog:
judeknightauthor.com

Subscribe to newsletter:
judeknightauthor.com/newsletter

Bookshop:
judeknight.selz.com

Facebook:
facebook.com/JudeKnightAuthor

Twitter:
twitter.com/JudeKnightBooks

Pinterest:
nz.pinterest.com/jknight1033

Bookbub:
bookbub.com/profile/jude-knight

Books + Main Bites:
bookandmainbites.com/JudeKnightAuthor

Amazon author page:
amazon.com/Jude-Knight/e/B00RG3SG7I

Goodreads:
goodreads.com/author/show/8603586.Jude_Knight

LinkedIn:
linkedin.com/in/jude-knight-465557166

www.ingramcontent.com/pod-product-compliance
Lightning Source LLC
Chambersburg PA
CBHW061240210726
48293CB00003B/847